A TENDENCY FOR VIOLENCE

PETER S. LORD

ISBN 978-1-9990359-8-3

Sterling Publications

ALSO BY PETER S. LORD

PROLOGUE

The bat was sick for five days before it died, spending its final hours shivering under the eaves of an abandoned equipment shed in West Texas. It suffered and died in isolation, like untold billions of animals before it, and it intuitively isolated itself from the rest of its colony.

The sickness, a virus that attacked the tissues of the brain and nervous system, produced an aggressive inflammatory response. The bat could not eat, it could not fly, and its body was wracked by seizures. Early on the sixth day, it fell to the hard-packed ground where it spent its final torturous hours.

Two days later, a wild boar came across the carcass and ate it. The boars had voracious appetites and ate everything they came across, plants, bird eggs, dead animals. The boar became sick as well, but the virus was not deadly to its species. The animal continued to forage along with other members of its herd, furthering the propagation of the contagion. Initially, the spread was limited in scope because the primary mode of transmission was through blood, fecal matter, and saliva. However, deep within the boars' cellular structure, the virus mutated, taking on features that began to affect other parts of their bodies, including their respiratory systems. Once the members of the original herd began to sneeze, the virus quickly spread among its ranks and into neighboring herds.

The wild boars were highly nomadic, and the virus was transmitted throughout Texas and into neighboring states.

The virus also developed characteristics that allowed it to be communicated to other animals with a close genetic match. That close genetic match was tested four months later when an infected boar was shot by a hunter. The hunter, an undocumented worker by the name of

Hector Villas, introduced the pathogen into his system when he carelessly wiped his hand across his nose while field-dressing the two-hundred-and-twenty-pound boar.

A virus previously unknown to humankind found its way into his bloodstream. His immune system kicked into action, but there was nothing in his hereditary database to effectively deal with the assault.

Hector Villas, thirty-five, unmarried and uninsured, became Patient Zero.

Hector was cared for by his employer, an oil executive by the name of John Scranton, a man who maintained a certain profile in the local Texas society. Despite his wealth, Scranton did not take his worker to the hospital, preferring to move him into the main house instead. Hiring undocumented workers was not uncommon in his part of the state, but he could do without the scrutiny and unwanted attention this disclosure might bring. He also did not take any precautions while around his wheezing, coughing, and headache-suffering employee. Within forty-eight hours, Scranton also developed symptoms of what was to become known as the Texas Wild Boar Flu.

The disease could have petered out at that point if Scranton had stayed at home with his hired hand. The contagion might have been relegated to nothing more than a near miss, like a large asteroid that passed between the Earth and the Moon. But Scranton worked in the oil sector and had been invited to the wedding of the daughter of one of the leading oil barons in Texas. It was a large wedding, even by Texan standards, and was attended by a great number of family members and representatives from the oil industry who had come from far-flung parts of the world.

He was still quite ill on the day of the wedding, barely able to catch his breath. Hector, a smoker, suffered even greater respiratory distress, and there were days when Scranton wondered what he would do if the man died.

Scranton was determined to attend the wedding, however, and prepared for it by consuming quantities of cough medicine and Tylenol that were far in excess of the daily recommended maximums. He didn't really care about the wedding itself, but the networking opportunities it afforded were too important to miss.

Not all the attendees with whom he interacted became infected, but there were many who did. They, in turn, passed the sickness on to fellow travelers at the airport, other passengers and flight attendants on the planes in which they flew, and acquaintances in their home cities.

The contagion spread throughout the world within days. It was a distressing infection to incur, with a fatality rate of approximately 3%. The formal name was Viral Hemorrhagic Pneumonia (VHP-25), although some countries, especially China, gleefully continued to use the colloquial term. They had not forgotten *The China Virus* or *The Wuhan Virus*. It was doubly pleasurable that it had *Texas* in the name, a state that had been so vociferous in its condemnation of China after the previous pandemic.

Some of those who contracted the disease coughed up dramatic gouts of blood and drowned in their own bodily fluids. It did not spare the rich, a specific race, or those affiliated with any one political party or religion. It primarily killed the very old, the very young, and those who were already infirm. For all the others, it was a very unpleasant experience, resulting in the hospitalization and intubation of millions. The people of the world were terrified.

The development of a vaccine for VHP-25 was swift, and even those who were formerly reluctant to receive any type of inoculation were eager to line up for shots. Seeing friends, family members and relatives in blood-soaked sheets made a dramatic impression. The vaccine was almost as effective as the one for measles immunization, effectively eliminating serious infection in those receiving the treatment. Although there were waves of variants, each one was less severe than the one before, and by the beginning of the third year, few people paid any attention to Texas Boar. No one had considered the possibility that a cat by the name of Tiger could change the course of history.

In most ways, Tiger was a typical domestic short-haired tabby, one who loved to roam through the woods outside its owner's house. It loved to hunt, and its favorite prey were birds. But on one occasion, Tiger made the unwise decision to take on a Great horned owl, which resulted in the cat contracting an avian virus that made it feel miserable for several days. The cat was also working its way through a bout of VHP-25, possibly contracted via one of the neighborhood children.

Tiger was owned by a thirty-four-year-old man by the name of Jeremy Findlay, who would likely be appalled if he realized the carnage the cat left in its wake during its outdoor adventures. Jeremy was five days away from a long-planned trip to Rome when he started to feel unwell. He spent the first three days sick in bed, cuddling Tiger, unaware that the cat was the source of his illness. In a rare case of zoonotic transmission—a sickness passed from animal to human—Tiger had infected him with a slightly altered version of VHP-25.

By the fifth day, Jeremy felt sufficiently recovered to begin his trip, if not *fully* better. He felt a little guilty about traveling while sick. Going anywhere while ill had been thoroughly vilified during the latest pandemic, and Jeremy was not immune to societal shame. But he really, really wanted to go on this vacation, and Texas Boar was no longer considered a serious disease, not for anyone vaccinated. He would be careful, and he would wear a mask when he was around other people.

But Jeremy did not wear a mask, not once in ten days. And during the course of his travels, he came in close contact with 2632 people, at the airports he visited, on the planes in which he flew, at the museums he toured, on the subways and buses between venues, and at the restaurants he frequented. Approximately one in five of those people became sick. Those first-generation contacts interacted with hundreds of thousands of additional people in the next week. From there, the number of individuals exposed increased exponentially. After just three weeks, the number of sick people who could trace their path back to Jeremy Findlay was in the hundreds of millions.

Jeremy remained oblivious to his role in the spread, thoroughly enjoying his time in Europe.

Tiger received lavish attention upon its master's return, and over the next four weeks, no one seemed overly concerned about the emergence of yet another VHP-25 variant, this one designated Beta IV.

CHAPTER 1

New York City

If Mike Richards stood and walked just five feet to the left of his desk, he could see a tantalizing hint of green from Central Park. He did this a lot. Something about the sight of that green eased his mind and lowered his blood pressure a few notches. It helped that he had a job as a creative consultant where the act of looking out the window was indistinguishable from doing actual work. Like the bulk of the proverbial iceberg, ninety percent of what he did took place out of sight, in his brain. The remaining ten percent, the work of transforming his vision into reality, was mostly about communicating his ideas to the graphic arts people.

He stood and stared out the window at this green anomaly in a sea of grays and blacks and blue-tinted glass. Then he leaned forward and looked down at the street scene below him. There were plenty of cars and people, but not a single tree.

He was adequately compensated for his work, which was primarily dedicated to the development of marketing campaigns. But the job came with punishing deadlines, and the stress that accompanied the position hovered above him like an avenging spirit. He used to drink away his lunch hours, trying to dull the sharp edges, but the liquor also dulled his mind. It gave him the illusion of facility with words and ideas, but it was only that, an illusion. When he reviewed the work he produced after drinking, he discovered that the slogans and print copy were not fit for publication. That lack of professionalism was unacceptable to both him and his employer.

Almost by accident, he discovered that the simple act of walking through the park during his lunch hour was a far more satisfactory way to combat his stress. This was surprising to him since he was a city boy born and bred. His father had been raised in the country but fled the city almost immediately after his wife—Mike's mother—died of a brain aneurysm.

Mike always assumed that those who really appreciated nature had grown up surrounded by it and would miss it when they moved to the city. He now believed this to be inaccurate; almost everyone needed nature whether they were aware of it or not. It was something innate in the human experience. Being amongst the trees and grass and flowing water was soothing and primal, even if it wasn't *true* nature, just a reasonable facsimile.

Central Park in New York City was in the middle of a concrete jungle, literally surrounded by roads and traffic, and swarms of people. The architects of the park had done their best to conceal this fact by using cleverly designed flora. There was an outer perimeter of trees and thick hedges in some sections that could partially or fully block out the sights and sounds of the traffic. Paths led to the interior of the park and many culminated in grassy sections that surrounded the two major bodies of water, The Reservoir, and The Lake.

Mike's preferred path was to travel through the Ramble, a byzantine maze that allowed him to imagine that he was walking in the woods — albeit with hundreds of other people. His route always culminated at The Lake. He didn't know which elements of the nature walk gave it the effect it did — whether it was the sight of the green grass and plants, the sound of the wind through the trees, the organic smell of it, or the water — but he thought he needed it all. Today was no exception.

As he made his way to his destination, an attractive young woman came jogging toward him on the trail. She was clad in running shorts, a white sports bra, and a pair of high-end running shoes. And earbuds, of course. Her gait was smooth, and her blond ponytail bounced along behind her. Mike glanced at her, but she maintained that rigid, eyes-fixed-forward stare of a native New Yorker. Unfortunately, it was the same reaction he always received. To be fair, he didn't think it was personal. Avoiding eye contact was a defensive mechanism he had seen most female runners adopt. They would otherwise need to fend off hundreds of stares during their runs. At least he *hoped* he was not the only one she ignored. If she were to glance his way, he knew exactly what she would see: an early thirties white guy in a dark suit and tie, average build, average height, dark hair, clean-shaven, unremarkable looks. In other words, a clone of any one of a thousand other men in this part of the city. He liked to think he was different—everyone did, but he worked at an anonymous job at a generic advertising firm, and he didn't have much of a life outside of work.

As he exited the trees that grew at the periphery of the pond, he was pleased to see that the area was not overcrowded. He liked to sit on a bench if one was available and watch the swans. The birds were sleek and majestic and serenely unperturbed, and their noble bearing had a calming effect on him.

Mike could feel the sponginess of the grass under his feet as he walked toward the water, and he longed to take off his shoes and socks and walk barefoot. That sense of touch would complete the illusion. A person could pretend, just for a while, that they really were in nature. He would never do it, of course. Anyone seeing a man in a suit walking barefoot through the grass in Central Park would think he was unhinged.

There were a multitude of benches facing the water, but only one was free. In many other cities and parts of the world, sitting down at a public bench with a stranger was considered innocuous. In this city, it was considered an intrusion, possibly even a threat. He was pleased that he did not have to share.

Fat white swans swam close to the water's edge, begging for food. More crowded in toward him and he held out his empty palms to let them know they needed to look elsewhere. Most moved on, but a few stragglers swam in circles and watched him with their small black eyes, ever hopeful. He made a mental note to bring some bread the next time he visited.

Five minutes later, he got up to leave.

He had only walked a few steps before he noticed something that drew his attention. There was a man with dark hair in a black suit standing about thirty yards away, staring at something. No, that wasn't quite right. There was no focus to his gaze and his face was utterly void of expression. He was very still, like an expertly rendered exhibit in a wax museum, Businessman in a Park. The man was not someone who Mike would typically notice—he was white, well-dressed, and had an expensive haircut. An older version of himself.

Mike normally lived by the credo of big city life; don't make eye contact, do not engage with anyone, and generally ignore what is going on around you. And most importantly, the prime commandment, do not under any circumstances get involved. Other people's business was other people's business. But something about this fellow raised the hairs on the back of his neck, his body's feeble and completely inadequate attempt to make him look larger and more aggressive. It just made him want to loosen his tie.

7

The man was not situated directly on the path Mike needed to take for his return trip to the office, but it would take him closer to the guy than he wished. Something was off about the man, and Mike was not in the mood to be harassed by anyone today. Walking by the guy seemed like an invitation for an interaction. He looked behind him, scouting for an alternative route. He could take the loop around the pond, but that would add at least another half mile to his walk.

This is ridiculous, he thought. The man was just zoning out, everyone did it once in a while. Plus, he didn't have time to make a detour around the pond. Nevertheless, Mike kept watching the guy out of his peripheral vision as he drew nearer, maintaining his gaze as steadfastly forward as the female jogger. He most assuredly did not want to make eye contact. He was almost fully by the man when the guy began to stride purposefully toward the water. Later, Mike would think about the term that popped into his head at that moment. *Switched on*. The fellow appeared to have been switched on.

The businessman walked to the edge of the pond, leaned down, and picked up a rock the size of a cantaloupe. He hefted it in his hand a few times as if to assess it for suitable size and weight. Apparently satisfied, he walked briskly toward the nearest bench, currently occupied by a woman with a baby stroller. The woman was well put together, nice clothes, skillful blonde highlights, expensive boots. The baby stroller probably cost as much as a cheap car.

Mike was frozen to the spot, watching the scene play out with horrifying predictability. But was it predictable? It just seemed too unbelievable. And if it was predictable, what did that say about him? He didn't even call out a warning before the man slammed the rock into the back of the woman's head. The impact made an alarming sound, as if the woman's head was constructed of wood. She pitched to the side, but even before she was lost from view, Mike saw blood bloom through those blonde highlights, shockingly red. Several women screamed. The man continued to pound away at the woman's skull, relentless, his face without expression. He paused for a moment, as if examining his handiwork, and then delivered a few more forceful blows. Mike could hear a sound like wood cracking and was grateful he could no longer see the woman's head.

There had to be thirty people within eyeshot of the incident but not a single person made a move toward the assailant. The bystander effect was on full display, with everyone waiting for someone else to intervene, including Mike. Granted, most of the people at the park at that time of the day were seniors, women with children, and the odd stoner.

A torrent of thoughts rushed through his head, some rationalizing his inaction. *She's likely already dead. Why isn't anyone helping?* And, more practically, *this man is crazy*, and everybody knows you can't fight crazy. Crazy people don't stop when you concede defeat. You can't tap out. People like this guy were just as likely to take that rock and keep pounding away at your skull until there was nothing left but pink jelly.

There was nothing to be done. He didn't even take out his phone. Someone had to have called 911 by now. That was the twenty-first century version of getting involved. That, and taking a video to post on social media later.

For a few seconds there existed a frozen tableau, thirty witnesses, a madman, and the woman he murdered. And her child. The man's gaze shifted to the baby carriage, and Mike heard someone let out a low moan of despair, as if the act had already been committed. Mike felt his legs carry him closer to the attacker as if by their own volition. He felt detached from what he was doing, walking headlong into a confrontation with zero plan.

"Hey," he shouted, but it came out weak because his saliva had dried up and he needed to clear his throat.

"Hey!" he said again, louder this time.

The man paid him no attention, his bland face now directed toward the baby. Blood dripped from the rock held between his hands, the object now resembling an organ of some type, as if he had ripped it from the woman's body. There seemed to be little question that he planned to use it again.

Mike broke into a run, his hard-soled leather shoes a poor choice for any athletic endeavor, and especially inadvisable for a confrontation on grass.

The man had made his way around the bench, unhurriedly, and was only several steps away from the carriage.

It was perhaps better that he ignored Mike. If he had turned that dead-eyed stare onto Mike in those last seconds, Mike may have balked or tried to talk some sense into the man. Judging from his previous actions, talk therapy was unlikely to be effective.

Mike had played football in high school, some fifteen years earlier, although his role was mainly to run away from other people. Some of those athletic skills remained, and he kept himself reasonably fit from weekly boot camp classes at a local gym. In his mind he saw what he would do; he would take a running leap at the park bench, step on the top edge of the back rest, and then push off forward in a flying tackle. It could have worked except that his shoes, an expensive pair of black Oxfords, had approximately zero grip on the lush grass that grew close to the water.

When he was five steps out from the bench, he already knew that he didn't have enough traction to make the jump. He could feel it in the way the shoes slipped just a little bit on each step, small warnings, like the sound of ice cracking under one's feet on a frozen pond. Forcefully jumping would not be an advisable action in this situation. So, he came to a skidding halt just short of the bench, so close he could have laid his hands on it. On the other side, less than five feet away, stood a madman with a rock, about to pulverize an infant.

Mike had lost all elements of speed, surprise, and momentum. There was no plan B. He looked around for potential allies, hoping that his actions may have inspired some other soul to lend a hand. Although no one in the immediate vicinity looked ready to take up the fight, his gaze did fall upon a surreal sight—a police officer approaching on a horse at full gallop. The rider was still too far away to intervene before the man acted, so Mike did the only thing that he could think of in the moment; he took off one of his shoes and threw it at the man's head. His aim was poor, and the shoe bounced harmlessly off the man's shoulder, but it had the desired effect. The man turned his head away from the carriage and faced Mike.

Shit, thought Mike.

Up close, Mike was able to get a better sense of the assailant. He appeared to be about fifty and had black hair with some grey mixed in around the temples. His suit was expensive and so was his haircut. A Rolex or similar quality watch was strapped around one wrist. He was clean shaven, had light brown eyes, and was wearing a tie with a Windsor knot, the epitome of an executive, perhaps a lawyer. Strangely, his shirt was misbuttoned, the collar somewhat askew. There was no hint of hate or anger or fear in his eyes or on his face. In fact, he regarded Mike with no more interest than one would give a fire hydrant. Somehow, this made it worse, this lack of emotion. It removed the human from the human being and made him seem foreign and alien.

Business Suit turned and began walking around the bench toward Mike, purposeful. The man ignored the large chestnut horse pounding toward them. Mike could feel the vibrations from the horse's charge through his unshod foot, a rhythmic pattern, the hoof beats so powerful that they sent seismic waves through the earth.

The horse was reigned to a halt about thirty feet away, its chest heaving. The animal had clearly been pushed hard, perhaps all the way from the other end of the park. The direction from the 911 operator, or the police dispatcher, would have been unequivocal. Aggravated assault in progress. Very aggravated.

The rider was a young female police officer, Black. She had her gun out almost as soon as her feet hit the ground.

"Police officer," she screamed. "Put down your weapon."

"Weapon" seemed like an odd word choice for a rock, but Mike guessed that the term was technically correct. He doubted she could distinguish what he was carrying but could not fail to notice that it was covered in blood and gore. The man ignored her and continued to advance toward Mike. The movement created an awkward angle for the officer since a stray bullet could just as easily hit Mike. He sidled away from the line of fire, never taking his eyes off the man.

"Stop or I'll shoot," the officer shouted, sounding increasingly distressed. Mike wondered if she had ever shot anyone. Perhaps she had never even drawn her gun.

The man took two more steps toward him, now less than six feet away.

There was no other warning from the police officer. A gout of blood erupted from the man's chest simultaneous to the sound of the shot. Drops of blood sprayed on the grass, the red and green reminding Mike of holly branches at Christmas. The man staggered but did not fall. He gurgled out a mouthful of blood as he resumed his advance toward Mike. Mike backpedaled, walking awkwardly with only one shoe. The sound of the shot woke the baby and it emitted wailing cries that bordered on shrieking. The cop fired again, once more hitting center mass. The man finally stopped, swayed on his feet for a few seconds, and then dropped to his knees. From there he toppled forward, face-planting into the grass, not even able to bring his arms forward.

The police officer kept her gun pointed at the prone figure as she approached, and Mike could see that her hands were shaking. Cops were people too.

Six other officers reached the scene before the first ambulance arrived, and they were busy corralling witnesses, including Mike. Because of his involvement, his statement was considered especially important. A forensic team followed shortly after and collected as part of the evidence an Oxford shoe, size- eleven, color- black. He hobbled his way to a waiting police vehicle that would transport him to the precinct for a formal statement.

Just as he was about to enter the vehicle, another commotion erupted. The husband of the dead woman bolted away from the officer accompanying him, and he alternated between calling her name and wrestling with several other officers as he attempted to get to his wife.

Someone wheeled over the baby, and he dropped to his knees sobbing as he looked into his daughter's face. Mike felt for the man, who just this morning had anticipated an entirely different life than the one he now faced. In an instant, it was cruelly and irrevocably changed by the fickleness of fate.

CHAPTER 2

By the time Mike left the precinct building, it was almost nine in the evening. He had been offered food early on by the investigating officers, but the thought of eating at that stage was unappealing. Now, with some time and distance from the incident, his appetite came roaring back. He had not eaten since breakfast, as he had planned to pick up something on his way back to the office from the park.

There were still plenty of restaurants open at this time of night, but eating out by himself was always an option of last resort. It was a too-blatant reminder that he was single, and sitting at a table by himself felt vaguely embarrassing. If he was going to eat alone, he wanted to do it in private.

He took a taxi back to his place.

Mike cracked open a beer almost as soon as he entered the door to his apartment. He did not normally drink during the week, but tonight was going to be an exception.

An Uber Eats driver delivered a meal of Thai food about thirty minutes later. Mike tipped the driver handsomely. He reminded himself that he really should learn how to cook, even something basic. The amount of money he spent on eating out and ordering in was staggering, although he made just enough money to continue this practice without too much concern about his finances.

His phone signaled an incoming call just as he was setting out a plate and utensils for his food. Perfect timing, as usual. He stared at his father's name on the call display as the phone rang once, twice, three times. A conversation with his father could last an hour or more based on previous history, and he was definitely not in the right headspace for it. But it was after 10 p.m., a time when his father was normally in bed for the night. That meant it could be something serious. He tried to sound cheerful as he answered the phone.

"Hi Dad," he said.

"Mikey, how are things?"

Mike hated that his father still called him Mikey. *Mikey* was only appropriate for the kid who ate Cheerios for breakfast every morning and then skateboarded to Hillsdale Elementary School.

"Fine, Dad."

This was untrue, of course, but Mike had no intention of reliving the entire episode over the phone. He attempted to inject a note of humor into his voice. "Isn't this past your bedtime? I'm surprised to hear from you at this time of night."

"Oh, I'm just checking in. So, are you still liking your job? Have you met any nice girls yet? My gosh, it's been really warm lately."

Mike looked over at his slowly cooling food. He needed to hurry this along. His father could keep this going all night, asking questions, complaining about his annoying neighbors (not that he had any close by), and checking on Mike's non-existent love life.

"The job is fine. Speaking of which, I have an early day tomorrow, so I can't stay on the line too long. I haven't even had supper yet."

"Oh, sure, sure. Sorry for the late call." He paused for a long moment. "I had a bit of a fall two days ago. Broke my damn leg."

There it was. True to form, his father could not lead off the conversation with the most pertinent point, the reason Mike presumed he called in the first place.

"Oh my God, Dad! Are you okay?"

"Yeah, yeah. But I'll be in this goddamn cast for eight weeks. The docs tell me that old bones don't heal quite as quickly."

"You're not *that* old. I'm sure you will be as good as new once the cast comes off."

Mike knew that this was not even close to being accurate, but he wanted to keep things positive. His father had never been very good at keeping himself in shape, and it was likely he would need extensive physical therapy to rebuild what little strength he had. Mike also suspected what was coming next. His father would never call just to tell him about his broken leg.

"So, are you still on track for the visit?"

The visit, as his father termed it, could be more accurately described as a detour. Mike had a business trip scheduled for this weekend, and the

14

location was only eighty miles from his father's rural home. Mike had let slip about the trip, not presuming that his father would ask him to visit. He did ask, though, immediately and with enthusiasm. Mike felt compelled—perhaps guilted was a better word—to honor his father's request.

Prior to the events of today, the plan had been to fly to Savannah, take care of the meeting, and then head to his father's place. He budgeted for a three-hour stay with his dad, just long enough not to be rude. Then back to the airport, catch a late flight home, and be done with it for another six months.

His father was speaking again. "Perhaps you could help me set up my place? I can't get down to the basement, and I'll probably need a few modifications to the bathroom."

Mike was aware that his father was heavily reliant on a huge freezer in his basement, and losing access to it was like losing his independence. He closed his eyes and tried not to sigh into the phone. This was a complication he did not need.

"I don't know, Dad. I may have to reschedule."

This was met by silence on the other end of the line, a silence that conveyed more than anything else his father could say to him.

He was supposed to fly out tomorrow after work, but the thought of the trip filled him with weariness and dismay. He tried to quash an ember of resentment. The company treated him well, but he did not want to see anyone or go anywhere right now. Unfortunately, there was no one else at the firm who could provide an update to the clients on such short notice.

He normally took the Monday off after these business trips, so that would give him the better part of two days to deal with his father's situation if he arranged to head there immediately after the meeting.

"I'll see what I can do," he said.

He stuck his now-cooled food in the microwave and zapped it long enough for it to reach a reasonable temperature. However, a meal of this type was never quite the same after being microwaved. It seemed as if some food items in the container absorbed more heat than others. What resulted in a satisfactory temperature for one item caused the other selections to be thermonuclear hot.

Mike only managed to eat a small amount of food before he spotted something in his peripheral vision, on the underside of his left shirt cuff. He turned his hand palm up and stared at a drop of blood that had hit his white shirt and then bloomed into a Rorschach-shaped blot. A psychiatrist would have been disappointed in his interpretation since the only image that came to mind was the bloody rock used to commit the crime.

There was no question in his mind that the blood had come from the man in the park. The bullets must have ripped through his chest with such violence that the spray traveled another six feet before landing on his shirt. The idea of the man's blood on him was repulsive, and he stripped off his shirt and threw it in the hamper. Chances were that some of the blood also landed on his jacket and trousers. His suit, shirt, and tie might all have to go, along with the remaining shoe. He could send the items to a laundromat, but they would never be truly clean again.

He returned to his now-cooled food and discovered that he was no longer hungry. The remainder of the meal went into the refrigerator, but it was unlikely he would ever eat it. He grabbed another beer instead.

He then pulled out his personal laptop and doomscrolled through various news stories while he drank, taking in the major headlines of the day but not seeing anything about the murder. There were stories about a coming heatwave, an uptick of violent assaults, a new variant of Texas Boar making its rounds, and a political scandal involving a congressman and a sixteen-year-old girl.

Those stories held no interest for him. What he wanted to find were more details about the man involved, particularly the presumed reason behind the attack. Mike wanted to learn if the man had been suffering from a severe mental illness or was in the throes of a drug-induced psychotic break while in the park. He *needed* for it to be something of this nature. The alternative was just too disturbing. Because if today's attack was due to some garden-variety grievance—like jealousy, or anger over child support payments—then it suggested that any given person was capable of such savagery. He hated to think this was true, but part of him believed that it was possible, that deep inside every person existed the potential to perform horrible acts if sufficiently motivated. What he most desired was an acceptable excuse, something largely beyond the man's control, an explanation that could bring some order back to his world.

The police had been resolutely tight-lipped at the station and would not reveal any details of what they learned, not even the man's name. Perhaps they had learned nothing beyond that; the man was dead after all and might take his secrets to the grave.

Mike was also curious to see if his actions had warranted any mention. But there was no news story yet of him or the crime, which seemed surprising. Perhaps the perpetrator was someone important, and there was an attempt to get the story suppressed. But that could only work for one news cycle. The incident was too big and too gruesome and there were multiple witnesses. A woman was dead, and so was her attacker. Someone was sure to have taken a video recording of the shooting, if not the attack itself. That had happened too quickly.

There were two other stories in the crime section that caught his eye. An eighty-three-year-old woman had attacked fellow passengers on a bus with her cane before being restrained. Several men and one woman needed medical attention.

"She didn't seem angry," one passenger was quoted as saying, "she just stood up and started swinging."

Probably dementia, thought Mike, although something about the incident nagged at him.

The other story was far more violent and considerably more disturbing. A hairdresser had killed a long-time client by stabbing her repeatedly in the face with a pair of scissors. The client had just finished having her hair washed and was seated in a chair when the attack began. Two of the hairstylist's co-workers were also injured as they attempted to intervene. There was no additional information from the police concerning a motive, although Mike intuited that the attack was highly personal. He was no criminologist or psychologist, but he did watch a lot of crime dramas. When investigators found a person who had their face damaged in this way, they almost always suspected an acquaintance, often a boyfriend or a husband. It usually happened during a domestic dispute, especially if there was infidelity involved. There were certainly more efficient ways to kill a person. It was faster and more effective to stab them in the heart or the neck. Stabbing someone in the face, destroying the very thing that made that person unique, was a sign of deep-seated hostility.

This was quite a different circumstance compared to a domestic dispute, of course, an attack in a business setting while surrounded by other staff and their clients. What could have transpired between the two to trigger this type of rage killing? Perhaps the hairdresser suspected the client of cheating on her husband. The attacker had been wounded by the police when she advanced on them with the pair of bloody scissors held in a striking pose above her head. The report indicated that she had been sent for a psychiatric evaluation, and the police had not yet been able to interview her.

That made three attacks by three unlikely assailants, although Mike didn't know enough about the scissor attack to group it with the other two. And really, he could not be sure that the man with the rock and the woman with the child were strangers. There was simply not enough information based on his observations. New York was a big city with a huge population. Incidents of violence happened every hour, around the clock. One could find all sorts of patterns if one looked hard enough.

He checked the news first thing the next morning and saw that not only had additional details been added to the reports of the other attacks, but that the assault at which he had been present was the leading story. The perpetrator had been chief of oncology at Saint Mary's Hospital, just three blocks from the park. It was quite likely that he was now in their morgue. The man's biography, presumably pulled from the hospital's website, indicated that he was married, had three children, and was a member of many philanthropic organizations. He had been educated at Harvard and worked almost the entirety of his career at the hospital. The story also contained the obligatory interviews with his neighbors (impressively fast, thought Mike), who said the usual things.

"He was a great neighbor, and he seemed to love his kids," said Frances Henretti. "I can't believe he would do such a thing."

"He was a quiet guy, never said too much," said another neighbor, who requested anonymity. "It's the quiet types you have to watch out for."

Mike thought that this was an inaccurate assessment, except for serial killers. Most murders were perpetrated by loud and aggressive men who had short tempers and poor impulse control.

There was mention of an unnamed man, him, who had heroically intervened and saved the life of the infant. Mike did not feel like a hero. He had been scared shitless at the time, and his primary act of heroism had been to throw a shoe at the assailant. From the other side of a park bench. He wondered if his shoe would ever be returned to him and, if it were, whether he would want to wear it again.

Although he set his alarm with the intention of going to work, he slept poorly, reliving the event over and over in his mind. When he did finally sleep, his rest was interrupted by dreams in which the man in the park started chasing him. He always felt very slow in dreams, like he was running through water. Perhaps it was because his legs were trapped under the bed sheets, a situation poorly suited for high-speed locomotion.

Mike plucked his phone from its charger and called the Human Resources person at work. It seemed an antiquated way of doing things, but the owners of the firm were in their late sixties and did not approve of texting or email for certain types of correspondence. Mike thought their insistence on using the phone had to do with the psychology involved in person-to-person communication; it was easier to lie via text message.

Every employee was allocated one sick day per month and six personal days per year. In his first two years with the company, Jack didn't take *any* sick days or personal days. Part of the reason was to show that he was a healthy, dedicated, and productive employee and that this would put him in line for a promotion. A secondary but not insignificant consideration was that he rarely felt sick, and the idea of phoning in to provide a fake excuse made him extremely uncomfortable. But then he noted that almost everyone else in the company took these sick days regardless of whether they were sick or whether they needed them for another reason, although personal days were sufficiently vague that almost anything could apply. It amounted to a very substantial eighteen days per year, more than his meager two weeks of vacation.

He tentatively called in sick one day when he was feeling congested. Normally, he would soldier through it, but why risk infecting others? At least that was his rationale for taking the day off. The HR person hadn't blinked an eye (figuratively speaking, since he only talked to her on the phone), and he had thoroughly enjoyed the day. He had gone back to bed, slept late, had a wonderful breakfast, and then just relaxed all day. That had opened the floodgates for him. His previous conscientiousness had not resulted in him getting promoted, and he had foregone thirty-six days off in those first two years. Thirty-six! They did not roll over into the following year and were now gone for good.

He could never bring himself to use the entire allotment, although he had been legitimately sick in April and needed to take three consecutive sick days, the longest stretch he had been ill in his adult life.

The HR person picked up on the second ring.

"Precision Marketing Human Resources, Candace speaking," said Candace.

Jack had never met the woman, but generated a visual image of her, nonetheless. By the sound of her voice, he estimated that she was in her mid-forties, probably with sensibly short hair. In his mind, she was plain, wore glasses, and was losing the battle to keep her weight under control. Human Resources was a desk job and often involved a lot of stress. And people under stress often consume too many carbohydrates. She likely had a pet as well, for stress relief, and it would probably be a cat based on her hours. There would be at least one picture of said cat (or cats) in her workspace. He would have to drop by her office sometime to assess the accuracy of his predictions.

"Hi Candace, it's Mike Richards from Digital. I won't be coming in today."

He was not obliged to provide a reason, but he thought he might be able to finagle an extra day off from work that was not classified as a sick day, personal day, or vacation. It could exist in some netherland, where good deeds were sometimes rewarded.

"You may have heard on the news about the murder in Central Park, by The Lake?"

"Yes," she said cautiously, as if wary of hearing details that would make her life more complicated.

"There was a man who intervened to save the woman's baby. Well, that was me."

He had to admit, the composition and delivery of his story was pretty shitty for a guy who considered himself a professional marketing executive. He was assuming she knew the details, but many people never read through an entire news article. They sometimes read only the title and the subtitle. "Rampage in Central Park." "Prominent Doctor Alleged Killer." Or she could have read something equally abbreviated on Twitter. He refused to call it X.

"*You* were the guy who threw his shoe at the murderer?"

It sounded a lot less impressive when stated like that, but he heard a tone of respect in her voice. He hoped this little tidbit of information would find its way into the ears of the higher-ups at the company and contribute in some way to his advancement or, at the very least, get him an extra day off.

"Yes, that was me. I still don't have the shoe back." He tried to inject some humor into the statement, but there was nothing funny about what had happened in the park, and his voice reflected that.

"It must have been so frightening," said Candace. "Are you okay?"

She sounded generally worried about his well-being, the first person who really cared. The police had wanted information and his impressions regarding the attacker, but they had never once asked if he was okay. From their perspective, the absence of blood, or something equally obvious, was a sufficient assessment of his health. Her simple statement, that note of concern in her voice, triggered something in him. He started to shake and had a hard time formulating a reply. What followed was an uncomfortably long pause, but he waited until he could trust his voice not to break.

"I'll be fine," he said.

Sometimes the deepest wounds don't show at all.

CHAPTER 3

Bates Memorial Hospital

Nurse Jackie Winters was just one hour away from finishing her shift in the Acute Care ward when the biter arrived. He was being escorted by two policemen who seemed larger than life, inflated by their gear and tactical vests. Jackie had a nervous reaction to policemen, regardless of whether she was driving, working, or taking a walk along the street. She was generally a law-abiding citizen, but she did speed, was known to imbibe in the occasional joint, and had downloaded a pirated version of Game of Thrones. These were all minor offenses, but she still had an ongoing fear that the authorities would catch up to her someday, with their heavy fists banging on the door.

However, she had seen these officers before, so that tended to lessen her concern. The man they were escorting was casually dressed in black skinny jeans and a light blue golf shirt, untucked. The shirt was not in great shape. There were dribbles of what appeared to be blood all the way down the front. A reddish smear also marred one of his cheeks. He appeared to be about twenty-one, perhaps a university student. His face was completely devoid of any expression, and she wondered if he was under the influence of a drug, perhaps an antipsychotic. Those medications tended to blunt emotions.

The demeanor and actions of the officers stood in stark contrast to the placid man they were marching toward her. Even though the man's wrists were handcuffed behind his back, the officers walked slightly behind him and to the side and held his arms up at almost shoulder height, a position used to ensure compliance and control. She was sure it was quite painful, although this was not reflected in the young man's face. The cops were edgy and alert, the same way they acted when bringing in a violent meth head. But this kid looked utterly unremarkable, a sophomore student who perhaps had too much to drink. It could be her little brother.

"Guys, is this really necessary?" she asked.

Although she knew this question would antagonize the policemen, who hated to be told what to do or be criticized for their methods, she saw it as her obligation to call out any behavior she considered abuse. Although too simplistic for all situations, the term "silence is compliance" seemed to fit this scenario.

The first officer practically rolled his eyes at her, surely assigning to her a bleeding-heart-liberal designation. Which, to be honest, was not entirely inaccurate.

"Yes," he said. "It is. The guy's a biter."

"So, that blood..." she trailed off.

"It ain't his," the second officer said. The identification plate pinned to his shirt indicated that his name was Campbell. "We pulled him off some woman at the grocery store. Practically chewed her face off, like something a chimpanzee would do. She's probably already in surgery. Not here, though."

Jackie wasn't offended. There were better hospitals for that, and she knew it. Her gaze returned to the man. It was hard to reconcile the description of the assault with this seemingly passive individual.

"Bath salts?" she speculated, using the term commonly associated with synthetic cathinones. The drug had emerged in the United States in the late 90s and was infamously linked to gruesome assaults, some involving cannibalism. She hadn't heard any stories about them recently, but that did not mean they had disappeared from the scene.

"Doesn't seem like it. He's not agitated, he's just homicidal."

"Why are you bringing him here then? He should be in the Psych ward."

"Because we shot him, not that you can tell by the way he is acting. Hit him in the calf."

The black jeans had obscured the fact that he was bleeding, or had bled, into the fabric. But when she glanced down the corridor behind them, she could see a bloody heel print every four feet or so. She would need to call someone to clean that up.

"Okay, bring him into examination room three." She pointed toward a door midway down the corridor.

The officers began directing their prisoner along the hall, but had been lulled into complacency by the man's continued submission. As he passed by Jackie, he suddenly lunged forward and attempted to bite her on the face.

"Jesus Christ!" she shouted.

His teeth clacked together so hard and so close to her face that she felt the vibrations in her cheeks. His breath was rank, like spoiled meat, and her mind rebelled against the understanding of why that smell existed in his mouth.

Something is caught in his teeth, her mind suggested, and she thought she might be sick. She had seen a lot of terrible things in her career as a nurse, but there were still some sights and smells that could push her over the edge.

The officers responded to the attempted assault by simultaneously pulling the man toward them and pushing his arms up even higher, surely to the point where his muscles would begin to tear.

Jackie was somewhat less sympathetic to the man after the near miss, but she soon regained her professionalism.

"Bring a set of restraints to exam room three," she told an orderly.

The orderly was a new hire, inexperienced, and he was making a futile effort to blend into the wall.

"Which ones?"

"All of them, chest, wrists, and ankles."

"Don't you guys have a spit hood?" asked the burliest of the two cops. His name was Kiely.

"We don't use those here. And before you ask, the mask they used on Hannibal Lector doesn't exist either."

She made her way over to the nurses' station and had the attendant page a doctor. Jackie wanted this man out of the hospital as soon as possible, even if that meant giving him priority over some other patients.

By the time she got to the examination room, the orderly and the officers had the man seated and were working on getting the restraint around his chest. It was tricky due to the necessity of staying away from those teeth. That was going to be a challenge in a room this small. It was already feeling crowded with five people, and the doctor had yet to arrive. There was an examination table, but the orderly placed the man in a straight-backed chair, apparently considering it a superior option for attaching the restraints.

The room had multiple cabinets and shelves containing medical supplies, and Jackie quickly gathered all the items she knew the doctor would require. She would be there to assist, and she located scissors to cut off the man's pants and disinfectant to cleanse the wound. The pants would have been cut off regardless of the man's mental state, since dragging tight jeans over an already damaged leg was simply not good practice. For the doctor, she gathered gauze, forceps, tape, sutures, needles, and a scalpel, in case the doctor needed to cut away non-viable tissue.

All of the items were placed on a tray next to the patient. One officer held the man's arms behind his back while the orderly affixed straps to the man's ankles.

Dr. Indiri Gishar arrived just as that task was complete. He was a small man of about fifty-five with salt and pepper hair and wire-rimmed glasses. It was close to the end of his twelve-hour shift, and he appeared to be tired and even more rumpled than usual.

Jackie nodded for the orderly to leave.

"Dr. Gishar, this man has a gunshot wound to his left calf. He has demonstrated violent behavior, so it was necessary to restrain him. I believe the wound is superficial, although I haven't had a chance to do a proper examination."

The doctor sat on a small stool and then stared at the tray containing the medical supplies as Jackie spoke, not even acknowledging her or the four other people in the room, including the patient. The two policemen shared a glance, perhaps just a little put off at being so obviously dismissed. Jackie was surprised as well, since Dr. Gishar tended to be one of the more amiable physicians on staff, always greeting patients and nurses with a ready smile.

He continued to stare at the tray after Jackie finished speaking. An uncomfortable thirty seconds passed, feeling more like five minutes in the cramped room. One of the officers shifted his weight, no doubt restless to get the job done and get the prisoner into lockup.

Jackie hated to push the doctor before he was ready to act, but the atmosphere in the room was growing increasingly awkward.

"Dr. Gishar? Is there anything else you need?"

She wasn't sure at first if he heard her, but he reached over and picked up the scalpel. It was not the appropriate tool with which to cut open the man's pants, and she decided to be pre-emptive and squatted down with the scissors to assist.

At the same moment she squatted, Dr. Gishar stood, scalpel in hand. His face was blank, but he was now looking at the officers. With one deft swipe, he cut the carotid artery of the policeman closest to him, Officer Kiely. Blood sprayed cartoonishly, like a special effect exaggerated for laughs. The other officer hesitated a moment as if deciding whether he was the victim of an elaborate and grotesque practical joke.

Jackie knew it was not. As soon as she saw the jet of arterial blood, her brain immediately went into assessment mode. Even under ideal circumstances, a clean cut was often fatal, as the victim usually bled out before the hemorrhaging could be stopped. These were not ideal circumstances. Even as she processed the officer's likelihood of survival, Officer Campbell drew his weapon. It was a challenge within the tight confines of the room, and he stepped back, slipping slightly on the blood pooling on the floor. There was a shocking amount of it. A large man like Officer Kiely could hold six liters of blood in his body—and fully half of that seemed to be on the floor already. They would soon be sloshing around in it.

The doctor slashed at Campbell's wrist, severing several of the tendons. The gun clattered to the floor. Jackie could not help but notice that even in the midst of this savage attack, Dr. Gishar was using his knowledge of anatomy to inflict debilitating damage. He kept up his assault, slashing at the officer's face and hands and any other part of the man's body that was unprotected.

Jackie looked at the scissors in her hand, blunt-nosed and short-bladed, practically the antithesis of a weapon. They were *designed* not to puncture flesh. She looked for an acceptable alternative among the medical supplies, but the obvious choice was the officer's pistol. It was practically at her feet, sitting in a massive pool of blood. She set the scissors down, squatted, and picked up the pistol, which she believed was a Glock. The blood on the grip was still warm, and heavy red drops fell from the barrel as she lifted the weapon.

Jackie hesitated before firing, but only partly out of reluctance to shoot Dr. Gishar. The doctor was a slight man, and his back was practically at point-blank range to the pistol in her outstretched hand. She feared the bullet could pass straight through the thin doctor's body and strike the officer on the other side. She stepped slightly to the left, adjusted her aim, and fired. It was not something she wished to do, but it was necessary, like excising a tumor.

The shot was shockingly loud in the room, and her eardrums felt assaulted by the sonic wave. Dr. Gishar lurched forward as if hit by hurricane-force winds and fell to the floor, directly into the pool of blood.

Officer Campbell had his hands over his face as if trying to keep the flesh in place. It probably wasn't that far off the mark. Blood streamed out through his fingers, and it was quite possible he would lose his left eye.

Jackie spared a glance at the prisoner. His expression was still as serene as before, and she wondered if he was aware of what was happening.

The gun was still in her hand, sticky with blood. Instead of handing it to the officer, who was using his one good hand on his face, she deposited it in a locked cabinet away from the seated man.

The room was a scene of carnage. Two men dead, one grievously injured, one lightly injured. The air was heavy with the smell of cordite, blood, copper, and salt. It was almost too much for her brain to process.

"I'll get some help," she said.

Officer Campbell only moaned in response, the sound burbling out from between his fingers.

Her hand was shaking as she reached for the doorknob. It had not occurred to her until that moment that no one had come to see what was happening. There had been shouting and screaming and a gunshot. Of course, that last part may have prevented anyone from blindly rushing in. And although the attack seemed to go on and on, it was quite likely that the entire sequence of events took less than a minute — an eternity for those inside the room but not enough time for those in the hallway outside to get themselves organized.

She pulled open the door. Two nurses cowered away, one of them talking quickly and urgently into a cell phone. The other nurse let out an alarmed cry.

One of the women, a new girl named Serena, said, "Jackie?" The girl's eyes flicked down to Jackie's light-colored scrubs and then back up to her eyes.

Jackie looked down at herself and realized that she had caught a substantial amount of spray from Officer Campbell's carotid artery.

"Issue a Code Blue. And call 911."

A Code Blue indicated an emergency medical situation. That designation did not seem sufficient for the circumstances, but that was all they had.

"Serena, come help me. We have a couple of injured men in here."

Serena was extremely agitated, bouncing on the balls of her feet, looking like she would prefer to flee down the corridor instead. Jackie kept her voice both calm and assertive.

"I need your help *now*," she said.

Serena dropped her heels to the floor, took a moment to compose herself, and then followed Jackie into the examination room.

CHAPTER 4

Mike did not make a final decision regarding his flight to Georgia until almost three in the afternoon. He hated to fly, and the presentation he was scheduled to deliver to the clients was practically an anachronism. His role at the company was to create digital marketing; that was the entirety of his work. *Digital.* Meaning that everything that was to be viewed by the consumer would be seen through a screen. If ever there was a meeting ready-made for Zoom, this was it. But no, he was flying seven hundred miles to stand next to the company's clients so they could look at the screen together. Hopefully, he would get their approval. The absurdity of it made him want to scream.

Taking the morning off work had been a smart decision. He felt much better, almost completely rejuvenated. He went back to bed, slept until almost eleven, and then cooked up a huge breakfast. The television was on while he prepared and consumed his meal, but he intentionally selected a channel that was solely dedicated to classic movies. He studiously avoided watching the news and tried not to let his eyes drop to the constantly scrolling chyron at the bottom of the screen, with its litany of horror stories. He had lived it, he did not need to read about it or any of the other tragic events happening in the city.

Ultimately, he decided that getting out of town would do him good. Yesterday had been a deeply disturbing experience, even for a jaded New Yorker. The flight would be a welcome distraction, although it was unfortunate that Savanna was the destination. He had been there in July once before, and it was so hot and humid that he felt like he was drowning. Plus, there was the smell, like a bog full of dead flowers. He was not there to sightsee, however, so he didn't think he would have to spend much time outside.

The business trips always followed a familiar format: he arrived at his destination the day before, spent the night in a mid-level hotel, caught a cab to the client's office building in the morning, performed the presentation, had a working lunch to discuss any issues, made adjustments as needed, and then took the clients out for drinks. He always woke up the next morning feeling like hell, and then he flew home.

He was going to have to visit his father anyway, so he might as well have the company pay for the trip. The flight would get him ninety percent of the way there, and it was difficult to pass up the opportunity. His plan was to rent a car and drive the remaining distance on Sunday morning.

His father's house, which was really more like a cabin, was located in the southern part of the state of Georgia on the fringes of a wilderness reserve. It was a remote area, just twenty-five miles short of the border with Florida, and his dad lived there by choice, adopting a *no neighbors are good neighbors* philosophy.

Mike estimated he could drive there in less than three hours if he pushed it. He planned to push it. The sooner he got there and got his father sorted, the sooner he could get back.

The Uber driver who took him to the airport the next morning was an older man, a retiree, who talked non-stop about how the city used to be. Mike thought it a peculiarity of age that allowed a person to selectively filter all the negatives from the past, like the coffee grounds you didn't want to find at the bottom of your mug. What they were left with was a sanitized version of the past, where there was little crime, everyone had a job, you could buy a house for thirty thousand dollars, and people picked up after themselves. There was often a subtext of racism and anti-immigration woven into the story, convenient scapegoats for a bucolic past that never really existed.

Mike tuned it all out, focused on rehearsing the presentation he was to give. He eventually stuck in a pair of earbuds, a tacit symbol that he was no longer interested in what the driver had to say. He did not see the random acts of violence on the streets, or hear the cacophony of sirens, or acknowledge that something was more than a little off in New York.

The driver noticed but was too bewildered by what he was seeing to mention it. It was so prevalent and so widespread that it didn't seem entirely real; it was like a staged performance on a blocks-long movie set. He began to wonder if he missed the memo.

By the time he thought to mention it to his passenger, they were on the highway.

"Did you see all those people fighting back there?" he said. He was immediately annoyed by the *way* he asked it, with a *did I really see that* tone in his voice. He was already doubting the validity of his own recollections. The violent incidents had gone on for *blocks*, making it improbable that it was related to a single argument. And there was no consistency to it; there were blacks fighting other blacks, whites against whites, women fighting with other women, and every other possible combination.

The driver looked in the rear-view mirror, but his passenger hadn't even raised his head. *Typical New Yorker*, he thought, so consumed with his own concerns that he didn't pay any attention to the world around him.

His passenger just grunted a negative, his eyes glued to the screen of his tablet.

They arrived at the terminal ten minutes later. Mike rushed to get his bags and then darted toward the check-in. He always traveled light, wearing the suit he would use during the presentation and packing a more casual outfit for the evening activities. His case held little else besides toiletries and fresh underwear, and socks. The tablet doubled as an e-reader if he had any trouble sleeping, although this was uncommon after a booze-soaked evening.

This was only his second flight since the pandemic. The first excursion, an ill-advised trip to Toronto, had left him traumatized. Medical-grade masks were still required at the time, and due to a mechanical issue, the passengers had been left sitting on a hot, airless plane for hours before take-off. He did not do well in hot, enclosed environments and was practically out of his mind with discomfort by the time they departed. That episode had cured him of any further desire to travel for leisure during the intervening period.

The mandatory mask directives had since been lifted, but Stop the Spread posters and decals were still ubiquitous in stores, restaurants, and at this airport. There were various iterations of the messaging: Only YOU Can Stop The Spread, and VHP-25 Does Not Have Legs, accompanied by a cartoon image of a toothy virus hitching a ride on a clueless teenage. He thought the second one was a weak and confusing entry, but he guessed it meant that the virus couldn't get around on its own, that it needed help from its human carriers.

Some people still got mildly ill from Texas Boar, and most accepted this as a part of life. They considered it a fair compromise against the need to wear a mask for the rest of their lives. It was amazing how quickly things changed after they introduced the new vaccine. It was so effective that people forgot just how afraid they had been. Mike himself had stood in line at 4 a.m. one morning to get his shot. Those days now seemed like a distant memory.

He processed his boarding documents through an automated self-service machine and made his way to the screening area. Just before he arrived, two uniformed police officers ran by him at full pace, their faces red from exertion.

Seeing this caused his anxiety to tick up a notch, not because he was a nervous flier but because any delay could disrupt his itinerary. A serious incident that sparked a mandatory evacuation of the terminal would be the worst outcome since it would require everyone to renegotiate the screening area.

He turned to look down the long concourse but could not see any disturbances. There was an unsettling sound that reached him, something shrill, but he may have conjured that in his imagination, fostered by the crowded and noisy terminal.

After he suffered through the indignity of being patted down after removing his shoes and belt, like a potential suicide risk, he sat in the departures lounge. Being processed like that through security always made him consider ways to defeat the system. Not that he would ever want to, of course, but he was a creative person who was accustomed to problem-solving. The security measures were put out there like a challenge, and he was sure that some people spent a lot of time thinking about how to bring drugs onboard or even a bottle of sunscreen that exceeded the acceptable limit.

Things were different now when passing through the security checkpoint; it was mostly perfunctory, a bored routine. Although he had been a child when the 9/11 attacks occurred, he still remembered watching footage of the burning buildings after his school closed early that day. His family had taken a flight on Thanksgiving weekend that year and the level of scrutiny at the airport had verged on the ridiculous. People had their safety pins confiscated. Safety pins, of all things.

Mike visualized an agitated man shouting threats and brandishing a safety pin as a weapon in the weeks after 9/11. The guy would be lucky to escape with his life. Passengers would no longer sit quietly by and let something like that happen again.

He wiled away the time thinking about how he could obscure the shape of a weapon or conceal it in such a way as to make it seem innocuous. It would be an attractive occupation, if that type of job existed, to test the efficiency of airport security measures.

His flight was called five minutes later, Flight 206, and he left his hijacking ruminations behind. It was time to join the herd at the boarding gate.

The flight was full, and the office had not sprung for Business Class since the flight was less than a thousand miles, and the flight time was less than two and a half hours. The bean counters assumed that he could tolerate Economy for a brief period without damage to his mental health. Had they not flown recently? Economy Class was like taking the transit bus through the bad part of town. Mike was no snob, but the cheap seats on the plane were commonly filled with half-drunk rowdies with bad attitudes and little self-control.

Things had gotten worse since the pandemic, after the mandatory mask orders. Although masks were no longer required, it appeared that their introduction and the subsequent pushback against their use had changed the dynamic between passengers and flight attendants. In the past, passengers generally complied with commands to raise their seats to the upright position, buckle their seat belts, reset their tray tables, remove their headphones, and turn off their phones. Some travelers did it grudgingly, complaining under their breath, but it was a token resistance.

The masks had changed the game, however. Some passengers outright refused to comply with the request —the demand— to place the mask properly over their face. The rejection of this command was for a myriad of reasons, mostly invalid, but it created a new paradigm where an instruction from a flight attendant, any instruction, was often now treated as a suggestion rather than an inviolate rule. The flight attendants' role as enforcers of an unpopular regulation had the contrary effect of reducing their position of authority. They were now regarded in the same light as some people viewed police — as a force to be resisted at every turn. This did not often end well for the passengers, but the disrespect continued regardless, frequently resulting in confrontations that became violent.

These incidents were not solely restricted to economy class —people in Business Class could be contrarians as well— but it was certainly less common. Many of those traveling in Business Class were doing so on the company's dime, so they had to be somewhat more circumspect in their behavior.

Mike considered himself reasonably fortunate as he was seated on the aisle and had as his seatmates a young couple who appeared to be university students. They buckled their seat belts immediately upon sitting down, even before receiving instructions to do so. The girl, about twenty, pulled a heavy textbook from her bag and began to read it. The boy, about the same age, stuck earbuds into his ears and sat back with his eyes closed.

Mike glanced around to see if there were any troublesome passengers, but everyone seemed to be getting into their seats with a minimum of fuss.

Ten minutes later the seatbelt sign blinked on, and the captain introduced the flight crew. Mike always felt sorry for the attendants as they performed their obligatory safety demonstration, largely ignored, and he feigned giving them at least some of his attention. Most of the other passengers were either covertly examining their phones or had their eyes closed in anticipation of sleeping while in flight.

The trouble started quite abruptly about thirty minutes after take-off. Mike had tired of reviewing his presentation and was scrolling through the selection of movies available on the seatback entertainment console. There were several new movie releases, and he was in the process of calculating whether he had enough time to watch one when he heard a commotion coming from behind him. The rapid escalation of the incident was startling. It went from being almost serenely quiet in the cabin to complete pandemonium in a matter of seconds.

Someone shouted, "What the fuck?"

People also shouted versions of "Stop." "What are you doing?" and "Help!" in frantic and panicked voices.

Mike stood and turned in a crouch, with one leg in the aisle, and his head bumping up against the overhead compartment. However, he could not immediately see what was happening since a few other passengers were standing in the aisle and blocking his view. A flight attendant with a cart full of drinks and food was also between him and whatever was unfolding at the back of the plane.

Amidst all the shouting, a woman screamed, fear mingled with horror.

The flight attendant had to reverse her cart before she and her fellow crew members could make their way up the aisle to the incident. Mike pulled on the cart as it reached him, trying to speed up its passage.

There was an ebb and flow of people between him and the epicenter of the incident, and it broke just long enough for him to see two things. One was the battered head of a man, seated next to the window. There was not a spot on his head that was not covered in blood, and he appeared to be unconscious or dead. The second thing he saw was a fat man, apparently the victim's seatmate, wielding a laptop like a cudgel. Even as Mike watched, he drew back and smashed the sharp edge of the closed laptop against the man's forehead.

Mike's first thought was: someone needs to stop that guy. His second thought was: how can this be happening around me twice in two days?

He did not plan to intervene this time. In fact, it would be a challenge to get anywhere close to the assailant, considering the number of people between him and the site of the assault, but he felt compelled to at least bear witness to what was happening.

"What's going on?" asked the young woman in the window seat. She had twisted around and tried to see, but she couldn't stand up fully, and her view was completely blocked.

"Two men got into a fight," he said, deliberately downplaying the severity of the attack.

The girl was pretty and blond and gave him a nervous smile, the kind of reflexive smile one gives in response to a threat.

A number of passengers had pulled out their cellphones and were capturing the moment for posterity, an ugly incident that would live on through time on obscure websites. Mike believed the footage was likely too graphic to sell to the major networks, or even to play on YouTube for that matter. Perhaps they were capturing it simply because they were in the habit of documenting their lives online. The number of views and likes they received validated their existence. Mike was a child of the Internet and had never known a time when it did not exist. But social media was a newer phenomenon, and it had the ability to elevate average people to a level of visibility and fame that was once reserved solely for movie stars, singers, and politicians. It was a strange development. How did people judge their popularity before social media? He honestly couldn't remember.

Several men who were larger and braver than the rest emerged to restrain the laptop-wielding assailant. It should not have taken so long, but like the incident in the park, everyone waited for someone else to make the first move. And then there was the blood, of course; there was no way to avoid it. Many people were justifiably reluctant to expose themselves to potential pathogens.

Mike watched for several minutes as the men secured the assailant to his seat with a combination of luggage straps, duct tape, and lanyards. Mike could see a small rectangle of plastic attached to one of the lanyards, presumably identifying the wearer as an employee or as a participant at a conference.

The amount of bondage applied to the attacker was bordering on overkill, but Mike could hardly blame them. They were in the mix of it. He would likely do the same thing if he were located in any of the seats in close proximity. The man would have to be cut out of all those restraints once the police arrived on board, a process that could be lengthy. Mike groaned, regretting his decision to take this flight for a business meeting that he might need to cancel after all.

Although he appeared calm on the outside, his adrenaline surged with the first cry of alarm and had not dissipated even though the situation appeared to be well in hand. He was practically jumping out of his skin, and he decided he needed to move, even if it was just for an unnecessary trip to the toilet. Surprisingly, no announcement had yet been made by the captain, and there were no instructions for the passengers to remain in their seats. Perhaps the captain was still being briefed.

Mike threaded his way past a number of men and a few women who were standing in the aisle, either gawking at the man in restraints, taking videos, or wondering if they should make a show of offering assistance now that the real threat had passed.

The toilet was blessedly empty, and he closed and locked the door, relishing a moment of solitude. He stood with his hands on the little counter that housed the miniature sink. The temperature was always a little cooler inside these tiny washrooms, verging on uncomfortable. Perhaps it was to discourage loitering.

Either the light was poor in the room, or he looked terrible. He pressed the tap, scooped up some lukewarm water, and splashed it over his face, attempting to reboot his system to a lower stress level, perhaps to Defcon Three. He let out a long breath and used a paper towel to dry his face. His heart rate slowed, and he started to feel better, not yet calm by any stretch of the imagination, but his nerves had settled. There was an hour and a half left of the flight, and he sincerely hoped the attendants would come by and offer a drink. Maybe two. Unfortunately, considering the circumstances, he felt that this was quite unlikely.

He deposited the paper towel in the waste disposal slot and then reached for the latch to disengage the lock. At that moment, through the door, he heard a very unwelcome sound. It was a shrill scream, very close, an outpouring of pure terror.

CHAPTER 5

Bates Memorial Hospital

By the time Jackie attended to the two injured men and gave her statement to the police, she was practically catatonic with fatigue. It was not just a matter of the twenty hours she had been awake, but the adrenalin surges and roiling emotions that accompanied the timespan.

Her shift had ended four hours earlier, and she still hadn't managed to leave the building. Not only was she the sole available witness to the murder and aggravated assault on two police officers, but she was also the person responsible for the death of a beloved surgeon. That was how she viewed it. It could hardly be deemed self-defence since the doctor had his back turned to her when she shot him.

The police, of course, didn't see it that way and heralded her actions. They seemed determined to finesse her story in the best possible way for her to avoid any possible repercussions. It never even occurred to her that anyone could or would consider her actions as anything other than what was necessary for the given situation. But Dr. Gishar was married, and there was always the possibility that some ambulance-chasing lawyer would suggest that she should have attempted a non-lethal intervention first and sue her on behalf of the widow.

"We just want to ensure that a tragedy of this type never has to happen again," was the usual refrain. Nothing about money, nope; it was always about the protection of society or the vulnerable. However, the chances of something like this happening again in this type of circumstance seemed vanishingly remote. Nevertheless, the police crafted the narrative that she would repeat in her formal statement, one that would show that she had pursued the only viable course of action, a judgment call that saved the life of both her and the gravely injured officer.

She was currently in the nurse's lounge, mentally readying herself for the journey back to her apartment all the way across town. She normally took a series of trains, but it was almost beyond what she could face. Perhaps she should call a cab, or an Uber. It would be ridiculously expensive, but on this occasion, it would be worth every penny. She could regret it later.

Jackie was saving for a house out in the suburbs, and although she made good money, it was difficult to save as much as she hoped. She was doing it on her own and rent within the city was astronomical. She was not *intentionally* single, but sometimes it just worked out that way. Finding a good partner was tough, and she was a little picky. Her girlfriends told her that she was in a prime position to pick up an eligible young doctor, but doctors didn't often go for nurses, as a rule. Perhaps it was too much like taking their job home with them.

Jackie swapped her blood-spattered scrubs for street clothes but did not have a spare set of footwear. There was a rim of blackening blood around the white foam midsoles of her running shoes, like the high-water mark after a flood. There would be much more blood trapped within the treads on the bottom. She did not want to put them in her locker, and she certainly didn't want to wear them in an Uber. She took one last look at them and then stuffed them into a garbage can.

Many of the nurses left their outside shoes on a mat by the door, and she sorted through the selection, trying to find a pair in her size. She hoped that whoever was missing their footwear at the end of the shift would be forgiving.

She was just tying the laces on a pair of Nikes when one of the newer nurses at the hospital came skittering in through the door, practically sprinting. The nurse, Cara? Sarah? *Carrie*, that was it, slammed the door shut behind her and locked it with the deadbolt. She leaned against the door, breathing rapidly.

Jackie watched her in astonishment.

"What are—" she started, but Carrie waved her to be quiet.

"Something is happening," she said, in an urgent whisper. Her blond hair was pulled back into a haphazard ponytail, with errant strands now framing her face.

"What do you mean?" asked Jackie. She said this in a whisper as well, although she had no idea why she was whispering.

"Something. Is. Happening," Carrie repeated, emphasizing each word.

Someone rattled the doorknob. They both turned and stared at it. Jackie waited for the person to knock or to ask that the door be opened, but there was just silence. The knob was rattled again, aggressively. Jackie met Carrie's eyes, and Carrie just shook her head.

Jackie slowly knelt and looked under the door. She could see the bottom of a pair of running shoes, the kind that were commonly worn by the nursing staff. Although the door was thick, the sound of distant gunfire reached her. The shoes hurried away in the direction of the shots.

Carrie turned her head as she tracked the receding steps, as if she could see through the wall. She waited for a few more moments and then seemed satisfied that the person was gone.

She took a deep breath before recounting her tale.

"People started going crazy. It was busier than usual in the ER, especially for a Thursday. We were already getting a ton of people coming in with injuries, the type of injuries you get from assaults or fighting. Blunt force trauma, knife wounds, bullet wounds, bites. We were overwhelmed. And then all of a sudden it just started. There were people attacking other people right in the ER, random people. One of the first to start it was a guy waiting for his wife. He had been sitting there by himself for an hour, and then he got up and smashed some woman on the side of the head with a chair. The woman was in for a badly sprained ankle. As far as I could tell, there had been no interaction between them prior to the attack. Luckily, there were still some cops around after everything that went down up here."

Carrie was considerate enough not to mention the specifics, like the fact that Jackie had *killed* someone.

"That was the first. Then it was an *orderly* attacking a *patient*. There was no reason for it that I could see. I mean, how could there be? The guy was on a stretcher! Came in from a car accident." She hung her head and put her hands over her face. "The hospital is going to get sued out of existence."

She seemed to realize that that sounded uncaring (it did) and then added, "The patient is alright. There were a couple of family members there and they took the orderly down pretty quick."

"So why did you leave? It sounds like everything was getting back under control."

"Those were just the first. There were at least two more attacks after that, probably more. I heard screaming coming from another wing, and I just ran."

"You abandoned your patients." Jackie said this as a statement, but there was more than a hint of reproach in her voice.

"You don't understand. Something is *happening*."

"What do you think it is then? A toxin? Drugs? Multiple people don't go crazy on their own."

"Well, *going crazy* was the wrong way to describe it. They weren't out of their minds; in fact, they were very deliberate. What they were *doing* was crazy, but they seemed emotionless, vacant. They didn't appear to be angry, they just wanted to hurt people as bad as they could, kill them."

Jackie thought about this for a moment, shocked at how closely it reflected what she had seen with Dr. Gishar. Cold indifference but with a purpose. His use of the scalpel. How could there possibly be a connection between all these people? Their demeanor and behavior were strikingly and terrifyingly consistent. She had done a stint as a psychiatric nurse at a hospital upstate and knew that the combination of flat affect, formed intent, and extremely violent behavior was very, very rare. The individuals here were all acting, to some extent, like people with psychopathy— except people with psychopathic tendencies usually tried to conceal the worst of their behavior.

She was still convinced that it had to be a drug or toxin of some type. "Did you notice if they were drinking out of the same water fountain or getting food or beverages from a vending machine?"

Carrie shook her head. "Those are still shut down from the pandemic, remember? Besides, I was getting water from the taps during the entire shift, to make coffee or just to fill my bottle."

"It could be that whatever is affecting these people only acts on certain individuals," Jackie suggested.

Carrie shrugged. "Well, there will be plenty of blood samples to check once things get back to normal."

Jackie listened at the door. "I don't hear anything. And I really want to get out of this building and go home."

She was motivated to leave for several reasons. She was exhausted, she believed the hospital could become even more dangerous over time, and last but not least, she had a hungry cat at home. The cat could make it another eight hours on its own, but she needed to rationalize her decision.

"Leave? Are you insane? We are better off right here. There could be any number of crazies roaming the halls looking for people to kill."

"That's—" She was going to say *ridiculous,* but realized that it wasn't ridiculous at all. "I'll call 911. We'll get an escort."

But the call to 911 did not go through. An automated voice stated that all the lines were busy and to wait for the next available operator. Jackie looked at her phone in disbelief. She didn't think that the inability to get through to 911 was a real thing, just a dramatic device used in movies to create tension. She held the phone away from her ear to let Carrie hear the recording.

"So, I guess we're staying here," Jackie said.

There was food in the refrigerator, water, and a toilet— all they needed for a lockdown situation. Jackie had just lain down on one of the two sofas when something occurred to her. She sat up again and turned to Carrie.

"Most of the supervisory nurses have keys. Plus, the janitorial staff. Maintenance and security as well."

"So?"

"So, the people experiencing this… *syndrome* are not running around like zombies. It's hard to tell for sure, but they seem to retain their ability to think and make decisions. And if they can think, they can certainly use keys to enter a locked room where there are people to kill. We are not safe in here."

"Damn. You're right."

"Look, we're only thirty feet away from the stairwell. From there, we can walk all the way to the bottom and exit into the parking garage."

The parking garage was a four-story structure attached to the hospital. Once they reached it, they could take two different exits, one to the east or one to the west. Both emptied onto wide, well-traveled streets.

Carrie chewed her lip, clearly conflicted about leaving the relative safety of the room but also recognizing that this safety could well be an illusion.

"Okay. Let's go." She grabbed Jackie's arm and looked her in the eye. "We need to run when we get outside."

They both listened at the door but could hear nothing. Jackie turned the deadbolt, opened the door, and looked both ways. The hallway appeared to be empty.

"Go, go!" implored Carrie, practically pushing her out of the room.

They were only three steps from the stairway door when Jackie sensed someone behind them, maybe from a scuff of a shoe on the tile floor. She dared a quick glance behind her.

"Oh, thank God," she said.

Carrie stopped walking when she heard Jackie speak, and they both turned and watched as a uniformed police officer made his way up the hallway toward them.

Jackie called out to him. "We've been trying to find a safe place. Can you tell us what is happening?"

The officer abruptly stopped walking, unholstered his weapon, and held it in front of him in a shooting stance.

Jackie was alarmed and wheeled around to see who he was targeting behind them. She had not heard anyone approach.

The corridor was empty. As she turned back, the officer fired his weapon and shot Carrie in the head.

CHAPTER 6

Flight 206

The woman's scream was somewhat muffled by the toilet door, but it clearly came from the opposite direction to where Mike had been seated. His first thought was that the fat man had escaped his restraints, made his way up the corridor, and was now in the process of assaulting someone else. But that was ridiculous. Not only was the man bound up so tightly that it would require multiple people to free him, but there were also many capable men who could stop him before he got far. No, this was something else, something he was not keen to see or experience, but he couldn't very well stay in the toilet for the remainder of the flight.

He unlocked the door and pushed it open, looking first to his left, toward the man who had been restrained earlier. As Mike expected, he was still in the same location. When he turned his head to the right, he saw that there was already a huddle of people standing in the aisle next to a row of seats. Despite this, he had a clear view of what was happening. A woman with long red hair had both hands pressed against her face, and there was blood streaming between her fingers. A girl who appeared to be no older than twelve clutched a bloody pencil in her fist and was being restrained by several men and a female flight attendant. The girl also had red hair and was almost certainly the woman's daughter. The flight attendant was holding the girl's wrist so tightly that her fingers were white from the tension. The woman's face displayed a teeth-baring grimace, as if she were in a fight for her life. Perhaps she was. Mike predicted that the attendant was likely doomed to a lifetime of PTSD and visits to a psychologist.

Mike really wanted off this plane, by parachute if necessary. *What the actual fuck?* This made *three* instances of extreme violence that he had witnessed in less than forty-eight hours. There was nothing for him to contribute to the current situation, so he made his way back to his seat, ignoring the questions asked by anxious passengers. It was not his role to supply answers or provide reassurance, and there was little reassurance he could give.

Finally, finally, the captain broke his silence and made an announcement. Passengers turned their faces up to the speakers with a much greater level of attention than they had greeted the safety procedures.

"On behalf of the co-pilot and the rest of the flight crew, I would like to thank those who provided assistance to contain the disturbances we experienced. We will be diverting to Stanton to obtain the assistance of medical personnel and local law enforcement."

There was a collective murmur through the cabin, and although Mike could not distinguish the comments of any single person, he could hear tones of annoyance, anger, relief, and acceptance.

"We apologize for any inconvenience."

Mike thought the captain might be done, but the speakers crackled and hissed as if the button on the audio system was still engaged. When the pilot did resume his announcement, his words were halting, and it was clear that he was struggling mightily to find the right tone and the right words to convey the information.

"We will try to get you on your way as soon as possible, but there are, ah, complications on the ground. The reports we are getting are incomplete, but it appears that a number of cities are experiencing what could be regarded as terrorist attacks."

The murmur in the cabin escalated to a cacophony, and Mike missed what the captain said next. *For Christ's sake people, get a hold of yourselves,* he thought. When he could next discern the voice of the pilot over the hubbub of voices, the words filled him with worry and fear.

"...passengers must remain on the plane until we can determine if the terminal is secure."

It could not have been easy to make the decision to land at an airport that might be experiencing a terrorist attack. The captain would have had to weigh the risk to the remaining passengers against the need for urgent medical care for the victims of the assaults. That would be the only real consideration. The passengers and crew were not in any imminent danger from the fat man and the little girl. He presumed that the girl would also be restrained, although he suspected she would require far fewer straps and other bindings.

Mike was not surprised by the decision to land at a different airport, since the Savanna/Hilton Head International Airport could be considered a prominent target for terrorists. But surely the captain could not be concerned about the status of an airport in Stanton? It was a fraction of the size of the Savanna Airport, with a runway barely able to accommodate an aircraft of their size. Perhaps the captain was just being overly cautious. It was beyond the realm of possibility that *every* airport in America was experiencing these threats. There had to be many hundreds of these airfields, perhaps thousands.

Regardless, the plane could be waiting on the tarmac for a long time if the situation was uncertain in the terminal. His entire trip was screwed anyway, so it ultimately didn't matter to him where they landed. If not for the injured passengers, his preferred option would be for the pilot to pull a full one-eighty and head back to New York.

He sat back and resigned himself to the fact that this situation was out of his control, so he might as well go along for the ride and avoid subjecting himself to additional stress.

After another thirty minutes during which he blankly looked at the flight progress screen, he heard a change in the pitch of the engines and could sense the beginning of their descent. The captain switched on the seatbelt sign and made a curt announcement that they expected to land in approximately twenty minutes.

Mike could sense the rapid descent in his ears. They were dropping altitude more quickly than usual, perhaps something permitted under FAA regulations during an emergency. It was damned painful though, and he yawned repeatedly, trying to equalize the pressure in his ears. He watched the graphic of their progress on the entertainment system, perhaps left operational to distract the passengers. It showed a representation of a plane in descent with information on speed, altitude, and the estimated time of arrival. He felt the plane bank slightly to the left and could make out the lights of the airport in the distance.

At least we'll be safe on the plane, he thought, *out on the runway*.

It was a reassuring notion, and it had no sooner entered his head than a man seated toward the front of the cabin began shrieking.

CHAPTER 7

Bates Memorial Hospital

The sound of the shot from the officer's weapon was still reverberating through the long hallway as Carrie collapsed to the floor in a disjointed heap. What was left of her head made a sharp cracking sound as it connected with the tile.

Blood from the exit wound on the back of Carrie's head spattered onto Jackie's face and clothes. Some of it also landed in her mouth, hot and coppery.

Jackie hesitated only a moment and then wheeled around and ran the few remaining steps to the stairwell. A bullet dug into the drywall next to her. The sound from the discharge of the weapon was louder than she expected, perhaps exaggerated because the gun was pointed directly at her. She was through the door an instant later, taking the stairs down three at a time with one hand sliding along the railing, like controlled falling. There were only eight flights down to the parking level, and she was past four of them before she heard the door bang open above her. She didn't look up even as a shot whined past her. The angle was poor from the shooter's perspective, and she was moving fast. Apparently, the officer realized this as well and set off in pursuit of her.

She didn't gain any ground from that point on, but didn't lose any either. The door at the bottom was painted with large white letters against the dark gray paint. They said: "Emergency Exit Only."

Vehicle owners were meant to walk along a corridor to access the proper exits at each end. Taped to the door was a laser-printed sign that read: "Do NOT leave this door propped open." No one paid any attention to either sign, and Jackie always wondered about the capitalization of "NOT." It made her think of a parent with a misbehaving child, the way they emphasized the "not" when they spoke. Do NOT throw your food on the floor.

The door was propped open with a piece of wood. The cleaning staff, the majority of whom were smokers, came out here on their breaks. The smokers always seemed to be the people who could least afford it. Some nurses smoked as well, a fact that appalled Jackie.

She burst through the door, looked right, and then left. The distance to the staircase down to the next level seemed impossibly far. The car park was dimly lit and only half full at this time of night. Three long seconds ticked by as she considered her options. In that span of time, she heard the footfalls from the cop draw noticeably closer.

She ran straight ahead to a line of cars parked nearby. Hospital staff were as lazy as anyone else and parked their cars as close to the stairs as possible. She ducked down and slowed her walk once she was among the vehicles, mostly compact cars. The officer would make it to the door in a matter of seconds, and she was determined not to be seen. She got down on her hands and knees as she worked her way to the outer edge of the structure.

The door from the stairwell creaked open, a drawn-out sound, like a castle door in an old horror movie. There was a small *crunch* as the officer stepped on a gravel pebble sitting on the concrete. Jackie hunched down as she crawled forward as quietly as possible. It did not sound very quiet to her ears.

The parking garage was open to the elements and had a concrete wall about four feet high around the perimeter. That was her destination.

A lone SUV, facing out, was parked a few feet away from the wall. She squeezed in between the wall and the back of the vehicle and leaned against the concrete, trying to slow her breathing. The cop would not know which way she had gone or whether she had access to a car. He could check every vehicle, she knew, but he would also be considering the possibility that she had managed to get to the stairwell and was now working her way down to the street. What would she do in a similar situation if *she* were the hunter? People turned right more than they turned left, so she would probably head toward the stairway to the right and listen for footsteps.

It was a risk, but she stood up and tried to peer through the windows of the SUV. They were tinted, of course; nothing could be easy. It was dark though, and there was very little backlight, so she eased her face around the edge of the vehicle, just her left eye. Jesus, the cop seemed to be staring straight at her. She tried to remain perfectly still. The human eye is sensitive to detecting motion and a cop's eye is even better trained than most. But his gaze eventually drifted away, and he turned and re-entered the stairwell, obviously unconcerned that she may have escaped even after witnessing him murder a nurse in cold blood. Jackie wondered what was happening in the brains of the afflicted, in their minds. It was unlike anything she had ever heard about or read about, something completely new.

The parking garage was reasonably warm, but she was sitting on concrete with the bumper of an SUV just a foot away from her face. It was far from comfortable. However, she planned to wait as long as necessary to ensure that the cop wasn't trying to trick her into showing herself. When she was ready, she would make her way down the stairs and onto the street and grab the first cab she could find.

The sirens of the various first responders—police, fire, ambulances—meshed together in an asynchronous symphony, the sound of a major emergency. The sound should have been alarming, but to her, it was reassuring. However, to her surprise and disappointment, she realized that the sirens were not converging on the hospital. Whatever was happening was not localized, as she had once believed. The hospital was not the epicenter; it was clearly just one of many sites across the city where serious incidents were playing out. Calling 911 was no longer a sure thing, and if the policeman roaming the halls of the hospital was any indication, it could make things even worse. She was on her own.

After another ten minutes, she considered it safe enough to leave her hiding place. She could have stayed there until morning, of course, but she somehow doubted that things would improve much in the interim.

Home beckoned to her. Once she was home, she would hunker down and stay there until this was resolved. It was probably delusional and unrealistic of her to believe that this situation would blow over quickly, but she didn't want to think about that right now. She needed short-term goals. Get home, feed the cat, feed herself, shelter in place, and watch the news.

The city appeared visually normal from the fourth floor of the parking garage. There were no fires visible, the power was still on, and the traffic lights at the end of the block cycled through their various signals. But there was the persistent sound of gunfire, some very distant, some relatively close. It was not uncommon for her to hear the occasional gunshot in Stanton; this was an experience shared by almost every resident of any large US city. However, this was not a typical Thursday night. There was often less than a minute between gunshots, sometimes only seconds, and it went on and on.

Jackie leaned out over the concrete wall and peered down at the street. A woman passed under a streetlight, running. It was the inefficient gait of someone who had likely not run since they were a child, short strides with zero knee lift and arms held straight. Jackie caught a glimpse of a pale face as the woman looked behind her. Less than ten seconds later, another figure passed through the corona of light, this one taller and moving much more quickly. Predator and prey. Jackie was reminded of an episode of a nature show from Africa, with a lion running down a baby antelope, and the inevitability of the outcome. It would be no different here. She was surprised that the woman did not yell for help. Did she sense that could place her in more danger? Were the afflicted individuals acting together? There was no way to know, and Jackie did not want to find herself on a darkened street trying to walk home with no weapon and no way to call for help. She needed a car, and she knew who had one: *Carrie*. Carrie, who was currently lying four floors above her with half her head missing, but just feet away from the stairwell. Carrie, who had slipped her car keys into her purse just seconds before the two of them exited the nurse's lounge.

Jackie had to go back inside.

CHAPTER 8

Flight 206

Mike had good reason to remain in his seat and would be fully justified in doing so. The plane was coming in fast for a hard landing, and everyone was already securely buckled into place. Remaining in his seat was the prudent thing to do. If it wasn't for the screams, that is. The man screaming was clearly the one being attacked, not the attacker. The screams were of pain, not of anger or of madness. He could sit there and do nothing, of course, but that seemed impossible. It was no different than if he were on the side of a busy road and failed to scoop up a toddler who had wandered into traffic. In this case, he was goaded into motion by the inaction of his fellow passengers, many of whom were closer to the man than him.

He reluctantly undid his seatbelt and stood. The aisle was pitched downward, and he needed to place his hands against the seat backs to maintain his balance. He could see the source of the screams and a couple of bobbing heads over the seat-tops, but he was unable to discern the nature of the attack itself.

The banning of knives and guns, and screwdrivers eliminated only the obvious weapons. But anything sharp or heavy would suffice, as the laptop and the pencil had demonstrated. What other innocuous items could be used? Most pens, especially if they were metal. The edge of a heavy, hard-cover book. Stiletto shoes. Bags for suffocating, straps for strangling, spoons for gouging. The list seemed endless. If you really wanted to kill someone, you only needed a little imagination and, Mike presumed, sufficient motivation. That's where this whole series of events left him baffled. What was motivating these attacks? They seemed completely random, strangers attacking strangers. A child attacking her mother. It was senseless and mystifying.

Mike made his way down the aisle on shaky legs, unsure of why he was doing this or what he hoped to accomplish once he reached the site of the attack. The man had stopped screaming, an ominous development that made Mike reconsider the wisdom of his actions. The absence of any further sound suggested that the attacker had completed his or her original mission and could very well be in the process of selecting a new target. Showing up outside that row of seats at this precise moment could put him at the top of the list. However, after passing the halfway point to his destination, he felt compelled to continue. A young girl to his left repeated, "I want to go home, I want to go home," as she rocked in her seat. Mike knew how she felt. The girl's mother was shushing her, as if afraid of drawing the attention of the attacker.

The aisle seat next to the attacker was empty, presumably vacated soon after the assault began. The passengers in the rows of seats directly behind and beside the site of the attack cowered in fear, like children hiding under their bed sheets at night. Someone whimpered quietly. There were no flight attendants in sight; perhaps they were steadfastly adhering to the seatbelt protocol for a rapid descent.

As Mike moved closer, he could see the head of the person in the middle seat, a woman in her seventies with her white-grey hair done up in a bun. The man seated next to the window had knitting needles poking out of his eye sockets. Blood and gore covered his face and his formerly white shirt. Several thoughts occurred to Mike in rapid succession. *What happened between them that resulted in such a vicious attack? How the heck did she get those needles past security? And was she still dangerous?*

It was difficult to assess anything from his current vantage point, slightly behind the row of seats. The woman appeared to be simply sitting and looking straight ahead. Mike leaned forward for a better look. In her lap was a cloth carry bag containing grey and black yarn and an unfinished grey mitten. There was a copious amount of blood on her folded hands, and the mitten was stained red. It will be seized as evidence, he thought, never to be finished. It was an unimportant detail for his brain to seize upon, grasping for a distraction away from the horror of the scene.

The woman, perhaps sensing his presence, turned her head to look at him. The eyes that affixed him were cold and aware, not the eyes of a person in shock over what they had done. He realized with a bolt of understanding that the reason behind her placidity was not remorse or shock or regret. She was resting, restoring her energy. She was not a robust woman, and the attack must have consumed a lot of her physical reserves. At least she was no longer armed with her knitting needles. That status was soon to end.

Apparently, she decided that she had rested long enough and reached over and tried to extract one of the needles (#9 gauge) from the dead man's eye socket. It dawned on Mike that she intended to use the needle on him. And if not on him, certainly on one of the other nearby passengers. He could not let that happen. He leaned across the aisle seat and grabbed her by the shoulder with his left hand. His other hand gripped her right forearm to prevent her from extracting the needle. The heat radiating off her was shocking, like she was burning up from a fever, although it could also be from her recent exertions. There was little flesh on her frame, and the shoulder beneath his hand was bony and frail, like the skeleton of a bird. His right hand completely encircled her tiny forearm. She may have been demented, but she was physically no stronger than most seventy-year-old women. He squeezed her forearm hard and felt the radius and ulna grind together. It had to hurt, but he was feeling unsympathetic toward her.

The knitting needle must have been embedded in bone because she had no success in removing it. Now, with his grip around her arm, she could not summon enough strength to close her fingers around the shaft.

"Give it up," he growled at her.

In response, she tried to turn toward him, but it was not difficult to control her. He didn't want to have to look into those eyes again, and he didn't want to have to contend with her teeth, although they could well be dentures. It was distinctly unpleasant to be this close to her. She had that old lady smell, something that was difficult to define. The odor was both musty and organic, with a hint of dead flowers and talcum powder. It made him want to gag.

The captain chose that precise moment to make a rough landing, and Mike lost his balance and fell into the space in front of the seat. He held onto the woman for a couple of milliseconds before deciding that he did not want her landing on top of him in the footwell. As it was, he was on his side, his face only inches away from the woman's feet. She was wearing sensible black leather shoes with a low heel. Flesh-toned nylons puddled around her bony ankles.

He squirmed out backward, into the aisle, not wanting to find out if she was able to use the diversion to retrieve a knitting needle or two. Someone managed to open one of the emergency exits over the wing, and he felt a whoosh of air sweep through the cabin.

Idiot. The plane was still traveling at a hundred miles an hour, and the slide that deployed would likely be destroyed before anyone had a chance to use it. Thankfully, there were more exits available. He could hear shouts from other passengers who were arguing for and against the immediate deployment of the chutes. Activating these before the aircraft was completely stopped made no practical sense, but the actions of the elderly woman had thrown everyone into a panic. Those who were not close to the seat were probably in a worse state since they had no idea what was happening, only that it was terrible.

Mike was immediately trampled by people surging up the aisle toward exits that were not yet available. They walked on his body like he was a piece of discarded luggage, stepping on his legs, his buttocks, and his back. Someone rolled their suitcase over the entire length of his body. No good deed goes unpunished, he thought. Sometimes he hated people, fucking hated them.

After he managed to turn onto his side, the other passengers generally walked by him instead of on him. However, he was still getting pummeled by both handheld luggage and small suitcases on wheels. No one stopped or offered to help him.

"Let me get up!" he shouted, but his voice was drowned out by the wind and the shouts and cries of those attempting to leave. The plane was slowing quickly, and so was the flow of passengers along the aisle. No one was quite brave enough to leap out of a moving aircraft with the exit ten feet off the runway. Plus, it was dark outside, which made it impossible to see the ground.

A woman standing next to him started to scream. She was in her early forties, heavyset, and wore a blue business suit. A leather attaché case dangled from her left hand.

Mike saw that the elderly woman had succeeded in her attempt to extract a knitting needle from the man's eye and was now stabbing at the woman's neck with metronomic precision, like a demented wind-up toy. The needle was long and narrow, and it was only a matter of time before it hit something vital. Drops of blood fell onto Mike's shirt and jacket. The businesswoman raised her arm to shield her neck and tried to lean into the opposing row of seats. The elderly woman followed her, stabbing her arm through the suit. Mike could sense the blows losing power though, and he knew his opportunity might come soon. The old woman was practically tripping over him in her efforts to reach the businesswoman and finish the job.

He pushed up onto an elbow and drew his knees up toward his hips in anticipation of climbing to his feet. The businesswoman had fallen across the three empty seats, which momentarily put her out of range of her attacker. That was fortunate for her but unfortunate for Mike. His efforts to get to his feet had drawn the elderly woman's attention, and she was currently looking down at him with those flat eyes. Before she had a chance to act, he scrambled to his feet and drove into her on his way up. The move didn't have a lot of power, but the woman was light, and Mike was able to push her back toward her seat. She sprawled across the man she had killed earlier.

The line of passengers started to move again, people fleeing in both directions away from the latest assault. Another over-the-wing exit chute had been deployed, and a second one at the front of the plane.

Fight the woman or leave? Those were his two options.

"Fuck this," breathed Mike. He had performed enough heroics for the past two days.

The businesswoman was trying to get to her feet, and Mike lent her a hand. She looked to be in rough shape. Blood poured from the wounds in her neck, and her right arm hung limply by her side.

The old woman was also struggling to stand, but Mike had absolutely no intention of helping her.

"Go, go, go!" he urged the woman. She was progressing all too slowly along the aisle, her attaché case catching on the seat backs as she walked toward the exit. He had an ungracious thought about the woman's body weight and the handicap it presented in an emergency. Mike looked back and saw that the old woman had managed to regain her feet but did not seem inclined to aggressively pursue them. Perhaps she needed a nap first.

The woman waddled ahead of him, walking at half the speed he would expect her to manage considering the circumstances. When they finally reached the emergency exit, with its already deployed chute, the woman balked.

"I'm afraid of heights," she said.

Mike resisted the urge to push her. Instead, he said, "Just sit on the top and slide down. You don't have to jump."

The woman gingerly lowered herself onto the top edge of the ramp with a slowness that made Mike want to scream. He should be more sympathetic, he knew. The woman had puncture wounds in her neck that still dribbled blood, and her right arm was only semi-functional.

He looked back up the aisle and was alarmed to see that Granny Terminator had closed half the distance, apparently refreshed enough to resume her attack. She was approaching with that creepily emotionless face and a bloody knitting needle in her hand, like a scene from a geriatric horror movie.

The businesswoman was still sitting on the top of the slide. Mike took one more look up the aisle and then placed his foot between the woman's shoulder blades and shoved her on her way. She screamed and her good arm flailed to the side as she descended the chute. Once she reached the bottom, true to form, she just sat there.

There was no time to wait. Jack leaped onto the slide and plummeted toward the bottom.

He yelled, "Coming down!", and hoped the woman would get out of his way. She was slow-moving moving though, and he struggled to decrease his speed before he hit her. They ended up in a tangle on the runway. The pavement was still warm from the sun it received that afternoon, and he was tempted to lie there for a while and soak it in.

"You could have waited," she spat.

Mike didn't want to get into it with her. He was done with this woman, and the only thing on his mind now was getting a ride to a hotel. Unfortunately, that was fantasy. He was going to be tied up with the police, again, and his dream of having a shower and a good night's sleep before he headed home in the morning was verging on impossible. The meeting would have to be postponed, of course. And continuing the excursion to visit his father was out of the question. As for his return trip to New York, he intended to rent a vehicle and drive. He didn't care if it took him sixteen hours.

Although the pilot mentioned potential complications on the ground, Mike still expected some type of shuttle service to take them to the terminal. He could see the sprawling, brightly lighted structure about three-quarters of a mile away. They couldn't very well be expected to walk; it was very dark, and they would need to traverse other runways. He imagined getting halfway across the broad expanse of a runway and seeing the lights of a fast-approaching plane coming in for a landing. No thank you.

"What now?" asked a middle-aged man. He didn't direct the question to anyone in particular; it was more of a musing out loud.

"They'll send a shuttle," Mike said, with a degree of conviction he did not feel.

No one said anything for a few moments as they stood in small groups ranging in size from family units of four to huddles of twenty or more. The people who gathered in the larger assemblies appeared to be strangers, but there was still an instinctive desire to come together as a group when there was a threat, especially in the dark. The herd mentality.

A young woman cried out and pointed at the aircraft. The old woman stood peering out at them from her perch at the edge of the emergency exit. It seemed absurd to be afraid of her now, out in the open. Even if she did manage to negotiate the slide, most of the passengers could outpace her with a brisk walk. Nevertheless, Mike would keep an eye out for her.

"Why aren't the pilots down here?"

It was the same man as before, asking a very legitimate question. Why weren't the pilots here? Come to think of it, there were no flight attendants on the tarmac either. He could, perhaps, excuse the pilots. There could be shutdown procedures of which he was unaware. Or they could still be receiving information from the tower. But where were the flight attendants? Were they not responsible for the passenger's care and safety until they were securely inside the terminal? There was no guidance here at all; the passengers had been left to fend for themselves. Something about the flight crew's absence made him very uneasy. They could be privy to information that the rest of them had been denied. There had been no instruction to leave the aircraft but what other choice did they have? There was a homicidal woman on board who was completely out of control.

Mike said, "They may be waiting for permission to leave the plane."

There was a murmur through the crowd, and the tone could best be described as incredulous. Or perhaps they were simply scoffing at his suggestion. Mike wished he had kept his mouth shut.

"I think I see something," a woman said.

Indeed, there were lights from a vehicle that appeared to be headed their way. As it drew closer, Mike saw that it was a luggage cart speeding toward them. Retrieving his luggage was the least of his concerns, and he wondered who on Earth thought it was a good idea to send this vehicle out here. He briefly considered whether this could be an alternate method of transportation if all the other shuttles were tied up.

The bright lights on the vehicle hauling the luggage cart sent long shadows arching along the runway. They also illuminated a group of about eight people who decided to start walking toward the terminal on their own. Some in the group put their hands up in greeting. The cart did not slow, and most of the passengers either did not react or reacted far too slowly to do any good. The vehicle cut the first people off at the knees before rumbling over top of them. Mike imagined he could hear bones breaking.

"No..." he moaned. The brutality of the act left him numb with disbelief.

Other passengers screamed in horror.

One man bellowed, "Stop, stop!" as if the driver had run down the passengers by mistake.

Mike knew deep in his soul that this was not a matter of driver inattention or poor visibility; this was deliberate. Whatever was happening to make these people so aggressive was widespread, and its prevalence was accelerating.

CHAPTER 9

Bates Memorial Hospital

Jackie was still sitting behind the SUV a full fifteen minutes after deciding to go back inside and retrieve the keys to Carrie's car. She kept second-guessing her decision and came close to talking herself out of it several times. Inertia was easy. She could stay exactly where she was until help arrived, tucked in between the vehicle's bumper and the wall. The dissenting opinion suggested that this was a bad idea for a number of reasons. It would grow light in a couple of hours, making her hiding spot much less tenable. She would also need to eat and use the toilet. And could she reasonably expect help to come? The parking garage at a hospital would be a low-priority location to search. At some point, she would have to go *looking* for help. She supposed that someone might eventually come down to retrieve this vehicle or some other, and she could get a ride. But how would she know who she could trust? If an afflicted person could accurately fire a weapon, they could certainly drive a vehicle.

At the heart of the matter was this: she desperately wanted to be at home. The pull of it on her was overwhelming. Her cat, her things, her bed. The only aspect that gave her pause was the fact that she was relatively new to the city, had never driven a vehicle here, and was not entirely sure of the route. Despite that, it seemed worth the risk.

Getting the car keys would not be complicated; she would climb four stories, just eight flights of stairs, carefully enter the corridor, and grab Carrie's purse. It would take less than five minutes, and then she could be on her way. She was encouraged by the fact that not a single person had come through the emergency exit door over the past thirty minutes. The likelihood of her meeting someone coming down the stairs in the next few minutes seemed very slight. She squinted at her watch. 2:37 a.m. It was time to go.

She uncoiled from her seated position, not even feeling the stiffness from sitting on a hard surface for thirty minutes. Thank goodness for adrenaline. She covered the thirty yards to the doorway in slow, careful steps, ready to flee at the merest hint of a sound. On the face of it, the slow but steady strategy seemed sound, but it would also double her exposure time. She quickened her pace. The running shoes she borrowed had thick foam soles, a necessity if you were walking home from work after being on your feet for twelve hours. The soft treads made little sound against the concrete. She stopped and listened at the door, like a mouse wondering if a cat had abandoned the chase or was merely more patient. There was no sound, and there was no *sense* of anyone either. She wondered if humans possessed other senses that might only awaken during life-or-death situations. It seemed possible, but it would be difficult to prove scientifically. How could a researcher (ethically) elicit the necessary emotional reaction in a lab to test this premise?

The door opened with only the tiniest of squeals, short-lived and just as plausibly caused by a gust of wind as by a human hand. She waited, not breathing, listening for a sound that didn't belong. The afflicted seemed uninterested in subtlety, and waiting quietly in a stairway for prey to emerge did not fit the profile. After a few more seconds, she started up the stairs. She reached the first floor and listened at the closed door for a moment, but couldn't hear anything. Three more floors to go. She was just steps away from the second-floor doorway when it swung open, and someone surged through. She screamed involuntarily, a short shriek, and flattened herself against the wall.

The man who burst through the door looked at her with terrified eyes, as if expecting her to attack *him*. He leaned back against the door and placed a hand over his heart when he realized that she was equally traumatized. The hand over the heart was more of an affectation than a legitimate cause for concern. The guy couldn't have been more than thirty-two and was tall, but slim. He was wearing a white lab coat and looked vaguely familiar, possibly someone she would see in passing once every couple of months. There were hundreds of employees at the hospital, but she personally knew only a fraction.

His name tag read: *Martin Howard*. He had a blue backpack slung over his shoulder and was carrying a metal canister with a biohazard symbol pasted on the side. It looked heavy.

"What is going on?" he said urgently, keeping his voice to stage-whisper volume.

Jackie shook her head. "I have no idea."

"Well, we have to get out of here!" he said. "I've been hiding in my lab for over three hours with the lights off."

He looked at her as if noticing something for the first time. "Wait, are you heading *inside*?"

"Just to the fourth floor."

He appeared mortified by the idea. "Are you crazy? We need to *go*."

She looked up the stairwell again and was seized by a hopeful thought. "Martin, do you happen to have a car in the parking garage?"

He shook his head. "I took my bike to work today."

"A bike. Well, I'm not going out on the street without a car." She paused. "It's not just happening in the hospital." She put up her hand to forestall any more questions. "I know where I can find a set of keys. They are just inside the door on the fourth floor. You can wait here, or you can come with me."

He peered down the stairs, up the stairs, and then back at her.

"I'll wait here." He said this mostly to his shoes as if he could not bear to meet her eyes.

Jackie left him without a word, moving quickly and almost silently up the stairs. She wanted to get this over with. She was only slightly out of breath by the time she reached the fourth floor. The door was designed with one of those horizontal bars that you could press with your hip to free the latch if your hands were full. There was no quiet way to do it, but she made the least noise possible. The *clack* sound it made seemed to echo down the entire stairwell. Jackie could imagine Martin looking up in alarm.

She eased open the door a fraction of an inch at a time. Of course, she could only see in one direction, but there was no one visible. Once she had opened it far enough to get her head through, she checked the opposite direction as well. Clear.

She stepped out and quickly made her way over to Carrie's body. She intended to just grab the purse and hunt for the keys later, but the strap for the bag was clasped in fingers stiffened by rigor mortis. A stronger pull only succeeded in shifting Carrie's position. The movement of her head produced a dark red smear on the white floor, and there was a slight ripping sound as hair peeled away from where it had adhered to the tile.

Jackie grimaced and stopped pulling. She stooped and worked at the purse's uncooperative zipper. It finally opened, revealing all manner of items —a wallet, tissues, loose change, a pack of gum, an N95 face mask, and a small bottle of hand sanitizer. She only cared about the keys. At the exact moment her hand closed over them, she detected motion at the end of the corridor.

The police officer was back, forty yards away, and already reaching for his weapon. Jackie sprang to her feet and whirled toward the door. She hit it at a run, and as soon as she was through, she yelled down to Martin.

"Run!"

She heard him say, "Oh, Jesus."

She couldn't see him, but she could hear his footsteps, and they were moving far more slowly than hers. She caught up to him just as he reached the exit door into the parking lot, the heavy metal canister bumping against his hip. Her hand was on his back as they pushed through.

Jackie spun around with the car fob in her hand, listening for the beep. Luckily, Carrie followed the general pattern of behavior and had parked her vehicle just five spaces away. The car was a dark green Toyota Corolla, a very sensible automobile. Jackie remote-unlocked the doors as she ran.

She yanked open the door and jumped inside. Her hands were shaking so hard that she had trouble getting the key in the ignition.

The stairway door slammed open, and the officer exited with his gun drawn, eyes rapidly scanning all the vehicles. Martin was *still* only halfway into his seat, a slow-ass impediment to her safety.

She started the engine, and the car lurched forward and stalled. She had not even noticed that the car had a manual transmission when she climbed inside. This time, she depressed the clutch before the engine roared to life. The windshield splintered, and the hot whine of a bullet passed by her head. She gave the car too much gas before releasing the clutch, and the wheels screamed and smoked as she did a burnout, barely avoiding a concrete pillar.

Two more shots rang out, shattering a side window and the rear window. The officer may have been crazy, but he was a hell of a shot.

She was probably traveling at least 45 mph when she drove by the 10-mph maximum speed sign. One could safely drive twice the speed limit in the parking garage, but going four times as fast was pushing it. Still, she negotiated the turn with only minimal body damage to the Corolla.

However, the cracked windshield was a major issue. She had to lean to one side and peer through a dinner-plate-sized patch of clear glass. The parking garage was well-lit, making the job manageable. However, as soon as they drove outside, snapping off the barrier adjacent to the automated checkout, navigating became much more difficult. After they had slowly driven two blocks and were out of sight of the garage, Jackie asked Martin to kick out the window. He looked at her as if she were out of her mind.

"*Kick it out?*" he said, incredulous. He looked at the windshield as if he had just become aware of its existence.

"I can't see where I'm going. And it will get worse once we meet other cars. The glare on all this fractured glass will make it impossible to see."

"I don't think —I mean, how would I even do it?"

"Lean your seat back, put your feet up, and kick."

Jackie may well have been saddled with one of the least athletic and graceless representatives of the male species. Martin's kicks were weak and ineffectual, the action more akin to stepping than kicking.

"Switch places with me," she said.

Martin looked aghast.

"We can stay in the car while we switch places," she said, although the car did not offer much protection, especially when they were stopped. One side window was completely absent, and the rear window was shattered. The front window would soon be among the missing if she were any more capable than Martin.

She was. After three hard kicks, the impacts of which she felt through her internal organs, a section of window ballooned out. Once it started to give, the rest of the windshield seemed to follow quite readily. After another minute, only ragged traces of the window remained. It would be a breezy ride, but it would be better than hanging her head out the window like a dog.

She reclaimed the driver's seat with little protest from Martin. The thought of him behind the wheel during an emergency made her especially insistent. It also meant that she had full control over where they drove. She intended to take the safest path back to her place, which was not necessarily the shortest. Unfortunately, because of her lack of familiarity with the different routes, she would need to rely on Martin to some extent.

She didn't know where Martin lived, and she had no intention of driving him there tonight. They could reassess the situation in the morning. She did not want to have a house guest, especially Martin, but extra driving would mean extra risk. If he did not wish to stay with her, she would not insist. There was a perfectly fine hotel only five blocks away from where she lived.

She pulled away from the curb, mentally charting the course home. It was daunting; seven miles through a densely populated city in a badly compromised vehicle.

CHAPTER 10

Stanton Airport

The remaining passengers scattered soon after the luggage cart ran over members of the group of eight, once it became evident that the initial incident had not been an accident. That fact was made abundantly clear when the driver of the luggage vehicle swung around to have another go at the passengers he missed during the first attack. The remaining individuals were better prepared this time, but he still managed to take down two more. One was still tangled up in the undercarriage, and the body left a dark smear on the tarmac as the driver made a wide turn.

No one waited for him to take aim for the third time. Some fled deeper into the night, and some set out along the runway.

The vehicle drove in erratic circles, seeking more prey. Mike found himself running in the general direction of the terminal. The headlights from the luggage cart occasionally passed over him, like a searchlight during a prison break. Every time it happened, he wanted to throw himself to the ground to avoid detection.

It was an every-man-for-himself type scenario, and he was not proud of his panicked reaction. At some point he realized he was on grass, likely safer, and far enough away from the runway and the aircraft to be obscured by the darkness. Hopefully, he was invisible to the crazed driver.

He slowed to a walk and allowed his ragged breathing to slow as well. It was still night, but he would not describe it as full dark. There were runway lights, taxiway lights, lights from other vehicles and buildings, and the terminal itself. Shadowy figures moved in concert with him in complete silence, all of them headed toward the terminal. It was a surreal feeling, like he was leading a squad of soldiers into battle in the middle of enemy territory.

The terminal complex may have represented safety and normality to the others, but Mike was less convinced. The violent incidents on the plane, and now on the runway, were unlikely to magically disappear once they crossed the threshold into the building. There would be more security personnel, but also many more people. Three passengers had gone apeshit on this one flight, with a manifest of approximately one hundred and fifty people. That was one in fifty. If this condition or syndrome or illness were widespread, there could be twenty of these people roaming through the terminal, perhaps more. He wondered if he and his group could completely bypass the terminal and the grounds surrounding it. It seemed unlikely, although the majority of the security measures were designed to keep people from *entering* the areas where they maintained the planes and handled the luggage. He would have to play it by ear.

The first thing he noticed was that there was no one looking out the windows of the departure lounge. A lot of people liked to watch the planes come in for a landing and there was always an assortment of observers standing at the windows, peering out over the runways. The ground crews also appeared to be missing. Those faceless people who refueled the planes and loaded the luggage, and moved the skyways into position. Mike already knew where one of their baggage handlers was located.

He and the six other passengers simply walked through an unsecured door and into a part of the terminal that was typically off-limits.

"Where is everyone?" whispered one of the men. He looked like a suburban father who had been fit in his youth but was now a few years into the complacency of a stable marriage. His shirt was tight over a thick torso, and a few grey hairs sprinkled his sideburns. He had a trim beard, also shot through with grey.

Mike scanned for an exit. "Evacuated, maybe? I don't know."

He led the group of six to an elevator, but it required a key card. The door to a set of stairs was propped open, probably against regulations. A chart just inside the door laid out the floor plan of the terminal. They decided on the Arrivals level, which should open out onto the street.

Mike found himself reluctant to open the door once they arrived at their destination. The calm and quiet of the operations area had allowed some of the nervous tension to dissipate from his body. He was not relaxed, not by a long shot, but the rats gnawing at his stomach had decided to take a break. Entering the terminal proper threatened to bring them back. But there was no other choice, really. He was certain that the quiet was just an illusion that would eventually end. In this moment, he could still pretend that everything was fine on the other side. He took a deep breath and pulled open the door.

The terminal appeared to be abandoned; that was the first word that came to mind. Not empty, because the detritus of prospective passengers was strewn everywhere. Lots of carry-on luggage bags, books, paper bags with lunches, disposable coffee cups, hoodies, and jackets. There were even a few laptops and cell phones. Mike considered the level of panic that would be necessary for him not to grab his cell phone before fleeing. Something horrifying, something so imperiling that it overrode normal brain function and delivered a single imperative: *Run.*

"What the hell happened here?" asked one of the men. He was a big guy with a loud voice and an unsuccessful combover. Presumed occupation: used car salesman.

Mike shook his head in response. Something bad.

They followed the signs that directed them toward ground transportation. Mike held out little hope of finding a taxi or a shuttle. The mass exodus would have overwhelmed the system, and no taxi driver was going to return to the airport under the current conditions.

A section of white tile floor was thick with blood, drag marks, and red handprints. No one could take their eyes off it as they walked past. The smell coming from it was strong, and Mike felt his gag reflex kick in.

The little group stuck so close together they were practically tripping over each other, especially since they were constantly scanning their surroundings, assessing it for threats.

They all jumped as one as a loud voice shouted, "Hey! You can't be in here!"

A uniformed police officer, possibly one on permanent assignment to the airport, approached them with his hand on the grip of his weapon.

All seven men raised their hands in the air in unison. It would have been comical under other circumstances.

"The terminal has been evacuated," the cop said. "You need to get out."

"That's what we are trying to do," Mike said. "I think we came in on one of the last flights."

The cop eyed each of them in turn. Apparently satisfied that everyone looked both terrified and compliant, he took his hand off his weapon.

"What happened here?" asked one of the younger guys. He had apparently descended the chute carrying his backpack, a breach of the rules that was likely never to be punished.

The cop didn't look like he planned to answer at first, but the eagerness with which the assembled group looked at him must have weakened his resolve.

"We don't know. It may be terrorism, domestic, but it's impossible to say for sure. It seems random, but I've never heard of so many random attacks happening at the same time. Perhaps it was just made to *look* random."

The suggestion had a tinge of conspiracy theory to it, and Mike was reasonably confident that this was a personal conjecture from the cop and not a serious line of inquiry the police were pursuing. He was equally certain that the attacks were *not* coordinated.

The young guy echoed what he was thinking. "I don't think it's terrorism. I saw a little girl stabbing her mother in the face with a pencil. That's not terrorism."

"Well, whatever the hell it is, it's working. All flights are grounded. And you need to leave."

They all heard it at the same time, the *click click click* of hard-soled shoes on a tile floor.

Mike thought he recognized the woman heading toward them as one of the passengers, a small blond woman in her mid-thirties. It was not unreasonable that some of the others would have found their way inside the terminal as well, and she seemed to be the first. She didn't appear panicked, just like she wanted to catch up to them before they moved on. Mike thought he saw a glint of something in her right hand.

The cop watched her approach but did not seem overly concerned.

"Ma'am," he called out, "You need to exit the building."

"Ah, I think she has something in her hand," Mike intoned to the cop.

She was less than twenty yards distant, eight seconds away from reaching them. The cop hesitated, clearly not wanting to draw his weapon. Mike surmised that he had not directly encountered any of the afflicted. The woman's face was completely blank, showing no anxiety, or anger, or aggression. Police officers are trained to read people, and this cop was either interpreting her lack of expression incorrectly or underestimating the threat the woman might pose. Unfortunately, Mike was becoming all too familiar with the look.

"Careful," he said, all he could manage in the brief span of time.

The cop's hand wasn't even on the butt of his weapon by the time the woman reached them. There was no hesitation on her part whatsoever; she didn't even slow her stride. The knife came up and then was plunged down toward the officer's chest the moment she was within range. Her speed carried her into him, and the cop staggered back.

"God!" shouted one of the older men. He practically tripped over his feet as he backpedaled away.

The officer was wearing a standard-issue Kevlar vest, and the knife did not penetrate it. The woman raised it again and stabbed at his neck, but he twisted away, and the blade sliced into his shoulder instead. The cop bellowed in pain and anger and pushed the woman away with his good arm. The woman tripped and fell.

Technically, the officer had a choice between the TASER on his left hip or the pistol on his right side. Had the woman not stabbed him in the left arm, he may have chosen the non-lethal alternative. However, Mike suspected that the officer was not particularly interested in the woman's well-being at that instant. She was still in the process of scrambling to her feet when he shot her five times in the chest.

The smell of cordite was heavy in the air as the group remained completely frozen, in a state of shock over the sudden violence. Mike wondered if his heart could survive the repeated strain from the adrenalin being dumped into his bloodstream on a regular basis.

The cop approached the woman, gun still drawn, and kicked the knife away from her hand. It skittered across the tile floor and came to rest against a wall. He knelt and laid his fingers over the carotid artery in her neck, although Mike could tell from the placement of the shots that this was a formality.

The cop regained his feet with a grimace. Blood dripped from his fingers onto her chest and mixed with her own blood, like some kind of pagan ritual, a bond that they would share forever.

He reached up and activated the mic for his radio. "Officer in need of medical assistance. Arrivals Level." He peered around for a landmark. "I am next to the Starbucks."

Mike wondered where the woman had acquired the knife and suspected that when the shops and restaurants were evacuated, they had not been secured. Anyone could go in and select whatever they wanted, including sharp-edged knives. It made him consider the possibility himself, but wandering through the airport with a knife in his hand might not be a prudent course of action after this incident.

They waited for reinforcements to arrive, and it did not take long. The three responding officers moved quickly but were also observant, checking all around them as they ran. They arrived red-faced and out of breath. One was carrying a basic first aid kit, the kind one might find in the trunk of a car. Two of the officers attended to the stricken cop, who had since developed the sickly pallor of ash from a bonfire. The adrenaline must have worn off in him as well, and shock was a distinct possibility. The third cop made multiple calls, one for an ambulance and another to someone who sounded like a supervisor.

Mike and the other men stood watching, shifting uncomfortably from foot to foot. There was nothing they could do, but they also did not want to stray too far from the protective knot of officers.

Finally, the oldest of the men from the plane turned to the others and asked, "Does anyone have a car in long-term parking?"

It was a dumb question since the flight had been diverted to an airport other than their original destination, but Mike answered anyway.

"No one has a car here. We will need to find some other type of transportation."

The old man nodded slowly as if absorbing complex information and then approached the officer who had been speaking on the phone.

"Are you going to take us into the city now?" His voice had the querulous and tremulous quality of one whose faculties are beginning to erode.

The cop looked back at him impatiently. "We have a full-blown emergency on our hands. You will need to find your own way home."

"It's your duty to protect us!" the man said angrily.

"The terminal is secure, and the exit is only seventy yards away. Once you get outside, you're on your own anyway." He crossed his arms over his chest in his best move-it-along cop pose. "We're not here to babysit you."

The old man flushed red but did not say anything further.

Mike walked over to him and laid a hand on his arm. "Come on. We'll all go out together."

The man muttered, "Our tax dollars at work." But not loud enough for the cop to hear.

The area outside the main entrance was eerily quiet, with not a single person or taxi in sight. He hadn't expected a cab, but he hoped someone would be there to provide some information. Mike checked his watch. 4:34 a.m. *Christ.* He'd been up for almost twenty-three hours.

"What now?" asked one of the other men, a guy with longer-than-average hair, skinny jeans, and tortoise-shell glasses. He looked like he might be a schoolteacher, or work in a library.

Mike rubbed his hands over his face. He was crashing from the latest adrenalin rush and had an intense desire to lie down and go to sleep somewhere. There was no chance of that happening any time soon.

"Give me a second."

He checked his phone. Three bars. He had received a few spam-type emails but nothing personal, and no calls or texts. That was disappointing. Did he warrant so little consideration that no one cared enough to check on him? He hoped it was because there were few people awake at this time of night, and even if they were awake, they might not grasp the full extent of what was happening. Who should *he* call? Work? His father? His sister and brother-in-law? He decided on a group text.

"I am fine, got diverted to Stanton. Will call later."

Sadly, the wording worked equally well for his family and for his employer, so he copied the text and sent it to Precision Marketing as well.

"Let's check the car rental places," he suggested.

At one point along their journey, they walked past an atrium-like structure that permitted them to see down into the concourse that led away from the baggage claim area. There was more activity here, with crime scene investigators placing evidence markers amongst three bodies, two of which were still uncovered. A police photographer was taking pictures of the bodies from different angles. The other body was covered in a white sheet, with blood clearly delineating its shape, like the Shroud of Turin.

There were a number of car rental operations at the airport. In a normal situation, the customer would make the arrangements inside and then travel to the parking garage to accept the vehicle. They were going to skip the middleman.

There were a lot of cars in the parking garage, their owners likely trapped in some faraway city. Unfortunately, no one in the group had any idea how to steal a vehicle, regardless of the year or model.

Only one of the rental booths had a light on inside. Typically, just a couple of employees worked the late shift, one to do a walkaround of the car with the customer, the other to process returns and hand out keys.

They all stopped short as they walked around to the side of the booth. A pair of legs extended out of the open doorway, clad in blue jeans darkened with blood. They could not see the rest of the body and were not sure they wanted to. Mike edged closer and peered inside. He wondered then if his mind had a limit to how much horror it could witness before suffering irreversible psychological damage. Would he begin to sense it as the limit approached, like a person walking perilously close to the edge of a cliff? Or would it happen suddenly, like a massive stroke that would leave him catatonic and drooling? He hoped he would have some kind of warning, because he was certain he had not seen the last of horrible things.

The man inside had been beaten to death with a small fire extinguisher.

The bottom of the extinguisher had been sharp-edged and left overlapping, crescent-shaped cuts on his face and skull, depressions that were now filled with blood. What was left of his face was askew; the bones underneath shifting and sublimating from the repeated blows. The perpetrator had set the fire extinguisher neatly on the ground beside the man's head.

Mike finally wrested his eyes away from the corpse and examined the rest of the office. It was a small space with chairs in front of two computer monitors, sheaves of forms, a landline telephone, a small washroom — and a cabinet that was a quarter full of keys on hooks.

Mike turned back to the others. "The keys for the rentals are in here." He paused. "I'll get them, you don't have to come inside."

A few looked anyway, but the rest stood back.

Mike collected seven key fobs, one for each person. His feet made sticking sounds as he made his way out, like disengaging strips of Velcro. There was no way to avoid stepping in the blood on the floor, and the bottom of each shoe left a distinctive print. He realized, belatedly, that he was not only disturbing a crime scene but was leaving tread patterns that might be traced back to him. The shoes would have to go, at some point, along with all the other soiled clothing he wore. He exited the booth and handed out the sets of keys. The old man looked uncertainly at the key fob.

"Isn't this stealing?"

"It's borrowing. If you want to pay for it later, you can send them some money."

"But shouldn't we stick together?"

That was the real issue, Mike knew. There was an argument to be made in its favor, strength in numbers, but he did not want to be saddled with a group. Soon enough, once the imminent sense of danger had passed, they would begin to disagree on where to go and what course of action they should pursue. He would be trapped in a minivan with six strangers with different agendas. That was not his way. He preferred to go it alone.

The old man looked at each of the men in turn.

"You can come with me if you like," offered the used car salesman. He did not appear keen to be by himself either.

The old man practically sagged with relief. He handed his set of keys back to Mike and then walked off with the salesman in search of their vehicle.

Mike decided to keep both keys and take the better car. He had grabbed the sets at random without examining the tags.

The rest of the men separated with barely a word. Now that an avenue of escape was available to them, they were anxious to leave. Mike was as well. The fob for the first set of keys was for a sub-compact. He kept walking. The second set was for a Dodge Challenger, a muscle car that he was surprised and grateful to find. He expected something like a Honda Civic.

The interior of the vehicle had a pleasant new car smell, like leather and teak. It was something you could now buy in a can, but he suspected that the scent was legitimate for this car. Rental companies rarely kept vehicles for longer than two years, and this one seemed practically brand new. The engine started with a satisfying throaty roar, and he backed it out of its parking spot.

The others had already left by the time he reached the exit, and the twinkling lights of the police and emergency vehicles receded into the distance as he headed toward the city.

The city was still miles distant, but as he crested a hill he could see it laid out before him. It was much darker than he expected, more like the dying embers of a fire than a beacon of hope.

CHAPTER 11

Stanton

Traffic was light at half past four in the morning, but the drive across the city without a windshield was uncomfortable and dangerous. Jackie's eyes streamed with tears as she drove, making it very difficult to see. And yet, she could not slow down. Once, when they had come to a stop at a red light, someone ran up to the car and attempted to get inside. Jackie floored the accelerator and shot across the empty intersection. Since then, she only slowed enough at red lights to ensure she would not be t-boned if she crossed before the light turned green.

Aside from that one incident, the city appeared normal. A lot could be happening just out of sight. The darkness acted like a magician's cloak, obscuring and distracting. Who knew what daylight would reveal? And, she supposed, even deranged murderers had to sleep sometime. For now, she was satisfied to experience a brief period of normality.

"What's your theory?" asked Jackie. "I'm sure you must have one."

Martin had been stiff with fear at the beginning but was starting to relax now that they were making good progress toward their destination. He didn't even complain when Jackie informed him that he would be spending the rest of the night at her place. She also shared with him everything she knew about the situation, and he was able to fill in a few missing pieces. As a resident pathologist, he was well-placed to provide an opinion.

"Viral, probably. It could be causing inflammation somewhere in the brain or triggering a neurological disorder."

"Not a toxin or a drug?" Jackie asked.

"Most drugs *are* toxins, to an extent, but I don't think it's that."

"Why not?"

"Well, for one, the initial toxicology screens I ran came up negative. Of course, that's for known drugs and their variants. This could be something completely novel. But what possible connection can there be between a cop, a surgeon, some college kid, an orderly, and a man waiting for his wife? And those are just the ones we know about. Drugs just don't fit the profile. People who randomly murder other people are usually high on methamphetamines or PCP."

Martin was a different person when he was talking about his specialty. Gone was the skittish and inept man who jumped at every shadow, replaced by a professional who was confident in his knowledge.

"What about prions?" she asked. "Like Mad Cow Disease."

Martin shook his head. "That's a very slow disease process, and it would happen at different rates in different people."

"How about meningitis then? That can affect people at a faster rate. Could it cause people to act this way?"

"In a word, no. People with meningitis may exhibit unusual behaviour but they are also very sick. Headaches, nausea, lethargy. They are usually not at all interested in running around indiscriminately killing everyone they encounter. That's the really strange thing about this... condition. The people don't appear to be sick."

"Well, they are not exactly normal either," she said. "Obviously, they are violent, *extremely* violent, but they also have a flat affect. And I've never heard one speak, although I've only seen two, so that is not a definitive characteristic."

"Flat affect," Martin repeated, as if this were a clue. "Do you think it's that they don't *show* emotion or that they don't *have* any emotions? It could tell us which part of the brain is affected."

Jackie thought about this for a couple of moments. "Part of me thinks that they must have emotions to attack people like that. It's impossible to say for sure. Even psychopaths have emotions; they just don't have any empathy or remorse. That's the closest to what I am seeing here, but the flat affect is making me question that diagnosis. Plus, people don't just become psychopaths. Dr. Gishar was one of the sweetest men I know, and I'm sure it wasn't an act. I don't think anyone could sustain that façade for years without letting it slip."

Jackie saw Martin give a slight nod of his head. "That's the thing, though. We don't know what their motivations are. Maybe they aren't based on emotion. There are other reasons for killing someone beyond hate, anger, and fear."

"But what in the world could motivate a respected surgeon to take a scalpel and attack a police officer? Dr. Gishar *knew* what he was doing. It wasn't blind rage. He selected the appropriate implement and used his knowledge of anatomy to produce damage that would be almost impossible to repair unless the person attacked was already in an operating room."

"Perhaps he was acting under some type of delusion?" Martin speculated. "I still think the cause is viral, but I've never heard of a viral disease that produces this type of effect.

Dehydration and edible products such as hallucinogenic mushrooms can cause delusions, but then we are back at the drug hypothesis again. It just doesn't fit."

"Has there been any type of outbreak?" Jackie asked. "We haven't seen an increase in any unusual illnesses at the hospital —at least not until today."

Martin thought about it for a few moments. "The only thing worth mentioning is the variant of VHP-25, Beta IV. It showed up in both Europe and the US about four weeks ago. It's been mostly unremarkable except for the fact that it has one of the highest transmission rates I've ever seen, an R_o of 8.2."

"8.2!" Jackie exclaimed. She didn't need Martin to explain the significance of the number. A virus with a transmission rate of 8.2 meant that, on average, every infected person transmitted the virus to eight others. It did not take a math whiz to surmise that the variant would quickly spread throughout the entire world.

"Could it be that?" she asked.

"I can't see how that is possible. There have been tens of millions of cases across the U.S., at least. And the vaccine is working as it should, although this strain is causing some breakthrough symptoms, such as elevated temperature. But nothing too concerning. That's why you wouldn't have noticed a change at the hospital; very, very few people need to be hospitalized."

"Wasn't the vaccine supposed to eliminate these symptoms?"

"In theory, but every mutation takes it another step away from the vaccine developed to combat it. The typical trajectory for a new virus is for it to produce less severe symptoms while simultaneously becoming more contagious. So, even while the vaccine becomes less effective, it often balances out with the disease becoming less dangerous. If the balance is off, a new booster is developed, but the CDC does not seem overly concerned with the latest variant. The vaccine is still producing a very robust response from the immune system. Besides, VHP-25 primarily affects the respiratory tract, not the brain."

"But respiratory viruses *can* affect the brain, can't they? I remember seeing reports about "Covid Brain", people feeling foggy, memory issues."

"Sure, but violence? Never."

"We'll just have to wait for the biopsy analysis," he said. He held up the canister. "I took a sample from Dr. Gishar."

Jackie looked across at him. "Seriously?"

Although pathology was his job, the idea of sawing open the skull of a so-recently-deceased colleague seemed…indecent.

"That's why I left the lab. Believe me, I didn't want to. But I needed to get this to someone, a specialist in the field. Our lab is not equipped to perform any kind of in-depth analysis. The sample is stored in liquid nitrogen, so it should be okay for quite a while."

They drove on without speaking for a few minutes since the effort of shouting over the sound of the wind whipping through the car was exhausting.

Jackie came to a fork in the road with a sign indicating two choices; the old bridge or the new bridge. The qualifiers were strictly relative. Such was the age of the city that the Wilcox Bridge, which was completed in 1983, was still called the new bridge. Either one would eventually get her to her apartment, but taking the newer crossing would mean traveling almost twice the distance.

"What do you think? My place is in Peterborough."

Peterborough was a suburb of Stanton, just outside the city limits. People didn't live there because it was nice; they lived there because it was cheap.

"The Jefferson is the best way to go," Martin said without hesitation, referencing the old bridge. "There's hardly any traffic, so we should be okay."

Jackie had never driven in the city, but she listened to the daily traffic reports, nonetheless. The old bridge was always a nightmare during rush hour, and recent maintenance work had made it even worse, reducing traffic to a single lane in each direction. However, she hoped it would be smooth going since it was not yet 5 a.m. Still, it gave her pause even though she could not articulate exactly why. She flicked on her indicator for a right-hand turn and proceeded toward the crossing.

Traffic had been sparse for most of their journey but increased in volume now that the vehicles were being funneled toward the bridge. It was a major connection between the two sections of the city, and a surprising number of people were already on their morning commute, as if nothing out of the ordinary was happening. Jackie supposed that many of these people might have gone to bed early and not checked any news media prior to leaving for work. Although the violent incidents seemed to be escalating at a rapid rate, previous episodes of violence may have been shrugged off as anomalies.

In addition to the cars and SUVs, there were delivery vans, some larger transport trucks, and the occasional motorcycle. The traffic was squeezed over to the right, with barriers and construction materials occupying the entire left side lane.

The flow of traffic stopped before they were even a quarter of the way across. Jackie could smell the river as it passed silently below them. She craned her neck to see what was causing the delay, but the reason was not immediately evident.

"They shouldn't be doing any construction at five a.m.," she said, mostly to herself.

It was just bright enough for her to see a large truck stopped near the apex of the bridge, but she couldn't tell if this was the vehicle causing the disruption. No more than twenty seconds passed before they heard the sound of screams coming from the cars closest to the truck.

Martin moaned and sunk a little lower in his seat.

Jackie couldn't see properly through her rear window, so she leaned out and looked behind her. There were at least six cars behind their vehicle, and more were driving onto the bridge even as she watched. It would take time for them to realize that something was happening and reverse out of the way. She looked forward. About twelve cars ahead of her stood a very large man dressed in a checked lumberjack shirt and holding what appeared to be a crowbar. He swung it and smashed out the driver's side window of a black sedan. Pebbled glass showered to the ground, catching the light and sparkling like diamonds. The man then reversed the crowbar and used it as a spear to deliver penetrating blows to the driver.

"Oh my God," said Jackie.

Martin started to hyperventilate.

The man moved on to the next vehicle in line, smashing that car's window as well. He peered inside without reversing the crowbar. Perhaps the driver had scurried across to the passenger seat and was out of range of the man and his weapon. It would have been easy for the large man to reach inside and unlock the door, but he proceeded to the next car in line, as if the driver of the previous vehicle was not worth the effort.

The man with the crowbar wouldn't need to bother smashing the window of Carrie's car. He could come straight at them through the hole made by the missing windshield.

"We need to go," said Jackie. "Right now."

She did not want to leave it too late to run, since getting out of the car could draw unwanted attention. She looked over at Martin, who was staring forward and rigid with tension.

"I'm leaving," she said, and opened her door.

That seemed to break him out of his stupefaction, and he scrambled out the other side of the car to join her.

Jackie hoped that the lumberjack man would be so focused on the cars ahead of theirs that he wouldn't notice them exiting the vehicle. That was wishful thinking. As soon as she was fully out, the man turned toward her and started run to run. Martin produced a cry that was pitched halfway between a Guinea pig and a seagull and tried to catch up to her as she began running along the bridge toward the road.

She looked behind her to gauge the man's speed and was horrified to discover that he was much faster than he looked. They would never make it to the street before he caught up to them. It was a small consolation that he would reach Martin first. It was like that old joke about running from a bear. You didn't need to run faster than the bear, you just needed to run faster than the person you were with.

"Cut across," she shouted and pointed toward the opposite side of the bridge. The traffic there was still flowing freely, although not all that quickly. The drivers were rubbernecking the spectacle on the other side and perhaps reaching for their phones to call 911. Jackie zigzagged between pylons and other equipment to reach the median barrier, a concrete wedge about waist height. Martin was still working his way toward the median after traversing a section of broken pavement. He held the metal canister in his arms like a child, and it seriously hindered his ability to run.

"Leave it!" she screamed.

Martin either did not hear her or intended to ignore her suggestion.

The median barrier proved no challenge; she simply placed her hands on top and vaulted over. However, she had only taken a few more steps before rolling her ankle on a piece of loose concrete, like some overused trope from a horror movie. The ankle hurt like hell, and she could barely put any weight on it. Cars continued to roll on by, with the drivers as wide-eyed as deer as she hopped frantically past the safety cones. No one stopped to help.

Jackie crossed the median in hopes of getting into another vehicle, but that depended on the benevolence of the other drivers. So far, they were being steadfastly uncharitable.

The lumberjack was huffing along with crowbar in hand just ten yards behind Martin. Martin was literally running for his life and had closed on Jackie since her ankle injury. Neither had much time to get to safety.

Jackie waved her hand at another car, but the man behind the wheel just leaned on his horn and accelerated away from her. She screamed in frustration. A different driver gave their horn a short bleat, this one designed to get her attention. The vehicle was some kind of sports car, dark red with a black hood.

The driver shouted, "Get in!"

Jackie hobbled around to the other side of the vehicle since it was a two-door. She barely managed to get inside before Martin tried to squeeze in beside her in a space meant for one. The lumberjack was so close to Martin that the pathologist was in danger of being speared from behind. The driver pressed on the accelerator before Martin was fully inside or had the door closed. He was half on Jackie's lap and half in the footwell and one leg was still outside the car.

Jackie turned her body as much as the situation would allow and looked behind her. The lumberjack stood in the road watching them depart but did not give chase. Their car slowed and then stopped about a hundred feet away, once again facing some type of traffic jam.

The lumberjack turned his attention to the next vehicle in line and swung and smashed at the windshield as it passed by. The car swerved to a stop a little further down the road, and the huge man approached the vehicle to finish the job. However, the lumberjack's luck had run out. This being America, the driver leaned out his window and shot the big man three times in the chest before the fellow even had a chance to raise the crowbar.

Jackie turned back to look out through the windshield, then at their rescuer.

"Hey," he said. "Are you okay?"

"I think so. Thanks for stopping." She pushed Martin's shoulder out of her face. "This pile of sharp elbows is Martin. My name is Jackie."

The man nodded in acknowledgement. "I'm Mike. Nice to meet you."

CHAPTER 12

Once they got off the bridge and into an area where they could make a quick escape, if need be, Martin climbed into the back. Jackie was glad he did not put up an argument over who would get to sit shotgun. Sitting in the back seat with no door and the inability to roll down a window would have left her feeling trapped and claustrophobic. She didn't like sitting in the back under normal circumstances and certainly didn't want to sit there now.

After they made their introductions, they shared stories and theories.

Mike said, "The police thought it could be an act of domestic terrorism, coordinated over a number of cities."

Jackie gave a small *humph* from the passenger seat. "But you said one of the attackers was a young girl. And another was an old woman."

"I didn't say I agreed with him. In fact, I'm about 100% sure that the police are wrong. They can't help themselves; it's just the lens through which they see the world. A doctor witnessing a passenger sweating profusely while going through airport security might see a person who is having a medical emergency. A TSA agent might see that same person as a potential terrorist."

Jackie said, "Martin thinks it's a virus that is somehow affecting behavior. I am more and more inclined to believe this theory after hearing your story. I thought it could be a drug, a legitimate drug, but it would have to be something new on the market. However, there are far too many cases now, and the odds of three people on the same plane taking the new medication are extremely low."

"So, now what?" asked Mike. "If it's a virus, should we just avoid being in contact with other people until they come up with a vaccine or whatever?"

Martin spoke up from the rear seat with his typically fatalistic pessimism. "This isn't exactly like COVID or VHP-25. With those, all you had to worry about was breathing in too much of the same air that other people breathed or having someone cough on you. Everyone with this virus wants to stab you to death."

"Let's just get to my apartment first," said Jackie, "and then we can evaluate the situation."

The traffic thinned considerably once they were away from the bridge, and they made good time. Their surroundings lightened almost imperceptibly until the sun opened a bloodshot eye on the horizon, painting the eastern sky a crimson red.

"Red sky at morning, sailors take warning," said Martin, almost too quietly to hear.

Three minutes later, they came upon a man running in the street who was being pursued by a woman. The man glanced back frequently, but it was impossible to deduce the nature of their interaction.

Mike brought the car alongside the woman and gave the wheel a quick jerk to the right. The impact from the car's fender sent the woman barrel-rolling onto the sidewalk.

"Holy crap," said Martin. "How do you know he didn't just grab her purse or something?"

"That's a good point," Mike conceded, looking in the rearview mirror. "If that is the case, you didn't see anything."

The rest of the ride was uneventful, with Jackie ultimately directing Mike into the underground parking garage of her apartment building. She didn't have a car but had not relinquished her spot in anticipation of eventually owning a vehicle someday.

They left the car and crept toward the elevator as if they were about to commit a crime. Every dark alcove seemed to exude menace, but the afflicted did not appear to be the type to hide in the shadows. If they were there, they would have shown themselves already.

Jackie pressed the call button and the elevator arrived only twenty seconds later. They all stepped back when it arrived, not knowing what to expect when the doors opened.

The car was empty.

Jackie pushed the button for the tenth floor after they entered. All three tilted their heads back and watched the lights on the indicator panel with bated breath, praying not to hear the dreaded *bing* that would indicate that someone else had requested the car. Never had an elevator ride been so fraught with tension. Ultimately, the elevator ascended to the tenth floor without stopping, a minor miracle.

Jackie peeked out, looked both ways, and then hustled Mike and Martin to her apartment down the hall. Her hands shook as she attempted to insert the key. Once everyone was inside, she bolted the door, walked over to her sofa, and collapsed onto it. She did not realize just how much tension she had been holding in her body for such an extended period. Each of her limbs felt like they had tripled in weight the moment she sat down, essentially fixing her to the spot. She could have happily remained in that position for the next twelve hours.

She looked up to see Mike and Martin still standing, just looking at her. "You can sit down, you know."

Except when she looked around, really looked around, she saw her place through their eyes. She had been single for a long time and had not had any friends over recently. Things had slipped. There were clothes draped across every chair in the apartment, leaving only the sofa as a viable location. There were unwashed plates and pots in the kitchen sink. The cat's litter box needed cleaning, although she was normally scrupulous about this. Clothes over chairs did not bother her, but the smell of cat urine and feces was something she needed to attend to immediately.

The location of her cat was not immediately evident. The cat, a long and scrawny stray by the name of Slinky, generally hid from visitors.

Jackie hauled herself to her feet with a groan and waved the two men to the sofa. Mike immediately reached for the remote and clicked on the television, working the buttons until he found a news station, NBC. Jackie listened to the news reports as she dealt with the smelly litter box.

The incidents of violence they had all witnessed were not just an East Coast phenomenon, although this part of the country seemed to be experiencing the highest concentration of events. There were reports from all over North America and many places in Europe but just a handful of cases in Asian countries.

The media already had a name for it, of course. The usual depiction of a nighttime cityscape behind the anchorman's desk had been replaced by two words spelled out in enormous red letters: Rage Pandemic. In reality, it was sometimes impossible to parse between normal violence and the violence they were now attributing to an outbreak of illness. How would they know if a kid who shot up a school was among those afflicted? No one had any idea what they were dealing with yet. Not only that, but the term was both observationally and factually incorrect. For one, rage didn't seem to play any part in it. There was a distinct *absence* of rage. For another, it was currently just an epidemic, not a pandemic. That was probably splitting hairs, but Jackie was annoyed at the coverage, the sensationalizing of the horror she had witnessed. To be fair, it was almost certainly to become a pandemic within the next few days, spreading like cancer via international travel.

China and Japan had already suggested a ban on Americans flying to their countries, a suggestion that outraged the President.

There were the usual experts trotted out, like Dr. Anthony Brajio, made famous and infamous through his handling of the COVID crisis. He was now retired, but the media still liked to bring him out and dust him off any time a new contagion emerged.

"We've never seen anything like this before; we don't even know if it is a disease yet," Brajio said.

"What else could it be?" asked the anchorman performing the interview, a salty-haired man in his late forties.

"Mass hysteria, copycats, a Doomsday cult? We just don't know. And until we have some samples and patients to examine, any theory will just be speculation."

"Where do we stand on that, the investigation, the diagnosis? Could it be a variant of VHP-25?"

"To answer the first question, local hospitals are doing what they can, but it will likely require samples getting to the Centers for Disease Control in Atlanta before we know for sure. Finding the answer isn't as simple as looking at a swab under a microscope. They'll have to do RNA and DNA sampling and compare it to the database of known diseases. As for your second question, it seems unlikely to be a variant of VHP-25. The vaccines developed to fight it compare well to the most successful inoculations we have ever created. In addition to that, the symptoms of this illness are unlike anything we have seen with VHP-25. It must be something completely novel."

"What would be the next step after deciphering the cause? Developing a new vaccine?"

"Sure, but we would also want to determine the mechanism of action. Such as, how is it causing this change in behavior we are seeing? That may lead to an effective treatment as well. You can often treat the symptoms before you address the cause."

"*Change in behavior*," muttered Martin. "He makes it sound like these people decided to bike to work instead of taking their cars."

"What's the timeline for another vaccine if it is something new?" the anchorman asked. "I know the process has become much faster with mRNA work."

"It's all relative. Developing a vaccine is much faster than ever before, but it is still a minimum of ten months between identifying the virus —if that's what it is— and the development and testing and wide-scale distribution of a vaccine. Every vaccine is unique and needs to be tailored to the specific virus."

"It could be a long ten months," the anchorman said, adopting an appropriately grave demeanor.

"It could indeed," said Brajio.

They flipped through a few more channels and found that it was more of the same. No one knew anything for certain.

Mike said, "The report said that they are still using the original vaccine, not one specifically designed for the new variant. Maybe this new variant has a different effect, and the vaccine didn't work properly."

"Except it did," insisted Martin. "Jackie knows this as well. People get infected, the immune response is triggered, and then they get better again. I had it about three or four weeks ago. Barely a sniffle. We all want to blame the boogeyman of VHP-25 or the vaccines for this, but whatever is happening here may be completely unrelated."

Mike put up his hands in mock surrender. "I clearly don't have anything of substance to contribute on the topic. You guys are the experts— I make online ads for cereal. I guess I haven't been paying very close attention to advances in the medical field."

They took a break from the news and tried to watch a movie to take their minds off what was happening around them. It didn't work. There were regular emergency interruptions that advised them to stay isolated and informed them of the closure of various services. The messages seemed late in coming, but they could have been out there for a while. It wasn't like Jackie and the others had been sitting around watching television; they had been otherwise occupied with staying alive for the past twelve hours.

Jackie had had enough of this day and stood up so abruptly that she startled the two men.

"I'm exhausted," she said. "I've been up for over twenty-four hours, and I really need to go to bed."

They all had another bite to eat but none of them were very hungry. Mike took the sofa while Jackie showed Martin to a room that was technically a second bedroom but was not much larger than a walk-in closet. It had no windows and only a mattress pad for a bed.

"It's not much, but you'll have some privacy."

"It's great, thanks. I could sleep on a concrete slab at this point."

Jackie looked back and forth between the two men. "I'd say *good night* except it's 6:30 in the morning. Let's plan on sleeping until at least noon. We are not going to function very well or think clearly on anything less than that."

She retreated to her bedroom and shut the door. Slinky wormed his way out from underneath the bed about ten minutes later and stretched out alongside her as if sensing that she could use some comforting. She most definitely could.

CHAPTER 13

Martin woke the next morning feeling hot and disoriented. *Where the hell was he? Why was he lying on the floor? And why was it so dark?* It took his brain a few moments to come up to speed. There was just enough light coming into the room from underneath the door for him to see the vague outline of shapes around him, mostly boxes. The room was stuffy and airless, and he lurched up toward the door like a person trapped underwater.

He pulled it open to blinding sunlight coming through a window. As his eyes adjusted, he took in two people who were standing next to a kitchen counter, speaking in low voices. He thought he heard the woman mention him by name. It was odd that they would be talking about him since he couldn't remember precisely who they were. His brain felt hollow. Perhaps he was oxygen-deprived from sleeping in that room all night, hidden away like a troublesome child. Did these people put him in there? He couldn't remember that either.

The woman eyed him with a frown as he approached. "Martin, you look a wreck. Did you sleep at all?"

He didn't know how to respond to that; it was like she was trying to catch him out in a lie.

"Do you want some eggs for breakfast?" she asked.

Martin eyed her warily. "Eggs. Breakfast," he repeated slowly.

"Well, technically brunch, since it's well past noon. Almost one in fact. I have some milk and cereal and some bread if you don't want eggs. And there's coffee."

"Coffee. Coffee," he said.

"How did you sleep? Are you ready?"

"Fine. Fine. Tired."

The woman poured coffee into a large mug with a picture of a cat on the side and handed it to Martin. He stumbled out of the kitchen, away from the too-bright sun, spilling hot coffee over his hand. He acknowledged the burning sensation with a sense of detachment, as if it were happening to someone else.

The man and the woman followed him into the room, settling on the sofa.

"We've been watching the news but there really isn't anything to report except the extent of the spread and the number of cases," the woman said. "We've been talking about what we should do today."

Martin shook his head rapidly, like a dog shaking itself free of water. "We need to... we need to..."

In his hollow mind, some important thought floated just beyond his grasp. The television was on mute in the corner of the room, and he watched it, transfixed. The person delivering the news was clearly not human. Martin extended his arm and pointed a trembling finger at the screen.

The woman looked to where he was pointing but did not seem the least bit troubled by the obvious fake. There was no way the person on the screen could fool anyone, so these people had to be part of the scheme.

"What is it, Martin?"

Martin looked over at the woman who, although apparently a stranger, knew his name. There was something not quite right about her as well. The movement of her mouth didn't seem to mesh with the sound of the words being spoken, like he was watching a person in a poorly dubbed film.

The important thought swam again to the surface of his mind.

"We have to…" But as soon as he spoke, the thought submerged again, impossible to see through the murky waters of his brain.

"We need to what? Take the sample to the specialist?"

Martin blinked rapidly. Part of him wanted to tell this woman what he knew, while the other part, becoming increasingly dominant, suggested that this would be a mistake.

"Martin?"

Martin shook his head again, trying to clear away the cobwebs. How did she know about his sample case? Had they been spying on him, somehow reading his thoughts? He tried to focus.

"Dr. Sandoval, the university." He practically shouted out the words, a Herculean effort that exhausted all his remaining resources.

"Is he the guy you gathered the samples for? I suppose it wouldn't hurt to speak with him," the woman said. "Which university is he at?"

The man walked over to the windows and opened the drapes, flooding the room with light.

The act of opening the drapes seemed to be done for the sole purpose of inflicting pain on Martin, and he winced and cowered away from the new assault. He was so very tired. Was someone talking to him? Maybe he imagined it. Thoughts and memories and random images swirled in his brain. And something else, something he did not recognize or understand. Part of him, the very last of him, watched the interaction from a distance and listened to the words coming out of his mouth, words over which he seemed to have no control.

"Martin, which university?" the woman asked again.

"The virus is in the people who look like people. We must stop the virus."

"Martin?"

Martin observed the conversation as if looking through a round window that grew steadily smaller as he sunk deeper into his mind. He felt no real connection to this other Martin.

"People who look like people spread the infection," the other Martin said. "Without them, the disease dies out. No carriers."

"Okay, yeah," said the man, although he spoke as if indulging a young child prattling on about a play date. "Masks, keep your distance from other people, all that stuff."

"People who look like people are the carriers," Martin repeated.

"So, should we stay inside, or should we go to the university?" the man asked.

Martin's viewpoint narrowed to a pinhole, and he was too exhausted to keep watching the exchange.

He leaned his head back against the sofa and let the window close forever.

"Maybe it's the stress," Jackie said, although she did not completely believe it. "We should let him rest."

They moved back into the kitchen to refresh their coffees. The caffeine it contained created an illusion of wakefulness, a dyke holding back the storm surge. Jackie could feel it, just on the other side of a thin but flexible membrane that pushed into her brain at irregular intervals. The caffeine would hold it back for now, but the hurricane was building, and she would soon need to sleep again for real.

Mike said, "I really can't see the benefit of traveling all the way across town to learn something we already know. We would be much better off finding a supermarket and buying enough food and water to shelter in place. If we go to the university first, it will be too late by the time we get back. It may already be too late. I found that out the hard way during the last pandemic."

"What do you mean?"

"I'm sure everyone has seen the news. They may not have seen any actual violence yet, but you can be sure that as soon as people see reports of shoppers buying up cases of water, it's going to be a madhouse."

"Damn. You're right. We should go right now, as much as I hate the idea of leaving the apartment at all."

They wandered back into the living room. Martin was still on the sofa with his head back.

"Martin, we are going out to get some food. We'll need a hand."

Martin stayed where he was, and Jackie gave the sofa a kick to wake him up. He tilted his head forward and looked at her, seemingly without recognition. He then looked around the room, stood up, and walked to a side table on which sat an iron. Jackie didn't have an ironing board so used the little table as a substitute.

She gave a little laugh as he picked up the iron, at the thought of him feeling the need to press his clothes before heading out. His clothes were very wrinkled, as were Mike's, but they had more important things to worry about. They could purchase some new pieces of clothing when they went out looking for food. It was unlikely that apparel stores would be overrun with shoppers.

"Martin, we really don't have time for that."

Martin ignored her and walked over to where Mike was searching for his keys in his jacket pocket. He lifted the iron over his head.

Jackie cried out, "Mike!"

Mike turned just enough to see Martin in his peripheral vision. He started to raise his arm to deflect the impact but was only partially successful. The iron hit him with a glancing blow on the side of the head and Mike collapsed to the floor.

Martin turned the iron in his hand so that the sharp end pointed down. Water from the iron's reservoir dribbled onto Mike's head. It was clear that he intended to use the sharp end as a chisel for Mike's skull. Martin was taller and heavier than Jackie, but she had the advantage of speed. She threw herself at him and they both toppled to the floor. The iron flew out of Martin's hand and landed about six feet away. He clawed his way across the floor toward it with Jackie riding on his back. The iron had an extra long cord and it snaked behind them. Jackie grabbed it and wrapped it around Martin's neck.

There are some things a person can go through their entire lives not knowing and never wishing to know. These things one can only learn through personal experience. Such was the case at this moment, on the living room floor of Jackie's 10th floor apartment. Jackie discovered that the process of strangling someone to death is a very intimate and personal act. She was sprawled against Martin, her chest tight against his back, her hips against his buttocks, their legs entangled. She could feel and sense everything, his desperate struggle, his scrabbling hands, the heat from his body, the smell of his hair. She could even feel the pounding of his heart as it tried to deliver an ever-diminishing supply of oxygen to his brain. And then she felt his death, the sudden relaxation of the muscles, a slackness.

The muscles controlling Martin's bowels and bladder released when he died, filling the apartment with a stench that she knew would never truly disappear. Whatever the outcome of this crisis, it was a given that she would never again live in this apartment.

CHAPTER 14

Jackie immediately attended to Mike's injuries, trying to keep busy to avoid thinking about what she had just done and what she had just seen. She had looked at Martin's face, after. She should not have looked. The cord from the iron was still wrapped tightly around his throat, indeed so tightly that it disappeared underneath folds of flesh. But his face, *his face*. The skin on his face was as red and shiny as an over-ripe tomato, and it looked like it would burst open at the slightest touch. His tongue protruded about an inch outside his mouth, dark purple, the tongue of a deep-water fish. The whites of his eyes had turned red from burst blood vessels, and it lent him a demonic visage. Distended veins crisscrossed his forehead like letters in a Runic alphabet.

Jackie had a basic first aid kit but no sutures to sew up the wound. She estimated it would require about eight stitches, but there was little chance they would be able to visit an emergency room. Those would be overrun, possibly as dangerous as any other place in the city.

Once the wound was cleansed with hydrogen peroxide, she used butterfly bandages to hold the skin together. The procedure was not working very well, and the wound was going to leave a nasty scar.

Mike examined her face as she applied the bandages. "You didn't have a choice, you know. He would have killed me."

She didn't reply for a few moments. Finally, she said, "I know. It doesn't make it any easier. It should, but it doesn't. I have killed two people in the last twenty-four hours. Deliberately. I strangled Martin until I felt the life leave his body. I don't know if I'll ever get over that."

They moved the body back into the small room where Martin had slept his last hours.

"Should we be doing this?" asked Jackie. "Moving the body? It's technically a crime scene."

"No crime has been committed here, except for the one against me."

"I don't think that's the way the police are going to see it," she said.

"Jackie, the way things are going, I don't think the police are ever going to show up, even if you called 911 right this minute. They are probably getting a thousand calls an hour. No one is going to be concerned about a man killed in self-defense. No one is going to question it either, considering what is going on."

She looked at the door of the room again. "It seems wrong."

"There's a lot wrong with what is happening. Not calling the police to report his death is so far down the list it doesn't even register."

"So, what do we do now?"

"I think we stick with the original plan. Gather a lot of food and water and wait it out."

"What about... the body? We can't just leave it in there."

"I know you aren't going to like this, so I'll do it on my own. I'll take it outside when it gets dark and put it in a dumpster."

"No! You can't just throw him away like he's a piece of garbage. We'll... I don't know, leave him outside a hospital or something."

"That might put us at even greater risk. Look, I know it is a far from ideal solution, but I don't want to get killed trying to ensure that the man who just attacked me has a decent burial."

Jackie shook her head, disagreeing. "He was sick with something, out of his mind. It's like blaming a car accident on someone who had a heart attack."

"Not quite the same, but I get your point. How about this? —when we go out to get our food and water, we'll assess the situation and make a decision based on what we see."

Jackie rocked on her heels, arms crossed. "Fine. But I'm not going to change my mind."

Before they left the building, Jackie took Slinky to a neighbor who had previously done some cat-sitting for her.

"Just in case," she said to Mike. She hoped there was no reason not to pick up the cat in an hour, but the thought of her cat dying from starvation was almost worse than the fear of what might happen to her personally while she was out.

Ten minutes later, they exited the garage in the Dodge Challenger and Jackie directed him toward a local supermarket. Mike expected the situation outside the building to be bad, but it was even worse than he anticipated. There were signs of violence within three blocks. An abandoned car sat in the middle of the street with the driver's-side door open. As Mike maneuvered past, they saw a person lying across the front seats. Jackie made a noise that could have been interpreted as a desire to stop and help, but Mike pretended not to hear. And Jackie was not very insistent.

They saw another body on the sidewalk about two blocks further along. It was a brown-haired woman wearing a blue dress and black boots. There was no one attending to her and there seemed to be few people on the street even though it was two in the afternoon. The fact that there was no law enforcement or first responder presence at either scene seemed to confirm Mike's theory— that the police were overwhelmed to the point of complete dysfunction.

There *were* people at the supermarket, but Mike and Jackie did not go inside. A man in the parking lot was shooting at someone inside the store and the person inside was returning fire. It was unclear if they were among the afflicted or just aggrieved shoppers trying to kill each other. Both possibilities seemed equally likely.

No police were in evidence here either, and they could not detect the sound of sirens in the distance.

"There's a Whole Foods about six blocks away," said Jackie, sinking a little lower into her seat.

The Whole Foods store had been picked mostly clean. They found a few cans and produce that had rolled under the shelving units but there were no beverages of any kind. The place still had a few scavengers, and Mike eyed them closely as they made their way around the store. There were random smears of blood on the floor and against some shelving. Despite this, the place smelled oddly tropical, probably because of all the trampled fruit.

They left with one bag of supplies; three-quarters full.

Once they were back in the car and Mike started the engine, he just sat there for a moment.

"I don't think there's much point in trying to go elsewhere," he said. "For what we are going to get, it's not worth the risk."

"We need more, a lot more," said Jackie. "I never buy a lot of groceries at one time, because I don't want the stuff to go bad. I only have about three days worth of food and that's only if we eat all the condiments as well."

Mike just stared out the window for a few moments. "We'll think of something," he said.

He put the car in gear and started back.

A man was standing perfectly still almost directly in front of the entrance to Jackie's underground parking garage when they returned. Mike could see him from a block away, and he slowed the car as they drew nearer. The man was facing in their direction, but he was too far away for them to get a good look at him and assess his intentions. His proximity to the front doors of the complex was also an issue, so they couldn't walk in either without being seen.

Mike brought the car to a stop about half a block away, the massive engine indiscreetly rumbling and burbling with power. Normally, he would enjoy the attention this might bring. Now was not one of those times.

"What do you think?" he said.

Jackie looked long and hard at the man, trying to judge whether he was waiting for someone, taking a rest, or about to explode into violence.

"I think he—"

The man's gaze turned toward them, and Jackie stopped talking. There was a brief, hopeful moment when they believed he might move along, and they could proceed inside as usual. But the man started running toward them, catching Mike off guard.

His body went into autopilot, going through the steps necessary to escape the danger. However, the problem with an automatic reaction when you are in a high-stress and dangerous situation is that it only works when one is in a familiar vehicle. Mike's hand reached for the gear shift and his foot searched for the clutch as he kept his eyes fixed on the man barreling toward them. Unfortunately, with this being an automatic transmission vehicle, there was no gear shift to be found, and his hand and foot groped in vain. His eyes developed selective blindness as he shifted his focus onto the unfamiliar controls. The man was only twenty yards away before Mike's hand finally found the gear selector, and he was able to slide it into reverse. Jackie screamed something in his ear, far too loudly given the proximity, and completely unintelligible. The essence of the message, however, was clear. *Go.*

Mike floored the gas pedal, and they shot backward at an imprudent rate of speed, a speed so great that Mike questioned the wisdom of engineering a car with this capability. Why would anyone need to drive sixty miles per hour *in reverse?* He felt the rear end start to fishtail and stepped hard on the brakes to prevent the car from spinning out. He slammed the selector into drive and whipped the car around in a tight U-turn. The man receded in the rear-view mirror, running hard after them even though he had no hope of catching the vehicle.

Mike's heart continued to hammer so hard that he would not be surprised to see his shirt bulge out over his chest, like a cartoon character in love.

He pulled over to the side of the road and relaxed his death grip on the steering wheel, peeling his fingers away one at a time. Jackie continued to look behind them as if she believed the man somehow possessed superhuman speed and was able to follow them for the entire mile.

"We could wait him out," said Mike. "Check back in an hour and see if he is still there."

"I don't want to be out in the open that long." Jackie dangled a set of keys. "I took these with me when I left the car on the bridge, the one that belonged to the other nurse, Carrie. It has her apartment key on there as well."

"Do you know where she lives?"

"Approximately. I remember her mentioning it because she made a joke about the name. Reichman Towers. She called it Rich Man Towers, as if she might find a good husband there."

Reichman Towers did present as an upscale apartment complex. It had thirty-three stories with a front terrace, landscaped gardens, and private tennis courts to the side. Both courts stood empty, and the streets and sidewalks appeared to be deserted.

Mike parked the car across the street and they both jogged over to the entrance, slipping inside less than twenty seconds after leaving the vehicle. Flyers and unclaimed newspapers littered the vestibule.

Jackie scanned the names on a board that sat adjacent to the intercom, finally locating C. Richards after missing it the first time through. Apartment 2806. Carrie would have had an exceptional view from the 28th floor. Jackie couldn't help but remember her in her last moments, and she tried to think of a better mental image than that of Carrie's head exploding from the gunshot wound.

The lobby door opened with the second key she tried, and they made their way over to the cluster of elevators. They looked at each other and came to a silent agreement. The twenty-eighth floor was a long way to climb if they took the stairs.

"I think the elevator is worth the risk," said Jackie.

"I agree. Less exposure time. Plus, well, twenty-eight stories."

Mike pressed the call button and waited nervously for the car's arrival. It now seemed like a naive and poorly planned decision to leave her apartment without any type of weapon whatsoever. What had he been thinking? Something as small as a steak knife would have given him at least some degree of comfort. Even the iron would have been better than nothing, but it was still connected to the cord wrapped around Martin's neck. Both he and Jackie had been reluctant to disentangle the cord from the folds of Martin's flesh.

They climbed into the first elevator that arrived and pressed the button for the 28th floor.

A generic pop song played at low volume on the overhead speaker, something about a boy loving a girl, sung by a boy.

The elevator chimed and then stopped when they hit the 10th floor. They looked at each other and then back at the door.

Jackie said, "What do we do if it's someone who is sick?"

Mike didn't have time to answer before the doors slid open. There was a man standing directly in front of them as the doors parted, blank-faced and dead-eyed.

CHAPTER 15

There were none of the normal behavioral indicators to allow Mike to predict what was going to happen next— no shouting or glaring or grimacing. No smiling or nods of acknowledgment either. Just that irritating pop song on the overhead speaker. The lack of verbal and visual cues made Mike hesitate. He certainly could not attack the man based on his lack of expression. The guy could simply have an emotionally bland face and be on his way to visit a neighbor on the upper floors. Mike was also relieved to see that the stranger was empty-handed. This was but a momentary relief.

In contrast to Mike, the man knew exactly what he wanted to do. He quickly strode into the elevator and reached clawed hands toward Mike's face. Mike had never been in a fight before, not really. Scuffling with some other boy for fifteen seconds in the fifth grade didn't count. It wasn't that he was afraid of physical confrontation; he had just never encountered a circumstance where it was necessary. Now, it was on. Amidst the life and death struggle floated the refrain from the insipid love song.

"My heart is like a flower, never able to bloom; it's your love that makes it happen, as soon as you walk in the room."

Mike brought his arms up and deflected the grasping hands, sweeping them to the side. He drew an arm back and punched the man hard in the face. Mike's fist felt shattered from the impact, like every bone in his hand was broken, but it had the desired effect. The man staggered back, momentarily stunned. He had his hands down, and Mike stepped forward and followed through with a roundhouse punch with his left hand. This one was not quite as powerful, but it knocked the man back another step, driving him into the floor selector buttons on the console.

The teenage boy's song continued to warble over the tinny speaker. *"My lips are like a desert, waiting for the rain to come; it's your kiss that makes it happen girl, you're the only one."*

The punches had to have hurt, but his attacker simply shook his head twice and then pushed off against the wall, coming in low. Mike was forced back a step, and then they were engaged in a strangely silent grappling match, straining, pushing, and pulling. The man seemed determined to bite Mike since he could no longer claw out his eyes. His neck cords stood out like piano wires as he forced his teeth toward the nearest part of Mike's anatomy, his nose. The man's breath was rank, like spoiled meat, and Mike strained to push him away. The illness did not imbue the sufferers with superhuman strength, but it did seem to supply them with extraordinary determination and resolve. Although they were temporarily locked in a stalemate, Mike sensed that he had a small strength advantage over his attacker. Or perhaps it was the additive effect of Jackie pulling back on the man's shoulders.

"Girl, you're my light, my love, my comfort when it's cold, girl, you're my angel, I'll love you till we're old."

The chime sounded again, indicating that they had arrived at the 28th floor. What had seemed like minutes was more likely in the range of twenty seconds. Mike wanted to get out of the elevator before the doors closed again. He brought his head back as far as possible and then snapped it forward, driving his forehead against the bridge of the man's nose. There was an audible crack and the strength seemed to go out of his assailant. Mike threw him sideways onto the floor and then backed out of the elevator, Jackie walking in lockstep behind him. The man's earlier collision against the console had caused a number of floors to be selected, and the elevator would descend again as soon as the doors were closed.

Mike watched the man closely, ready to intercede if he tried to get out, but the doors shut just as the man was getting to his feet.

"Jesus Christ," Mike said, and ran a hand over his face. "I hate that song."

"I'm sorry," said Jackie. "I wanted to help more, but I couldn't see how. There just wasn't time."

Mike lifted a hand. "It's okay. You already saved my life once today. Once a day is fine."

He looked at the door numbers of the apartments lining the hall. "Let's get inside and take a break. I don't know what kind of mental capacity these guys have, but I'd rather not be in the corridor if he remembers which floor we got off."

Carrie's apartment was a reasonably tidy one-bedroom with a spectacular view from the living room window. It was much nicer than Jackie's place and suggested that Carrie had been less interested in saving her money for a future upgrade. The unit had a small galley kitchen and an even smaller deck outside a set of sliding doors. The refrigerator and freezer were well-stocked, and it made Jackie feel lazy when she realized that Carrie appeared to prepare most of her meals from scratch.

Mike turned on the television set almost as soon as he entered the apartment. His cellphone had died, and the charger for it was still in his carry-on bag, sitting in the overhead storage bin on the airplane. He thought about taking Martin's phone, but the idea of going through the man's pockets, soiled with urine and feces, had been repellent. He would need to find a store that sold chargers when they were next out of the apartment.

The news had gotten worse, much worse, since they last checked. A red banner headline scrolled along the top of the screen: National State of Emergency Declared…Martial Law Being Discussed. That was a big one. It would be a difficult decision to make, knowing the nature of many Americans.

In a span of just forty-eight hours since the first suspected case of what they were now calling the Rage Flu, still inaccurate, there had been over seven thousand confirmed homicides in the continental United States, mostly on the East Coast. Mike knew that this was a vast underestimate, considering what they had seen and experienced. Bodies lying in the streets, attacks in private residences. The real number had to be much higher.

The anchorman, silver-haired and serious, was interviewing the national press secretary from the White House, a Black woman in her mid-thirties. The anchorman's questions echoed Mike's initial thoughts.

"Seven thousand is just the confirmed number of homicide cases, correct? Do you have any estimate of what the real figure might be?"

"It is impossible to get an accurate number. Police services at every level have been overwhelmed with calls and there is a lag in reporting. There could be three or four times as many victims."

"That's a horrifying number, Ms. Chalmers. What is the federal government doing to get this under control?"

"Well, as you know, we have declared a national emergency and instituted stay-at-home orders and mandated 8 p.m. curfews for all but essential workers. This is not only to keep the populous safe but to also help prevent the spread of whatever it is we are dealing with."

"How will the police enforce these curfews if they can't even respond to emergency calls?"

"It will be difficult. We are seeking to use the National Guard to enforce these edicts."

The anchorman produced a deliberate look of skepticism and then made a show of examining his papers. "Controlling the spread is an important consideration, of course, but what have the researchers at the CDC learned regarding the mechanism of infection and how the disease affects the body?"

The press secretary looked momentarily at a loss for words, a serious liability in a profession such as hers. "There have been complications."

"What kind of complications?" asked the anchorman, sensing that there was more to the story.

"I can't get into the details right now. The White House will provide another update in six hours."

With that, she removed her mic, stood up, and left the shot. It was a remarkable breach of decorum for a White House Press Secretary and suggested that things were even worse than they feared, if possible.

Mike wasn't interested in hearing a recap of the interview he just watched, so he kept on scrolling through various news sites. He soon came across a clip of a reporter interviewing a doctor who was standing outside the doors of a hospital. The doctor had short gray hair and wore wire-rimmed glasses and a white lab coat over a shirt and tie. The subtitle identified him as Dr. Theo Mudakis, Head of Neurology.

"What can you tell us about the disease?" the reporter asked.

"There is little that we know for certain. A person suffering from the condition almost always experiences an elevation in body temperature which may or may not be classified as a fever. We make the distinction between a fever, which is generally associated with fighting an infection, and a simple increase in body temperature, which can have multiple causes. The patient may or may not complain of a headache, but they consistently endure a phase during which they experience confusion and disordered thinking."

Mike nodded his head. The symptoms perfectly matched what they had seen with Martin. It would have been very useful to have had this information a day ago.

"So, are people coming to the hospital with fever and headaches?" asked the reporter.

The doctor hesitated. "No. These observations are based on patients who were already in the hospital for unrelated matters, so it has enabled us to see the progress of the condition."

"Do you believe they contracted the disease while in the hospital?"

"That seems unlikely, considering the care we take with infection control. In addition, no long-term patients have experienced this condition— all the cases we are seeing are in patients from the last two weeks."

"Have these patients attacked anyone?"

"These patients do exhibit a tendency for violence, but most are too sick or too injured— or pregnant— to follow through on their aggressive intent."

The thought of a fight to the death with a woman who was nine months pregnant was not something Mike wished to contemplate, even as a hypothetical.

He continued scrolling. Fifteen minutes later, he learned of the nature of the "complication" the CDC was experiencing regarding their investigation into the outbreak.

He had the sound off and initially thought the report he was seeing was some B roll for an unrelated story concerning the Centers for Disease Control, with the usual shots of the large blue and white CDC sign and distinctive curved façade of the building, and people entering and exiting. But the people exiting the building were hauling wheeled stretchers with body bags. Another scrolling headline declared that there were multiple fatalities inside the building, victims of a lone gunman who had been killed in a shootout with security.

The full extent of the tragedy only became apparent hours later, when authorities confirmed that twenty-two people had been killed and that the suspected gunman was a researcher at the CDC. How he had come to have a weapon inside the facility was not clear, although Mike had no idea whether the CDC was considered a gun-free zone.

Once, while clicking through the news stations, the screen displayed an empty anchorperson's desk with the station's logo situated behind it. Mike initially thought that the image had frozen, but there was some distant shouting in the background, picked up by the studio microphones. The screen stayed like that for a full twenty seconds before being replaced with a generic "Program Interruption" place card.

"This is insane," said Jackie. "This is worse than the Ebola virus. At least with something like Ebola, you can wear a protective suit, or simply avoid contact with the people who are infected. This is like a virus that hunts you down no matter where you go or what you do. And it can keep going until the person with the virus dies—and we don't even know if it's a fatal condition."

"So, what do we do?" asked Mike. "Stick with the original plan?"

Jackie assumed he was referring to the original plan of sheltering in place. "I don't know if this apartment is a safe option. What happens if the building superintendent catches the sickness? He or she has access to the keys to every apartment in the building. They could come in while we are sleeping."

"I think the odds are pretty long that they would get sick *and* make it to this apartment before someone stops them. Besides, we can probably reinforce the door. Your friend should have a few tools we can use, a hammer and some nails, or screws."

Jackie looked at him for a long moment. "What happens if one of us gets sick? We don't know the incubation period for whatever this is. Then you or I would be trapped in here with the other person."

Mike seemed both startled and dismayed at the notion. "That's the road to madness right there. Paranoia and madness. If that is the strategy we're following, we'll soon be handcuffing ourselves to our beds. We would have to be on guard 24/7, especially with anyone new."

"Still, I think we have to be observant, and that's not the same thing as being paranoid. Martin's illness came on quickly, but there were signs if you knew what you were looking for."

"Disjointed thought patterns, the repetition of words, confusion," suggested Mike.

"He seemed a little feverish as well. And then he nodded off, although that may not be a common symptom. The last couple of days have been grueling, to say the least."

"The lack of emotion comes later," said Mike, "after they are fully sick."

"So, how are you feeling?" asked Jackie, giving him the slightest of smiles, as if she were joking but not really.

Mike waved off her question with his hand. "Fine. You?" His eyes were fixed on her face, and she knew that he was serious about the question as well.

She gave him a thumbs-up in response, but she knew that from now on, he would be watching her more closely. And she would be watching him.

The building was quiet to the point of eeriness, as if every person was holding their breath, waiting for something to happen. Jackie could imagine people with their televisions muted, standing at their hallway doors, and just *listening*. How long would it be before she and Mike started to do the same thing?

They had a light snack with some of Carrie's food and then tried to sleep even though it was still only late afternoon. Jackie took the bed, sleeping on top of the sheets, fully clothed, while Mike bunked out on the sofa. It was a restless sleep for both. Their discussion about whether to stay or leave had fizzled out when they went down the rabbit hole of possibilities, but it remained on Jackie's mind throughout her attempts to nap.

She gave up trying to sleep and climbed off the bed to get a drink of water. Her clothes were sticking to her, and she was uncomfortable and hot, but not feverish. She hoped.

She exited the bedroom to find Mike looking out the window. He was as still as a statue, his hands by his sides, and she watched him for a full minute before deciding to speak.

"This was a bad idea," she said into the quiet. "This apartment in particular."

Mike gave a slight jump when she spoke, which she thought was a good sign. He turned away from the window and faced her. "What? Why?"

"We're too high up and we'll eventually run out of food. There are too many people between us and the exits. If those people start to get sick, we'll be trapped up here. They'll be in the elevators, the stairwells, and the lobby. What if someone decides to set fire to the entire complex? We'd never get out."

Mike appeared to be annoyed. "This was your idea," he said, sounding much as he looked. "*I* wanted to wait the guy out and go back to your apartment."

"How was I supposed to know Carrie lived on the 28th floor?"

Mike didn't answer, he just turned to look out the window again. Jackie walked over to join him. The city looked deceptively normal from this high up, and Jackie thought of astronauts in orbit and how all the borders and cities seemed to disappear from their perspective. It would be nice to forget about all this for a while and just pretend that everything was okay, but she did not believe they had the luxury of time.

"Look, I'm sorry, but I think we should leave," she said. "While we still can."

"It seems safe here. And I am exhausted. Can we at least stay the night before we go?"

Jackie glanced out the window. The day had become overcast, making it seem later than it was. She was exhausted as well, and it was easy to be swayed by Mike's request.

"Fine, but we set an alarm and leave early. Okay? We need to be on the road before everyone else wakes up and tries to kill us."

"I second that plan."

At 2 p.m., emerging from the depths of sleep, Mike heard knocking. It was faint at first, and he tried to ignore it. He may have even drifted back to sleep; such was the depth of his fatigue. His bone-deep exhaustion overwhelmed even the warning bell that his subconscious mind was trying to ring. Then came a knock on *their* door. Mike came fully awake in an instant, his heart thudding painfully. There was not much light in the room, that high up. The drapes were almost fully closed, clouds obscured any moonlight, and any light from the street level had mostly dissipated by the time it reached the 28th floor. A red LED light from the power button on the television set was the only illumination produced within the apartment.

He jumped when Jackie spoke from the darkness.

"Is someone at our door?" she whispered.

The knocking was all that more dramatic because it accentuated just how preternaturally quiet the building had been since their arrival.

Before he could answer, the sound came again, slow, and deliberate, *tock...tock...tock.*

The very tempo of the knock made them freeze with fear. It was off, just like everything else in this messed up situation. Jackie switched on the living room light, a very human response to a threat, but not a very prudent one. The person in the hallway might notice the light spilling out from under the door, confirming the occupancy of the unit.

They looked at each other and then back at the door.

Jackie leaned toward Mike and whispered in his ear. "Do you think we should answer it?"

There was a security peephole in the door and Mike mimed putting his eye up to it. He walked over but hesitated for a moment, remembering a scene from a movie that involved a peephole such as this. As soon as it was evident that the person inside was looking out, someone fired a shot through the peephole into the person's brain. He winced a little as he leaned forward and peered out.

A man was standing there with a butcher knife in one hand and a terrifyingly blank expression.

CHAPTER 16

Mike realized at the last moment that even if the man outside had missed the light coming from under the door, he could not fail to notice the darkening of the peephole as Mike moved his eye to it. Even so, there was no apparent reaction. The man was in his late thirties, dressed in jeans, a black t-shirt, and a black windbreaker. He was completely unremarkable, one of those many people you encounter in your day-to-day life who make no impression on you whatsoever.

Perhaps all the other residents *were* holding their breaths; Mike was certainly holding his. The man suddenly leaned forward to knock again and Mike reared back reflexively. Jackie gave a small pip of alarm and grabbed his upper arm. They waited, frozen in place, eyes so focused on the door that they forgot to blink.

After what felt like a minute, they heard knocking at a door down the hall. Mike let out a long pent-up breath.

"Jesus," Mike said. "It was a guy with a big-ass butcher knife, like something out of *Halloween*."

"Dammit," said Jackie. "We could be stuck here for a while after all."

The man continued to recede down the hall. Mike wondered if he would take the stairs once he reached the end or just keep to this floor.

A woman's scream shattered the quiet.

Remarkably, improbably, it seemed someone had opened the door without first checking to see who it was.

Mike ran to the door and then thought better of it. "I need a weapon."

He whirled around, considering every object in the room that he could conceivably use: an end table, the large flatscreen television, decorative bowls, the remote control, a collection of books and magazines, candles.

He ran to the kitchen and threw open some drawers. Inside were whisks, a spatula, wooden spoons, a meat thermometer, and a serrated bread knife. The blade of the knife bent to the side when he pushed against it. The only feasible weapon appeared to be a long metal fork with two heavy tines, the kind of utensil used for lifting a roast out of a pan. It felt insubstantial in his hand, more a talisman than an instrument of war, like he was going into battle with a crucifix.

The woman stopped screaming sometime during his search, a fact he tried to ignore, perhaps to absolve himself of the blame he felt for acting too slowly. He could have left the apartment weaponless, but would that have been enough to save the woman?

Before he reached the door, two shots rang out from a heavy caliber weapon. He stopped again, trying to decide whether this development was better or worse. He thought he heard someone speaking, so he decided it was worth the risk.

An older man, mostly bald with just a fringe of white hair, was still in a shooter's stance outside of an apartment three doors down.

"Goddammit, Mildred, why did you have to open the door?" the man asked. He flicked a glance Mike's way and then lowered the gun.

"I didn't think anyone would open their door," he said, as much to himself as to Mike. "Mildred, you foolish old woman. Goddammit, *Goddammit!*"

He seemed both distraught and guilt-ridden.

Mike edged his way closer. He glanced back and saw Jackie peeking out from the apartment. The attacker was sprawled on top of an old woman, presumably Mildred, and they were both covered in blood. There were two neat holes in the man's back, eight inches apart, ruler-straight. By virtue of their positioning, the bullets would have punctured both lungs and possibly the attacker's heart.

The older man continued to stare down at the bodies. "He knocked on my door, you know. I could have stopped him then, but that seemed wrong, like murder. I didn't think anyone would open the door for him. Mildred is a bit senile. Was. And lonely. I should have guessed she would open the door without looking. Goddammit."

"We're all trying to figure this out," said Mike. "The right thing to do." He did not mention that he had wasted a full minute trying to find a weapon instead of immediately going to the woman's aid.

The older man looked down at his pistol. "I was a cop for thirty-four years and this is only the second time I had to shoot someone. Jesus Christ, what a mess."

Mike made a gesture that included Jackie down the hall. "We are planning to leave in the morning." He looked at his watch. "Four hours from now."

The man turned and looked at Mike as if seeing him for the first time. "You're at Carrie Saunder's place. Is she there?"

"I'm afraid Carrie was killed yesterday at the hospital. My... friend, Jackie, is a colleague. We came here after we couldn't make it into her own apartment building. There was a man outside. These people are everywhere."

The ex-cop gestured to the man on the floor. "This guy was a tenant. I didn't know him, but I think he worked for a pest control company. There's no rhyme or reason to it."

"Carrie's colleague thought it was a virus. He caught it and attacked me this morning." He pointed to the bandaged area on his head. "He was fine the night before, acted a little weird when he first woke up, and then attacked me with an iron."

"You mean like a golf club?"

"No, an iron for ironing clothes."

"Damn, that must have hurt. So, what happened to him?"

Mike looked back down the hallway to see if Jackie was still there. Apparently, she had ducked back inside the apartment. He lowered his voice anyway. "Jackie had to kill him. It hit her hard."

The old man turned solemn. "Killing someone is never easy, nor should it be. The person you kill takes something from you when they die, a little part of what makes you human. You're never quite the same afterward." He looked back into the room, at the body, as if acknowledging that he was now forever diminished.

Mike hadn't known the old Jackie long enough to know if the killings had changed her and now, he never would. He hoped that she could make peace with the deaths.

"Are you going to stay in the building?" asked Mike.

"I have to. I have my granddaughter with me. Which is why I didn't do anything when this guy first came by. I didn't feel too good about leaving her alone in the apartment to go and deal with this, but she's a smart girl. She won't open the door to anyone but me."

He held out his hand. "Name is Foster."

Mike introduced himself and then glanced back down the corridor. Jackie had not yet made a reappearance. He nodded in her general direction. "Jackie made a good argument for leaving. If the shit really hits the fan, there are twenty-eight floors of people between us and the exit. If the power goes out and you run out of food, it's a long way down to the street." He paused for a moment. "You could come with us if you want."

The old man was a quick study, and Mike could see him analyzing the risks versus the potential benefits. Mike realized that he should consult with Jackie on this, but he thought she would agree. It was not a purely altruistic act. The man was old, but he had a gun, and he was a good shot. That was a huge plus.

"Give me fifteen minutes to get ready," Foster said. "We shouldn't wait until morning."

With that, he turned and walked down the hall.

Jackie was not altogether keen on taking the other two along. "An old man *and* a kid? We may have to move fast and having them with us could be a real handicap. I'm all for helping people but we can't save everyone."

"I think the benefits outweigh the liabilities. The guy is an ex-cop, he has a pistol, and he knows how to use it. We have a serving fork."

"Fine, but we can't allow them to interfere with our plans. We should get the brain tissue sample to the university. If it was so important to Martin that he would risk his life to get it this far, I think we should complete the job. Then we can decide what to do from there."

Mike heard Foster speaking to someone in the hallway, using the tone of voice that people use when talking to small children. Their new companions arrived at the door a few moments later, Foster now dressed in trousers and a dress shirt, as if heading off to a nice restaurant. At his side was a girl of about ten. She had long dark hair and a Hello Kitty backpack on her slim shoulders. She looked like any of a thousand other ten-year-old girls except for her glassy eyes and a face flushed with fever.

CHAPTER 17

Mike looked at Foster's granddaughter for a long moment and then caught Jackie's eye, wondering if she was thinking the same thing.

Mike asked, "Is she feeling okay, she looks—." In his head, he thought *infected*, but he said instead, "A little sick."

"Amy was running a fever yesterday, which is why I was reluctant for her to leave the apartment, but she seems a little better today."

Jackie walked over to him. "Hi, we haven't met. I'm Jackie." She then took his arm and turned him away from the little girl. "I'm a nurse at Stanton General. Listen, there's no way to be certain, but your granddaughter appears to be showing the early symptoms of the sickness that is causing these episodes of violence."

Foster leaned away from her as if she herself were contagious.

"Ridiculous. It's nothing more than a touch of the flu, not even that, a bad cold. As I said, she seems better this morning."

"That's the way it presents. Once the fever breaks, there appears to be a period of remission. But during that time, other symptoms emerge. Some confusion, and a decrease in communication. In the final phase, just before the violence, their faces go blank and slack."

"Even if that were true, she's ten years old for Christ's sake! What's the worst she can do to us?"

Mike said, "You would be surprised," remembering the mother with the young daughter on the flight and the extremely effective use of a sharpened pencil to inflict injury. To be fair, this girl was a good two years younger than the girl on the plane and small for her age, a tiny slip of a thing. But Mike was certain that a well-motivated ten-year-old could still do a lot of damage.

"You'll need to watch her, closely," said Mike. "Make sure she doesn't have anything in her possession that can be used as a weapon. *Anything*— pencils, an iPad, any item she can break and use as a stabbing or slicing tool."

Foster stared back at him as if he had lost his mind. "You're acting like she's a cutthroat murderer or something. She just finished watching *Frozen* for the thirty-sixth time."

"It doesn't matter," said Jackie. "This sickness makes them into a different person, and it progresses very rapidly. There's no way to know precisely when it will happen."

Foster appeared unconvinced but dutifully checked through the girl's backpack. He pulled out a set of colored markers that were thick and blunt and unsuitable as a weapon no matter what the age. These went back into the bag. The scissors that he found were small and had rounded-off blades and pink handles. Still, they could be used for stabbing, especially to the face and neck. When Foster raised an eyebrow at Mike, Mike shook his head. Foster gave a dismissive snort, but he stuck the scissors in his coat pocket.

The elevator did not stop once during the entire descent, although they did hear shouting and cries of alarm as they glided by the fifteenth floor. Foster moved as if to press the stop button, but Mike stepped in his way, not exactly blocking him but running interference just long enough to make pushing the button pointless. Mike suspected that this inclination to intervene was likely ingrained cop behavior rather than a true desire to get involved. He had his granddaughter with him now, and her protection overrode any obligation he may have felt to some random strangers in his building.

The lobby was also clear, although this was unsurprising at 3 a.m. Mike went to the front door and closely examined the street for a full minute before directing the others to join him. Foster kept his pistol in its holster, but his coat was undone, and he kept his firing hand free should he need to draw the weapon quickly.

They hustled down the walkway, over the sidewalk, and across the four lanes of Reichman Avenue. Mike didn't know what he expected but breathed a huge sigh of relief once he was seated behind the wheel.

Foster sat in the back with Amy the granddaughter, a potential ticking time bomb, all sixty-five pounds of her.

Jackie clutched Martin's sample case in her lap. She was glad she packed it when she left her apartment. It felt like something both highly lethal and yet potentially crucial to the survival of the species. She felt equally motivated to toss it out the window and protect it at all costs. Her main goal now was to simply rid herself of it by passing it off to the researcher, Dr. Sandoval.

She was likely putting too much weight on the value this sample would have on the outcome of the epidemic. In fact, she knew she was, but it made her feel less helpless. The chances of one researcher making a significant breakthrough regarding the infection seemed slight, but they were not completely absent. The doctor was very unlikely to have the resources of the CDC, but individuals, or partners, in the past had made world-changing discoveries virtually on their own. Louis Pasteur with penicillin, Banting and Best with insulin, Jonas Salk with the polio vaccine. It seemed a less common occurrence in modern times, for whatever reason. Maybe all the easy answers were taken and elucidation by simple observation was no longer going to produce the necessary results.

The ride across the city was surreal. Despite what had been suggested by the White House Press Secretary and the news media, it was clear that control had been lost. Scores of dead bodies littered the streets. There were crashed and abandoned vehicles everywhere. Vacant-eyed people watched them from the sidewalk, occasionally making a charge at them like a dog chasing a rabbit. Mike drove the vehicle past two men who were exchanging gunfire while standing just ten feet apart, barrels sparking like flashbulbs. The combatants were facing each other with their arms extended, and it reminded him of paintings of warships engaging in broadside cannon fire in the sixteenth century.

Mike did not stop for stop signs, red lights, or blockages in the road. Jackie conceded that he was likely a better driver than she, able to judge and adjust and change course based on what was happening in the next block. He seemed calm, but when she glanced at his hands, they were white-knuckled against the steering wheel.

Although the emergency broadcast system was instructing individuals to stay indoors, there were still a surprising number of people out and about. This was a given in America. *Being told* to stay indoors almost guaranteed that there would be people out in the streets, even if they had no good reason to be there. It was the principle of the thing.

They were most of the way to the university when someone ran into them from behind, hard enough for their heads to snap back in unison, like a strange piece of choreography. Mike had been so focused on what was taking place a block or two in front of him that he practically ignored what was happening behind him. Luckily, the hit had been straight on, so it had minimal effect on Mike's control of the vehicle. He looked in his rearview mirror only to see the vehicle behind him making another charge. As the vehicle passed under a streetlight, he could see that the driver was an elderly man wearing a fedora. The man's face was free of any expression, and it seemed that he and Mike made eye contact via the mirror, although this could have been his imagination.

The vehicle, a huge boat of a thing, crashed into the back of their car again. This time the rear end of the car shifted to the left and Mike had to fight the steering wheel to avoid crashing into a row of parked cars along the street. Mike cursed, Jackie screamed, Foster shouted, and Amy remained unnaturally quiet.

Mike floored the accelerator, and the huge engine responded with a sound that was uniquely associated with a sports car, half roar, and half anticipation. If an engine had the capacity to be excited, this was the auditory expression of that emotion. Mike could almost hear words in the sound, deep-throated and commanding: *Release Me.*

The car was released. It rocketed away at such a high velocity that everything in Mike's peripheral vision became a blur. It was terrifying and exhilarating, like riding a roller coaster car at night on an extremely steep decline. His attention shifted so frequently from the road in front to the rearview mirror that he completely failed to notice that the light at the next intersection was dark.

He hit a white minivan at almost eighty miles an hour and both vehicles spun wildly. There were sounds of breaking glass and squealing tires and plastic and metal disintegrating and people screaming. Multiple airbags deployed, like giant popcorn popping. And then there was silence except for the hissing of steam escaping from the radiator and the ticking of the cooling engine.

It took several moments for Mike's brain to reboot. He didn't think he had suffered a concussion, but it certainly felt like he had been in a fight, if only with the car. His body had been subjected to forces that were outside the realm of what a human being should ever experience, perhaps thirty times gravity. Sustained, these forces would have killed him. That level of force would also have killed him if it had not been dissipated by large bags of air. Even so, the shock of it left him stunned and momentarily unsure of exactly where he was or what he was doing. He was surrounded by white. Once he realized he was cocooned by airbags, he fought himself clear.

From the back seat came a groan, and he remembered. Foster, Jackie, and the little girl, who may or may not be infected with the virus.

"Is everyone okay?" It sounded like he was gargling water, and he cleared his throat.

Everyone was not okay. Jackie had been protected and Amy had the resilience of youth. But the back seats were not as well protected, and Foster was an old man. Something had wrenched in his back and in one of his knees and he was barely mobile.

"We'll have to walk the rest of the way," said Mike, even though this did not seem viable. The man needed a hospital, not a nighttime stroll to the university.

"We need to check on the other driver first," protested Jackie.

"Of course, of course," he said, holding up his hands. "I'll try to find something that Foster can use as a cane."

Mike didn't see anything nearby that looked appropriate, but there was a looted drug store partway down the block. Glass from a broken window had sprayed across the sidewalk and into the street. He crunched his way across the broken glass and climbed over a window ledge and into the store.

People had stolen medication and food and diapers, but they had left all the health aides behind. He found a walker on wheels with a built-in seat and carried it out of the store and over to the car. It had a brake lever on the handle, like a bicycle. Foster looked at it with distaste. Mike hoped he would not be too proud to use it.

"It's just until we can get you checked out," he said.

After determining that the person in the other vehicle would live, Jackie rejoined them.

"Okay, we can head out," she said.

Foster didn't move and stared up the street as if he had not heard her. "The police are not coming," he said, mostly to himself, almost in wonder. It must have been hard for him to accept, after years on the force, that society had reached this point, this quickly.

Jackie looked around at the broken shops, the wrecked cars, bodies in the street.

"No, they are not. Not for this, maybe not for anything else either."

CHAPTER 18

Foster's injury kept the group from moving very quickly. They could only move as fast as the slowest person, and Foster was *very* slow, as slow as an arthritic ninety-year-old. It was not so much that Mike was in a rush to get to the university; it was the time they were out in the open, visible to any infected person in the area. They tried their luck with many of the abandoned cars, but every single one seemed to have some kind of an issue. The vehicles were either out of gas, had drained batteries, were missing keys or were damaged beyond repair.

They hadn't run into anyone who wished to do them harm, but that felt inevitable, like repeatedly running across a busy street while blindfolded. You only got lucky so many times.

It now seemed almost criminally negligent to have brought a ten-year-old child into this environment, even if she was potentially infected. The car had insulated them from the brutal truth and given them a false sense of security. Now that it was stripped away, the true scope of their predicament hit Mike with full force. He was walking at a snail's pace in plain sight with an unarmed woman, a defenseless young girl, and an injured old man for company. Granted, the man had a weapon, but how effective would that be if they were attacked from multiple directions?

Jackie seemed competent and could handle herself, but Mike now regretted his arrangement with Foster. It left him feeling responsible for the safety of the man and his granddaughter in a very precarious situation. Mike could not help but notice that the girl had not screamed when they hit the other car. That was abnormal, but he didn't know what she was like before. Perhaps she was an especially chill young girl. The fact that she had not yet spoken a word was somewhat more telling. He didn't know any girls that age who didn't keep up a steady chatter.

Jackie knew the name of the building they needed to find but not the location. Unfortunately, a campus map had not been included on the website. They wandered the leafy avenues of the university grounds just as dawn broke, looking at the names of the buildings. Their current course of action was not very efficient, and strolling around the campus like tourists on vacation was inadvisable. Although they were off the main city streets, they were still very exposed and did not know where to go if they did run into a problem. If anything, they were less likely to obtain the assistance of municipal law enforcement on school grounds since most of the universities maintained private security.

Foster had to stop and rest his leg more and more frequently. Jackie did not believe anything was broken, but he seemed to have torn a ligament in his knee, which was almost as disabling as a fracture.

They came across a body along one of the footpaths, a young man whose face had been battered beyond recognition. Foster put his hands over Amy's eyes, but she didn't seem to be the least bit phased by anything.

A scream came from behind them, and they turned to see a man chasing a woman across a small parking lot several hundred yards away. They disappeared from sight, but the woman's screams could still be heard. Foster stopped, but his decades-long instinct to head toward trouble was severely impeded by his damaged knee and wrenched back.

Mike laid a hand on his arm. "You have to let it go. You're only responsible for Amy right now."

It was a hard truth to accept. They had an important task to complete, one with the potential to save many more lives. Fighting individual battles was noble, but it would eventually get them killed. It was just a question of running the numbers. So far, few of the afflicted were armed with much more than what they had on hand.

Five minutes later they came across a campus directory just outside what looked like the athletic complex. Raven Dome was printed in large letters across the front, accompanied by the depiction of a raven coming in for a landing with its talons outstretched.

"You guys take a break and I'll figure out where we need to go."

He pointed to a bench under a large tree about forty yards away. No one argued with him.

The campus was huge, and the arrangement of buildings made it unlikely they would be able to find their destination by chance alone. Mike took out his phone to take a picture of the schematic, although it was more as a backup than a reference. The type on the diagram was small and the picture wouldn't do him a lot of good. He found the Thompson Centre for Science in the directory along the side of the chart and then scanned the grid lines for its location. Building 26, Section E5. He found the E grid and slid his index finger down toward the point where it intersected with grid 5. The map was covered by a yellowing plexiglass shield, and he stepped slightly to the left to get more light from the early morning sun.

The plexiglass splintered only inches from his hand, sending out jagged lines from a central impact point. He had the smallest fraction of a second to be startled by this inexplicable occurrence, like an act of spontaneous combustion, before he heard the shot. He jerked his hand away and spun around to look behind him. A gray-haired woman had a rifle aimed at him from about seventy yards away. There was little shelter available behind the directory and nothing else of substance within fifty yards.

He chanced a quick glance to his right and saw that Jackie was shepherding Foster and Amy into a hedgerow behind the bench where they could be concealed. He ran left, toward the athletic facility, to draw the shooter away from them. The rifle barked again but he couldn't tell how close he was to being hit.

He practically leaped up the low flight of stairs, only to find that the doors were securely locked. Two more shots came from the rifle, both hitting a glass door to his left. The glass splintered and cracked but stayed within the frame until he gave it a kick. It showered onto the floor inside the lobby, and he stepped through. Other shots hit the doors and windows, and he hurried deeper inside, grateful to be out of the line of fire but anxious about being trapped inside a building he didn't know.

He pushed through the turnstiles and tried to determine if there was another exit nearby. It would not take the woman very long to reach the front entrance and he needed to get out of sight. He continued through a set of double doors and discovered a corridor that led deeper into the building. Immediately to his right ran a line of black metal doors without windows.

He had almost decided to proceed along the hallway when he was startled by the appearance of a short woman with wavy blond hair. The woman was enormously fat, almost as wide as she was tall, practically spherical. She seemed to come out of nowhere and rushed toward him with jerky motions, like an animatronic doll.

He took a defensive stance, suddenly sure that she was infected and about to launch an attack. He looked at her hands to see if she was carrying a weapon.

"She's *inside*," the woman whispered, sounding absolutely terrified. She must have been watching the shooter's progress through a window.

The woman pushed Mike toward the black metal doors with the words "Track Entrance" printed on them in large yellow letters. It was not where he wanted to go, but there seemed to be few other viable options. The woman's pudgy hand gripped his coat sleeve with surprising strength, and she pulled open one door and dragged Mike through. In the few seconds that light came through the door, he took in the concrete surface for a rink at the lower level, and the stadium-style seating leading up to the balcony track on which they now stood. Outside the track were deep wooden benches against the walls. He guessed they were for runners to have a rest or to change their shoes.

The door closed, and they were swallowed by the dark. There were no windows whatsoever and no apparent electronics. There wasn't even any light leaking in from underneath the doors. He hoped that once his eyes adjusted, he would be able to see enough to navigate, however precariously that might be.

The woman walked him slowly along the outer edge of a track he could no longer see, where the benches were positioned. His leg would occasionally brush against them, and he guessed that this was how the woman navigated. That, and she appeared to know the facility very well. After they had walked for what felt like a quarter of a mile but was likely fifty yards, she yanked on his coat sleeve and whispered, "Under."

His hand groped until it felt the slats of the bench and he kneeled onto the track. The surface was rough, and he could feel little protrusions of rubber dig into his knee.

He crawled underneath the bench until he reached the wall, no more than three feet in. The floor had not been swept recently and his hands encountered what felt like dirt and empty chip bags and chocolate bar wrappers. He turned his body until he was lying on his side, facing out. The woman squirmed in directly behind him and had to squeeze underneath, barely able to fit even though there was a foot and a half of clearance. There was not much room, and they lay there spooning, like lovers. She was both hot and soft and he could feel her rolls of fat wherever their bodies touched, against his thighs, his stomach and chest, his shoulders, and arms. It was a strange sensation, like snuggling up against a huge mound of warm bread dough. It did not take long before he began to feel overheated and claustrophobic.

Just around the corner and out of sight, one of the doors opened. Whoever opened it kept it open for a good twenty seconds, perhaps using the light to scan the arena. Mike could not see much and truly regretted that he had allowed himself to be put in this situation. The only positive he could see was that there was now a formidable barrier of flesh between him and the afflicted. Although this technically provided him with some protection, it also made it impossible for him to make a quick and easy exit. The fat woman was wedged into the space in front of him as securely as a cork in a bottle. If she were to be killed, he would be trapped, at least long enough for the assailant to shoot him through the slats in the bench. Like fish in a barrel.

The infected woman released the door, and hydraulic hinges pulled the entrance shut, the light diminishing in degrees until there was nothing left but absolute darkness. His eyes became exhausted from straining to see through the shroud of black. And since his eyes could not see, his hearing and imagination filled in the blanks in the worst way possible. The idea that there was a deranged woman searching for them in the dark, in an enclosed space, was nerve-shredding. The boundary between the real and imagined sounds of her breathing became blurred and then disappeared altogether. The breathing was guttural and harsh, conjuring images of a being beyond the natural realm, inhuman and demonic. And she was definitely moving closer.

Breathing sounds rattled out of the woman's throat, far too much like the low rumble of a large predator, like a lion or a tiger.

The breathing moved closer, twenty feet, ten. Mike could feel his ears make subtle movements on the side of his head, like those of a fox, searching for the best angle to hear. Such was his focus that he sensed when the face of the person turned and looked in his direction, just the slightest change in pitch. He imagined the woman looking directly at him, perhaps with the ability to see in the dark.

The sound of her breathing abruptly cut off, as if the woman were also listening for any trace of sound. Mike stopped breathing as well and made his body like stone. He would have stopped his heart if he thought that would help. The slightest movement might cause one of the pieces of litter to crinkle and give them away. Remarkably, the woman against whom he was pressed was equally silent. Perhaps she had died from fright, and he was now intimately spooning a corpse. That was less disturbing than the unknown horror in the dark.

The woman could be anywhere, moving as stealthily as a cat. If a hand reached out and grabbed his ankle right now, he would scream like a little girl and not be ashamed.

After what seemed like a minute he heard the scuff of a shoe, and the rattling, raspy breathing sounds diminished into the distance.

Several minutes later the door to the arena swung open, but it was impossible to determine whether the woman exited or someone else entered. Mike waited five more minutes in almost unbearable discomfort, his shirt and face soaked with sweat. He prodded at the woman, but she gave no indication that she was willing to move.

"Let me out," he hissed.

"We don't know if she's gone."

"I haven't heard anything since the door opened," he whispered. "And I need to get back to my friends." He poked her in the back, hard. "Let me the *fuck* out."

The woman remained still for a few more moments and then began the laborious effort of dislodging herself from underneath the bench.

Mike followed as closely behind as he could, so eager to get out that he had to resist the urge to keep poking her. Once free, he started to make his way back toward the doors. He had enough of a mental map that he did not need the woman to help him find the exit, although he did struggle to find the door handle. He placed his ear against the cold metal of the door and listened. This was unlikely to be of any benefit unless the woman sporting the gun was making a considerable racket. All seemed quiet. In his mind he envisioned the woman standing outside with the gun pointed directly at the door, waiting to fire the moment he opened it. The details were crisp, right down to the black hole of the rifle barrel, the last sight he would ever see. He damned his too-vivid imagination and quickly pushed open the door and stepped aside, out of the way of a potential bullet. There was no gunfire. He leaned out and looked both ways. There was no one in sight.

He jogged toward the front entrance, reasoning that he would be more difficult to hit as a moving target even if he was headed directly toward the shooter. The grey-haired woman was nowhere to be seen. He never thought to thank the other woman for her help, and he hoped she would be okay. Judging from her fearful reaction, she might stay in the arena for some time.

Mike studied the area outside the front doors for several minutes. It had been quite a while since the shooter exited the arena and she could be anywhere by now. From his vantage point, Mike could see the bench on which Jackie and the others had been sitting and the area behind it. It appeared that none of them had stayed behind, likely departing shortly after the shooter entered the building. Finding a secure location would have been the prudent thing to do. Even so, he was torn between being relieved that they were safe, and a little peeved that they had not tried to help him. Perhaps it was an unreasonable expectation. Foster was the only one who was armed, and his priority was protecting his granddaughter. He would not abandon her to help a virtual stranger in this type of situation, especially when he was barely mobile. Jackie may have wanted to help but pursuing an armed and homicidal woman inside a darkened building would not have been a wise course of action.

So, where would they have gone? He spotted the directory again. Of course. They would have continued with the original plan.

According to the map, it should only take him five minutes to get to the building, but he moved very cautiously and avoided everyone he saw. There were not many people out in the open, and they all seemed as skittish as he was. The university classes would have been canceled by now, and any students in residence would be expected to stay inside. Mike thought that these residences were likely to become cauldrons of violence, with all the mixing that inevitably occurred among the students. Whatever was happening would spread like wildfire inside those buildings, a case study of close-contact infectious transmission. It would eventually spill out onto the campus, and he wanted to be either gone or inside another building before that happened.

There was no simple way of distinguishing the afflicted from the non-afflicted, especially from a distance. He had to treat everyone as a potential threat. So the attack, when it came, took him completely by surprise. The approach had been soundless and swift. The person leaped onto him from behind and hooked a thin arm around his neck. He staggered back a few steps and then fell to the ground, directly on top of the person attacking him. The arm around his neck loosened and he was able to twist around, ready to start pounding away at the person underneath him.

It was a young Japanese girl, slim and pretty. She tried to claw out his eyes. Mike grabbed both her wrists and stretched her arms over her head, lying on top of her to prevent her from getting free. For the second time in an hour, he found himself in intimate contact with an unfamiliar woman. Her breasts were pressed against his chest and as she bucked her hips, trying to dislodge him, he could feel the soft flesh of her pubis grind against his genitals. Under more appropriate circumstances, he would have been highly aroused.

He was not sure what to do. The woman would claw at his eyes and face the moment he released her and would keep following him even if he did get off her without suffering damage to his person. She lifted her head, her neck muscles straining as she tried to get her teeth close enough to bite. The effort only lasted a few seconds. The next time she tried it he was ready. He head-butted her, with as much force as was possible in the constrained space, but it seemed to work. Her eyelids fluttered closed. He got up and ran, confident that if he got out of sight, she would turn her attention elsewhere.

Mike arrived at the Thompson Centre for Science about fifteen minutes later, after consulting the picture on his phone a few times. A laser-printed paper sign taped to each of the doors said: Building Closed Until Further Notice. Mike tried one of the doors anyway. To his surprise, it was unlocked.

Getting inside the building was no guarantee of safety, but he felt more relaxed the moment the front doors closed behind him. He found himself in a spacious foyer with comfortable-looking sofas and lounging chairs arranged along each side, and large murals on the wall. The sofas and chairs sat next to large windows that ran from the floor to the ceiling. He could imagine students hanging out there between classes. The building still had power, and the floor indicator light for the elevator revealed that the car was at the main level.

A building directory was posted on the wall next to the elevator and indicated that each department was assigned to a different floor. It also showed the location of stairways that led to the upper floors and to the basement. Mike examined the directory for a few minutes before deciding on Epidemiology, 4th Floor.

He took the stairs.

CHAPTER 19

The lights were off on the 4th floor and the only illumination came from one window at the end of a very long hall. Mike wasn't sure where to go, and he wasn't even sure he had the correct floor. He squinted at the plastic panels adjacent to the doors that lined the hall, hoping for a clue. Some just listed room numbers, while others indicated that the spaces were allocated for storage or housekeeping. There was a washroom as well, but when he pushed open the door, he discovered that it was completely dark inside. He did not like the idea of using the toilet in the dark, at his most vulnerable.

He was almost to the end of the corridor when he spotted a sliver of light escaping from underneath a door. The glow came from an area only an inch wide, and he guessed that there was something blocking the rest of the light, perhaps a towel. The plastic plaque by the side of the door was barely readable. It said: Dr. Eric Sandoval.

Mike knocked and whispered, "Hello. I'm looking for some friends of mine."

There was dead silence from the other side. He could well be speaking to an empty room.

Then, a woman's voice, muffled by the door. "Who are you?"

"My name is Mike, Mike Richards."

The lock disengaged, and the door cracked open, spilling light into the corridor. Mike winced at the sudden brightness, but it wasn't so bright that he couldn't make out the faces of Jackie and Foster.

After they rushed him inside, they relocked the door and pressed a shirt along the bottom to block the light. The area appeared to be a lab of some type, with high-topped desks, cabinets full of chemicals lining the walls, and countertops holding numerous pieces of equipment. A man wearing a white lab coat stood behind one of the desks at the back of the room. He had gray hair, wore steel-rimmed glasses, and looked to be in the process of examining something on a laptop. Two younger people, also in white lab coats, stood on each side of him. Mike guessed they were lab assistants, graduate students, or possibly both.

Jackie gave him a full-body hug as if he were a long-lost brother instead of a recent acquaintance. He was not a hugger by nature, although this one felt right.

Foster shook his hand.

"Sorry, we had to leave. It was just too dangerous out there with Amy and all." He gave Mike an appraising look. "For what it's worth, I figured you would make it."

"Thanks. I know you didn't have much of a choice."

"I have been a wreck ever since we left you behind," said Jackie. "I was really worried that woman would find you, or that you wouldn't be able to find us again."

"It was an unpleasant thirty minutes," he said, remembering the claustrophobia and the heat and the fear. He glanced around. "Where is Amy, by the way?"

The man in the lab coat spoke for the first time. "She's having a nap on the couch in my office."

Mike caught Jackie's eye, and they shared the same thought. Martin also took a nap. What would happen when she woke up?

"I am Dr. Sandoval," the man said. He came around the desk and shook Mike's hand. "My students and I have just started the process of examining the samples Ms. Winters brought us." He gestured toward the man and woman behind the desk. "Thomas and Sherry are graduate students, and I am their advisor."

Thomas was tall and skinny and wore black plastic glasses on his thin face. He clutched a length of metal pipe in one hand as if not quite ready to believe that Mike was harmless. Sherry was small and plump, with thin brown hair and a nervous smile that flickered on her face like a faulty neon sign.

"As you can imagine, getting any samples has been problematic," said Dr. Sandoval. "We have not left the lab in two days, ever since this started."

"Have there been infected in the building?"

"That's hard to say. When we hear anyone in the hallway, we stay silent. I kept up on the news as long as I could, but the Wi-Fi connection went out sometime last night. What I see out the window tells me that this is far from being under control."

Jackie said, "That's why we felt it was so important to get the sample here."

Dr. Sandoval lifted his hands and dropped them again in a gesture of helplessness. "I don't have the resources here to find a cure if that's what you are thinking. I have a very narrow field of expertise. It's important, but it's only a piece of the puzzle. We can likely narrow down whether this illness is caused by a virus and how it may affect behavior, but we can't make a vaccine."

"Who can?" she asked.

"Most vaccines are created by pharmaceutical companies. People may love or hate these companies, but they are often the only ones who have the resources to create the necessary volume. But even large, multinational corporations cannot do everything. They need people like me to fill in the gaps. Like I said: pieces of the puzzle."

To Jackie, the challenge sounded insurmountable, with the situation deteriorating, communications disrupted, and infected individuals killing the very people who could help solve the crisis. She didn't think the last part was intentional, just circumstantial. There were probably many labs untouched by the crisis. So far. It was challenging even under ideal conditions to sequence the molecular structure of a virus and attempt to create a vaccine. These were about as far from ideal circumstances as you could get. It was a race now between the contagion and the cure. So far, the contagion was winning.

"Do you have any way of communicating information to other labs?" she asked.

"The landline still works," said Dr. Sandoval, "but I normally look up numbers on the internet. It's going to be a roundabout process without it. I'll need to contact people for whom I do have numbers and try to get the contact information for the other researchers in the field."

"You mentioned that you have a narrow area of expertise. What is it?"

"I study how viruses affect the brain. Not all of them influence the brain, of course, but I suspect this one does, for obvious reasons. And I believe that is why Martin was so intent on getting me the samples. He was a former student of mine."

"The samples are all brain tissue?"

"Yes. I won't ask how he obtained the tissue, but he thought it was vitally important that I receive the samples."

Jackie reviewed what she knew about the effect of viruses on brain function. It wasn't much.

"The people who are infected don't seem sick," she said. "Just hyperviolent. And it's not just that. They aren't wild and out of control. They are very deliberate in their actions, like the virus has turned them all into high-functioning killers without a shred of empathy or emotion."

Thomas, the lanky graduate student, spoke for the first time. "It's difficult to speculate as to what is happening without doing a proper examination of a person suffering from the illness. There may be different stages to the infection, with few initial indicators except for a high fever. That one is not very helpful. Fever is a common symptom for many, many illnesses."

Jackie asked, "How can it be so stereotypical? I mean, everyone seems to have the same response. I can see it happening at random, but it seems like every person we've encountered has exhibited violent behavior. Shouldn't some people get depressed or get migraines or strip naked and run down the street?"

"Well, we can't be certain that every infected person *is* having the same response," Thomas continued. "But for those who *are* exhibiting this behavior, the virus could be targeting a very specific area of the brain. For example, if it affected Broca's area, those who were infected might be unable to speak. Or if it hit the occipital lobe, vision could be impaired."

"What if we had an infected individual?" Mike asked. "What could you do?"

Thomas looked over at Dr. Sandoval, conceding the floor to the doctor.

"We would run an fMRI on them— functional magnetic resonance imaging. See what lights up when they are in an aggressive state. We often run these in conjunction with an electroencephalograph —an EEG— and other tests, like looking at their cerebrospinal fluid. That one can be somewhat uncomfortable."

Mike made eye contact with Jackie.

She shook her head. *No.*

Foster sat in a chair about six feet away, head back, eyes closed.

"We think we may have a candidate," said Mike.

"What do you mean?"

Mike looked pointedly at the office.

"The little girl," he mouthed.

Jackie said, "*Mike*," in a warning tone.

He looked at her. "You think it too."

"The decision should be made by her parents, not us," she said. "Especially if you need to do something like a lumbar puncture to collect cerebrospinal fluid."

Dr. Sandoval looked between Mike and Jackie.

"You think the girl is infected," he said.

"Pretty sure," said Mike.

"Well, of course, we would have to get permission from her father first," said Dr. Sandoval. He looked at Foster again. "Grandfather?"

"I think he'll be okay with it if you present it in the right way."

"What way is that?" asked the researcher.

Mike tried hard not to roll his eyes. Not all physicians understood people and human nature.

"You have to suggest that it can help cure her," he said.

"That's a problem then because I don't think I can do anything to help her. In fact, I'm sure of it. I'm like the x-ray technician who identifies a cancerous growth. I can't actually fix anything myself."

"Well, you could suggest that this process can *contribute* to a cure. That's not inaccurate, even if you cannot do anything to directly help her."

Dr. Sandoval gave a reluctant nod after apparently weighing this small white lie against the greater good.

Mike tapped the sleeping man on the shoulder. "Foster, wake up, we need to talk."

Foster had dozed off, and Mike was reminded of how old he was. His head snapped forward, but he was bleary-eyed and confused and didn't appear to know where he was.

"What? What is it?"

"Dr. Sandoval wants to run some tests on Amy." He paused for a moment. "He thinks she may be infected." At this juncture, it seemed wise to shift the burden onto the researcher, someone new and authoritative who could add weight to Mike and Jackie's opinion.

Foster stood. "This again!" He shook his head. "It's ridiculous. I would know if she was sick."

But he did not sound convinced, and the expression on his face betrayed him. He looked like a man who had already lost his granddaughter.

In the end, it did not take a lot of persuasion to convince the old man. He was a representative of a generation that still held doctors in high regard. That respect and confidence had waned in subsequent generations, as doctors publicly disagreed with each other on how to manage the COVID-19 pandemic, or had been caught shilling quack products, or been busted for writing bogus prescriptions for opioids. They were seen as fallible, sometimes morally corrupt. Human. When you were at the top of the proverbial ladder, it was a long way to fall.

Foster just wanted his granddaughter to be okay. His quick acceptance hinted that he must have suspected, even subconsciously, that all was not right with his ward. He would not sign off on the more invasive procedures but was comfortable with the doctor performing EEGs and examining her with the fMRI machine.

"I should go wake her," Foster said. "Where do we need to go?"

"The equipment is in the basement," the doctor said, sounding almost apologetic.

Mike made a face. "You might have mentioned that earlier."

"I'm not too crazy about the idea either, but we were going to have to leave at some point anyway to get more food."

"I don't suppose you have any type of weapons here?"

"I do, in fact. A Smith and Wesson .38 caliber revolver." He seemed pleased with the surprised looks he received, an uncool man trying to show how cool he was but not really fooling anyone. "It's a classic, a gift from my wife. With the increase in school and campus shootings, she thought it might be a good idea for me to have personal protection."

Although Mike highly doubted that this was the scenario his wife foresaw, the addition of another firearm was welcome.

"Where is it?" he asked.

A complicated series of expressions flowed over the doctor's face in quick succession, like time-lapse photography. Realization. Guilt. Fear.

"What, where is it?" Mike asked again, but he intuitively knew the answer. It was, of course, in Dr. Sandoval's office, along with a young girl who was very likely infected with a homicidal pathogen.

"I'll go get her," said Foster. "She is my responsibility."

The doctor piped up, "I'm sure it's fine. It's not like it's sitting out in the open. It's in the bottom drawer of my desk, all the way to the back."

As Foster took his first step toward the room, the door to Dr. Sandoval's office swung open and Amy walked out, a small girl with dead eyes carrying a large silver revolver.

CHAPTER 20

Everyone stopped. They stopped talking, they stopped moving, they stopped breathing. The moment seemed to stretch into infinity.

Foster spoke first. "Honey, you should put that down. That's not something you should be playing with."

Amy was not playing. Her head did a slow swivel, taking in everyone in the room, and then she raised the pistol and pointed it at Dr. Sandoval's graduate student, Sherry.

Sherry raised both hands in a stop gesture and said, "Whoa, whoa. You need to—"

Amy shot her in the head before she could finish her sentence. The recoil from the discharge caused the revolver to buck in her hands, but the little girl managed to keep hold of the weapon.

Things really went to hell after that.

Thomas, the other grad student, grabbed the metal pipe he had selected as his weapon of choice and launched himself toward Amy. It was both oddly heroic and horrific in the same instant, considering his intended target was a sixty-five-pound, ten-year-old girl. A shot rang out, but it did not come from Amy's weapon.

Thomas staggered and looked down in mystification at the red bloom forming across the breast of his white lab coat.

"Do not hurt my granddaughter!" Foster bellowed, his Glock still smoking in his outstretched hand.

In a complete absence of gratitude, Amy turned and shot her grandfather in the neck. Foster dropped his pistol, grabbed his neck, and started to make gurgling sounds. He sank to his knees, blood spraying out between his fingers like a faulty garden hose.

Mike's paralysis finally broke. Time was fluid, things were happening both too quickly and too slowly. It had only been eight seconds since the first shot and three people were either dead or dying.

Amy turned her body slightly away from him to locate another target and he took the opportunity to make a run at her. His body felt heavy and slow, as if he were running underwater. After just two steps, he knew he wasn't going to make it in time. Amy turned the revolver back toward him. A coffee mug hit her on the chest, bounced off and distracted her just long enough for Mike to make a diving tackle. He grabbed at the wrist holding the gun while at the same time driving his shoulder against her chest, like a linebacker taking down a quarterback. He probably hit her harder than was strictly necessary, but better safe than sorry.

He knew that he should not be angry at her, because she was sick, like a person with a cold. But people with colds were just annoying, blowing their noses into snotty tissues. They weren't walking around shooting people in the head. So, even though he intuitively knew that it was not her fault, it was difficult to make the leap into acceptance or empathy. He hit her so hard that her breath was knocked out of her when she hit the floor, and the revolver skittered away, coming to rest against the wall by the door.

For a moment, Amy seemed like a little girl again, gasping for breath and squirming on the floor in distress. Mike was reluctant to touch her, but he knew he must. He lifted her off the floor while she was still distracted and used cloth shopping bags to tie her to a chair. Within thirty seconds she was thrashing around trying to free herself. He found some medical tape and wound it around the bags. It would do as a temporary measure.

Dr. Sandoval had his hands on the top of his head, a picture of grief and torment. He kept repeating his students' names, "Sherry... Thomas," in a tone of voice that was half-moan, half-lament. He unquestionably blamed himself, at least in part for having an unsecured weapon in his office.

Jackie squatted beside Foster, holding her right hand over his neck, but he was already gray with death. The pool of blood in which she was squatting surrounded her black running shoes, twin islands rising out of a sea of red.

She stood up after a minute and used half a container of sterile wipes to clean every last remnant of blood from her hands.

Mike walked over to her after she was finished.

"What a fucking disaster," she said. "I'm sorry, I should have listened to you and pushed harder for Amy to be examined. A couple of minutes may have made the difference."

"You cannot and should not take any responsibility for this. No one could have anticipated this outcome. She was one little girl against six adults. I was worried that she was infected, but I didn't think we would have any trouble controlling her. And then there was Foster. Jesus Christ. He *killed* that guy."

Dr. Sandoval stopped his litany and was now staring at the corpses on the floor. Mike gave him some space. He knew the type; the doctor was going to obsess over this tragedy for a long time, probably for the rest of his life.

Mike walked over to Amy and stooped to assess her condition. She was now breathing regularly and had followed his approach across the lab with her dark eyes. Even though she was restrained, he was wary around her. He did not want to take the chance that she might be feigning passivity to catch him off guard. She did not have any other weapons, although she still had her teeth.

"What's going on in that head of yours?" he asked, not expecting a reply. Amy, true to form, remained mute.

He straightened and turned to Dr. Sandoval. "How much longer until you can complete the work on the samples?"

"I don't know if I can," said Dr. Sandoval, gesturing weakly at his murdered graduate students.

"You can't run the equipment, or you are not feeling up to it?" asked Mike. He didn't want to sound like an uncaring, unsympathetic asshole, but he also did not want these deaths to be in vain. So, he was going to be an asshole if it got things back on track.

Dr. Sandoval stood in silence for another forty-five seconds, Mike was willing to give him that.

He then gestured toward the lab equipment. "I'll help if I can. Just tell me what you need me to do."

Hours later —Mike had lost track of time— Dr. Sandoval stripped off his mask and gloves and sat heavily on a plastic chair. Despite Mike's offer, it was Jackie who assisted the researcher. Mike had barely passed high school chemistry.

He looked up expectantly at Jackie when she came over.

"Well?" he asked.

"Well, we know more than we did before, but we're not quite sure what it means."

"Are you saying that we are no further ahead?"

Jackie turned to Dr. Sandoval. "Not exactly. I'm going to leave the detailed explanation to the doctor."

The doctor appeared utterly exhausted, and it took him a few moments to rally himself before he delivered his findings. "The assay showed that the person from whom the brain tissue sample was taken had been recently infected with the VHP-25 variant and that there was a vigorous immune response. That the person was infected is not surprising, since we know that the spread of the variant has been rampant. But we also discovered that he had been previously infected with cytomegalovirus."

"I've never heard of that," said Mike. "But it sounds serious."

"It isn't, not usually. It is part of the family of herpes viruses. Most people who have it do not present any symptoms."

"So, what is the issue?"

"The two viruses have mated. We call the process *viral transformation*, where there is an introduction of new material into the DNA of an existing virus. Each of these viruses on its own has a relatively innocuous effect on the human body. However, the result of their mating, the bastard child, appears to be different."

"Do you have any idea what it is doing?"

"Not precisely, although it is clearly affecting the brain. It may be affecting other systems of the body as well, but we don't have the resources to confirm that."

"What are our options? Is there any other place in the city we can go for help?"

"Probably not. But we can take her to the fMRI lab," Sandoval said, nodding at Amy. "I think that could shed some light on what is happening."

Mike suddenly thought of something that caused his heart to compress, like a cold hand had reached inside his chest and squeezed.

"You said that the... the whatchamacallit virus didn't have any symptoms. How would I know if *I* have been infected by it?"

"The cytomegalovirus. We can run a blood test." He looked at Jackie as well. "We should all have the test."

Sandoval prepared collection tubules and Mike averted his eyes as the sample was taken. The doctor took Jackie's as well, and then Jackie collected blood from him.

He put the samples in an automated device that would do a complete work-up of their blood. It whirred to life as soon as he pressed a button.

"This will take approximately forty-five minutes."

Amy moaned softly in the chair across the room, and Sandoval shot her a quick, nervous glance.

"We should hurry," Mike said, "before she wakes up."

The doctor had injected her with his last remaining dose of a mild sedative after she became increasingly determined to escape from the chair. There was no parent or guardian to consult, and he rationalized his decision by concluding that she could harm herself if she continued to struggle. The sedative was normally reserved for patients who suffered from anxiety related to the lumbar puncture procedure and was not particularly potent. It was not intended as a general anesthetic, and the amount of time she would remain asleep was unclear.

Mike was the only one strong enough to carry the girl, which left Dr. Sandoval and Jackie with the burden of shooting anyone who appeared to be a threat. It was difficult to know how far the sound of the earlier shots may have traveled and whether any of the afflicted were tempted to investigate. That made opening the door into the hallway an unusually harrowing affair, like entering a habitat at a zoo that may or may not contain a very aggressive tiger.

Jackie stood ready, waiting for the doctor to open the door. She held Foster's pistol in front of her with both hands, police-style. She exhaled a humorless laugh that was tinged with nervousness. "I am having a serious case of imposter syndrome," she said.

Dr. Sandoval unlocked the door and pulled it inward. Jackie stepped out into the corridor and swept the gun right and then left.

"It's clear," she said, practically chuckling with relief. The tension was so high that all emotional states were bubbling about in a huge stew, some floating unexpectedly to the top when one least expected it. She could have just as easily begun crying at that moment.

They quickly made their way to the stairwell and went down, down, down, two stories underground. The lights flickered on automatically when they entered the hallway at the lowest level. It revealed a long, carpeted hallway stretching out some eighty yards.

"Where is the lab?" Mike whispered. He didn't know why he was whispering since their presence would not remain much of a secret as they walked along the corridor.

"It's at the very end," said Dr. Sandoval.

Of course, it would be.

Every few steps, Mike glanced down at Amy to ensure that she was still unconscious. Step, step, eyes closed. Step, step, eyes closed. Step, step, her eyes now stared up into his like they were coming from the deepest depths of a coal mine.

"Gah!" he said, purely involuntarily.

He resisted the urge to roll her out of his arms and onto the floor like a sack of hissing pythons. But the girl had her arms tucked tight against her sides, with several lengths of medical tape wrapped around her tiny frame. Falling onto the floor without the ability to catch herself would likely result in a serious head injury, possibly fatal. They still needed the girl reasonably healthy so they could assess her brain function in the fMRI.

Mike barely took his eyes off her as he walked the length of the corridor. Even though the girl no longer held a gun, couldn't grab at him, and could barely lift her head, he still didn't trust her. He postulated that the infected individuals would use any means necessary to inflict as much damage as possible to those they attacked. Indeed, as they reached a point only five feet from the door, she lurched up and took a shot at his throat with her teeth. He reared back like a startled horse and her teeth clacked shut on open air.

"Open the fucking door," he hissed, wanting to be rid of this bundle of bad intentions as quickly as possible.

Dr. Sandoval fumbled at the lock with infuriating slowness.

"I think it's this one," the doctor said, and then cursed under his breath and selected another key.

Mike clenched Amy's ponytail in his hand, trying to restrict her ability to bite at him.

The door finally swung open and Dr. Sandoval flicked on the lights.

Mike rushed into the room, walked over to a gurney, and dumped Amy onto it. She was not heavy, but he had been holding her limp body in his arms for a good five minutes and his muscles were fatigued. He barely had time to flex his elbows a couple of times to get the blood flowing again before she tried to worm her way off the table.

"Give me a hand over here," he shouted to Jackie. "Hold her legs."

Mike turned to Dr. Sandoval. "Let's get this done. How do we get her ready?"

"She will need to be situated on that table with her head restrained." He pointed to another gurney, this one situated on a set of rails. The rails extended into the tunnel of the machine and would permit the gurney to be slid inside, like a train on railroad tracks.

Mike and Jackie wheeled the gurney across the room and lined it up with the other table while Dr. Sandoval made himself busy at the controls for the device.

"Keep away from her mouth," Mike warned.

He was surprised to discover restraints on the second gurney. Perhaps Amy was not the only reluctant patient to be analyzed by this device.

Mike waited while Jackie did up her legs and then they jointly worked to cinch the belts around her arms and upper body. The head was next.

"Can we sedate her again?" Mike yelled across to Dr. Sandoval.

"Not if you want any usable results. This is a *functional* MRI, meaning that we need her conscious and processing information to determine which parts of her brain are being affected."

"Right. Shit." He had to remind himself that she wasn't a zombie and that although a bite might be painful, it was unlikely to be fatal. The head restraints still needed to be buckled, and he did not want to put his hands anywhere near those teeth. He walked over to a set of hooks and removed two white lab coats. He wrapped one of them around his left hand and had Jackie wrap the other around his right. After this was done, he placed his well-insulated hands on either side of Amy's head and held it in place while Jackie positioned a set of goggles over Amy's eyes and fastened a restraint over her forehead.

Amy fought and thrashed while they were in close proximity but dialed down her aggression once the goggles and restraints were in place.

Dr. Sandoval walked over when all the hard work was done and slid the gurney into the MRI, positioning Amy's head just so.

"This should not take long," he said.

They joined him behind the controls and examined the screen intently as he activated the machine.

He had to raise his voice over the sound made by the equipment, a series of rapid and oscillating vibrations and tones that reminded Mike of the electronic dance music he once heard at a rave.

"A standard MRI creates a series of static images that are then compiled into a three-dimensional image. An fMRI produces a more dynamic representation, assessing blood flow and oxygen use in the most highly active parts of the brain. I am going to present a series of visual and auditory stimuli to the patient to elicit a response."

"Her name is Amy," said Jackie.

Dr. Sandoval gave her a look that suggested he really didn't care to know anything about the girl at all. The girl had just killed one of his grad students and was a contributing factor in the death of the second. It was likely making it difficult to maintain professional detachment.

He shifted his attention back to the controls without comment. "I am going to show her a sequence of static images of rather benign objects to gauge her baseline reaction."

Mike and Jackie could see on the screen exactly what Amy would see with her goggles. The first images were of a tree, a coffee cup, a fire hydrant, and a seashell. The MRI machine thumped and warbled. There was little apparent reaction to these images in Amy's brain.

Sounds of phones ringing, doors slamming shut, sirens wailing, and birds chirping elicited no response.

The next series of images were those of animals.

"The responses to these are somewhat more difficult to predict in the general population. A picture of a dog may elicit feelings of affection in some patients but something completely different in others, fear, apathy, hostility. It depends a great deal on their life experience."

There were flashes in different areas of Amy's brain, reminding Mike of fireflies orbiting a large juniper bush.

Dr. Sandoval left the images and videos of men and women to the end. The first image was of a kindly woman holding out her arms as if about to greet someone with a hug.

"Oh, my," said Dr. Sandoval.

There were two distinct areas of Amy's brain that lit up; they were like those sprinkler sticks Mike adored as a child, the ones you waved around in the dark, spraying sparks everywhere.

"This is fascinating," said Dr. Sandoval. He pointed to the screen. "This area here," he indicated an area adjacent to the prefrontal cortex, "this is the spot most commonly associated with psychopathy. And the amygdala is less active than it should be. Those two need to communicate for proper social functioning.

"And this area," he pointed to another location in the center of the brain, "is commonly active in those experiencing psychotic episodes due to schizophrenia. I rarely see the two in concert with each other. I believe the transformed virus may be causing an autoimmune reaction in these specific areas."

"So, she is having some kind of delusion that makes her think she needs to kill everyone around her?" Mike asked.

"There is only so much you can deduce from a scan of this type, but yes, that appears to be what is happening. To them, their motivation to hurt or kill others may seem completely logical, even noble. The delusions that schizophrenics experience are often religious in nature, instructions either from demons or from God."

"But how can this be so widespread? There can't be all that many people who have been infected with cytovirus," said Mike. He knew the pronunciation was wrong when he said it, but he couldn't quite grasp the entirety of the word.

" Cytomegalovirus," corrected Dr. Sandoval. "Unfortunately, it is extremely prevalent in human populations, anywhere from 60-100% depending on which part of the world you live."

"Well, that's not good," said Jackie. "That means a lot of potential infected."

"Not only that," the doctor said, "but I believe we are just starting the see the first cases of this new condition. It appears there is a significant latency between the point of initial infection and the emergence of violent behavior, possibly in the order of three to four weeks. The amount of time may vary depending on the age of the person, the viral load they receive, their health at the time of infection, and a host of other factors."

"So, anyone who contracts the new variant of Texas Boar can start to lose their mind," stated Mike.

"*If* they have also been infected with cytomegalovirus. Which is why I thought it important to run the blood tests." The doctor looked at his watch. "The analyses should be complete. I'll run up and grab the results."

He started toward the door and then stopped. "These may not be results you want to know, but I believe it is important to have this information both for your sake and those around you."

The doctor left without another word.

Mike and Jackie did not speak for a few minutes as they absorbed the new information.

"This is like waiting for a doctor to tell you if you have an inoperable brain tumor," Mike said. "It's a life sentence, and in this case, the life sentence is only three weeks."

"Let's wait for the results before we start writing our obituaries. Besides, we don't know if it is fatal."

Dr. Sandoval was back quickly, holding several pieces of paper in his hand, examining them even as he walked into the room.

Mike felt like he might throw up.

The doctor did not leave them in suspense. "Mr. Richards, you have been recently infected with the new variant of VHP-25. However, you are among the roughly fifteen to twenty percent of the population who have not been infected with the cytomegalovirus."

He turned slightly and directed his next comments to Jackie. "Ms. Winters. At some time in the past, you have been infected with the cytomegalovirus, but you have not been infected with the new variant of VHP-25."

"Jesus, talk about dodging the bullet," said Mike.

"Except the gun is still firing," said Jackie.

"How is the cytomegavirus spread?" asked Mike.

"The *cytomegalovirus* is transmitted through bodily fluids —blood, saliva— even tears."

"Great," he said, "All I have to do is avoid being bitten or exposed to any blood. It's not like that hasn't happened six times today already."

Jackie turned to the doctor. "Assuming that your theory is correct, that the viral transformation is affecting the brain in some way, what can we do about it? And I don't mean just on a personal level. It's obvious that we both need to avoid getting infected with the other virus, but what about the people who are already infected?"

"That is a difficult question to answer because although I feel confident that the transformed virus is the cause of the problem, I am not certain of the mechanism of action. I suspect that it is an immune response. If the transformed virus has a close similarity to tissues in the brain, the antibodies created to attack the virus will also attack those tissues. There are tests that can be run —not here— to determine if the brain tissue in question is being affected in this way. If this is the case, it would be necessary to blunt or stop the immune reaction."

"Is it possible to do that?"

"Technically, yes. It's an imperfect remedy, however, and it brings to mind the old saying, 'The cure is worse than the disease.' Destroying the immune response is not only very difficult but can also lead to a host of other problems, including death from other diseases. Of course, the virus may be affecting the brain in a completely different way, such as causing the release of excess neurotransmitters, so no true action can be taken until more research is completed. That will take time."

Jackie sat down, looking exhausted and defeated. "I don't see a path to resolve this. There could be tens of millions of infected in the US alone. And even if the person hasn't become infected, they could well be murdered by someone who has."

The doctor sat heavily onto a stool, hands on his thighs. "Ultimately, the best strategy may be to avoid infection in the first place— and if a person is infected, to pharmaceutically neutralize them until we can find an effective treatment. And by 'we', I mean other researchers who are still alive and in a safe environment."

"Great," said Jackie. "By 'pharmaceutically neutralize them,' do you mean drug them into a placid state? Do I have that right? That could be a tall order."

"I did not say it would be simple," he huffed. "And I do not see you offering any viable alternatives."

Jackie realized that her comments were unhelpful. "I apologize, I'm just tired and overwhelmed— and you are correct; I have no idea how to fix this."

Dr. Sandoval shrugged. "There are no easy solutions."

"Could it burn itself out over time? What do you think will happen to those currently infected?"

"I don't know. I do not have enough data or observations to formulate a theory. Do the infected individuals eat and drink and take care of their basic biological requirements? Does the virus continue to damage their brains? That is the information we need to know. My best guess is that they will eventually die if they do not get treatment or take care of their needs. But it could take days or weeks from the point of showing symptoms. And I'm sure there will be new infections for weeks or months to come. This is not going away anytime soon."

"We can't stay here for months," said Mike. "There's hardly any food left."

Before Dr. Sandoval could reply, the power went off in the lab. Emergency lights kicked on after a few seconds, casting long shadows into the corners.

"Well, I guess that makes the decision a little easier," said Mike. "We should go now while we have the energy."

"What about Amy?" asked Jackie.

"What about her?" he said.

"Somebody has to take care of her."

"She obviously can't come with us; she'll kill us the first chance she gets."

"The only other alternative is to leave her here," said Jackie, turning to Dr. Sandoval, who looked back at her with a pained expression."

The doctor shook his head. "Just because you brought her here does not absolve you of your responsibility to her. My part in this is done. You will either stay here or take her with you, *those* are your only options."

"I hate both of those choices," said Mike. "How can we possibly take her with us? We don't even have a vehicle."

Dr. Sandoval thought for a moment. "Thomas's car should still be in the parking lot. I can get you the keys. There may be a place you can take her since hospitals are out of the question. I know of a private clinic that may have space. I will make a call; a friend of mine runs the place and he owes me a favor. It is a small center for people with severe mental disorders and addictions and should be secure."

He went off to a corner of the lab where there was a landline phone and began talking into the receiver in a hushed voice.

Mike and Jackie had their own conversation.

"I don't like this," said Mike. "

"I'm not crazy about it either," said Jackie, "but we need to get Amy ready to move as soon as we have a location. We can drop her off and then figure out what to do from there."

"That is not much of a plan."

"I'm good at improvising," she said.

Dr. Sandoval returned. "Great news, the clinic can take her. There have been a few recent… vacancies."

Mike could guess the nature of the vacancies and did not wish to pursue the topic. He was grateful for any suggestion that did not include the presence of a hyperviolent child in the back seat of the car. The stress of it would make him crazy, like having a bear snuffling at him through the thin fabric of a tent.

They approached the fMRI machine with Amy still strapped inside.

"I know you couldn't give her a sedative before the MRI, but *do* you have any?" Mike asked. "Just something to keep her from acting up before we get to the car?"

They had given up any pretense of following proper medical protocol regarding consent and best practices. Amy's immediate guardian was dead, they had no way of contacting her parents, and Amy herself was in no position to grant permission. Dr. Sandoval and Jackie were most at risk as medical professionals, but they also wagered that the chances of this coming back at them were slim.

"I do have something that might work. A few years ago, we were examining the effects of hallucinogens and other chemicals on brain activity. We still have a small supply of nitrous oxide –laughing gas– remaining from that research. It's not much, but it should make her easy to manage for fifteen to twenty minutes."

Dr. Sandoval used a flashlight and rummaged through some cabinets until he located a small canister and a mask.

They slid Amy out of the machine and looked down at her tiny face, half covered by the oversized goggles. She looked disarmingly serene and docile. The presence of the goggles made the procedure somewhat more difficult, but Dr. Sandoval preferred to have Amy oblivious to what was coming. He placed the mask over Amy's mouth and nose as best he could and toggled the valve on the canister. There was a slight hissing sound as the gas vented into the mask. Amy attempted to resist, but the restraints held both her body and head in place. After about fifteen seconds, she noticeably relaxed.

"Okay, clocks ticking," said Mike. "Let's get the keys and get out of here."

They undid the belts on the gurney and then positioned Amy in a wheelchair. Mike fashioned some temporary restraints for the wheelchair and gathered some material from a first aid kit to act as bindings once they were in the vehicle. The cotton slings he found would suffice, although he wished he had zip ties.

Mike stood by the exit and listened for a full minute before carefully and quietly unlocking the door and pulling it open.

The basement hallway was long and dark, lacking any form of illumination except for a tiny wedge of pale light that came through a small rectangular window on the stairwell door. The light was highly diluted after being filtered down a two-story underground staircase and provided only the barest of illumination.

He had just begun to push the wheelchair toward the stairs when he heard a curious rhythmic thrumming. Even as he became aware of it, the sound seemed to get closer and increase in volume. He flicked on the flashlight the doctor had given him and shone it down the hall. The source of the sound became immediately apparent. A young girl, perhaps eighteen, completely naked, was sprinting toward him at top speed on bare feet. Her small breasts bounced wildly, and Mike was momentarily transfixed at the sight. Her face bore no expression that he could discern, but it was difficult to justify shooting her without some degree of certainty that it was warranted.

"Stop," he yelled. "Or I *will* shoot!"

The girl continued without so much as a hitch in her stride. She was now only thirty yards away and closing fast.

He quickly angled the pistol upward and fired a shot. The sound was very loud in the narrow hallway, and dust rained down from a shattered ceiling tile. That should have been enough to stop any sane person in their tracks.

The girl kept on running though, completely unfazed. Ten yards now, a second away.

"Shit!" shouted Mike.

He lowered the revolver and fired three rounds directly at her in quick succession. Two missed, but one hit her dead center between her breasts. However, she had so much forward momentum that she slammed into him even after taking a bullet from six feet away. They both tumbled to the floor, her body splayed over his.

Mike could feel the blood from her wound through his shirt. It was shockingly hot, like he had spilled a cup of coffee on his chest. No doubt his mind was exaggerating the effect, knowing that it was blood, and knowing that it was too much for a person to lose. And knowing that it had the potential to infect him.

He pushed her off him, her nakedness and her youth compounding the distress he felt about taking her life. He climbed to his feet, pulling the wet shirt away from his chest, not wanting to feel her blood against his skin.

Jackie came over and stood beside him as he looked down at the girl.

"You did what you had to do."

It very closely echoed what he said to her after her struggle with Martin. Perhaps that was all there was to say.

Mike did not reply. He stripped off his shirt after donning a pair of rubber gloves and then used the dry parts of it to wipe away the blood that was smeared across his chest. The shirt went into a waste basket inside the lab, and he threw on a lab coat he found hanging over a chair.

After exiting the lab, he took another long look at the girl and then walked over to the wheelchair and began pushing it toward the stairs at the end of the hall.

Mike and Jackie navigated the wheelchair up the staircase and then waited by the exit while Dr. Sandoval went to retrieve the keys. He rushed back, flushed, clearly distressed after needing to rifle through the pockets of his dead graduate student.

"I don't know what kind of car he drives or where he is parked, although it is likely in the lot directly behind the building."

"You could come with us," suggested Mike."

Here he was, again, inviting another person along without consulting Jackie first. He hoped she would agree since it seemed to be the right thing to do.

Dr. Sandoval produced a sad and weary smile. "I'm afraid I will need to decline. You see, I also examined the results of my blood test. I had a mild bout of VHP-25 about two weeks ago and I also carry the cytomegalovirus in my system. From what we have discussed, the latency period between initial infection and the onset of the new symptoms seems to be somewhere in the range of three to four weeks." He paused and looked away. "I think it is best for everyone if I stay here."

"I'm sorry," said Mike. It didn't seem like it was enough, but nothing he said ever could be.

Dr. Sandoval looked at Mike and then at Jackie as if memorizing their faces.

"Find a safe place," he said, and then turned and disappeared up the stairs.

They watched him go, neither of them making an effort to convince him to change his mind.

Mike held up the key ring with the fob and several other keys attached, trying to determine the make of the vehicle. He didn't want to activate the unlock feature until they were closer, to avoid alerting any hostiles in the area. As he turned the fob in his hand, he discovered that it was sticky. He looked at his fingertips, red with blood.

"Shit!" he said, more out of concern than revulsion. One slight cut on a finger was all it would take for him to be infected with the cytomegalovirus. Perhaps he should start wearing gloves on a semi-permanent basis. He gingerly held the ring between two fingers as he used the cotton sling to wipe off the remainder of the blood.

"Let's make this quick," he said, as he started to wheel Amy down the ramp toward the sidewalk. There was an extensive network of pathways all over the campus and it took them less than a minute to navigate to the other end of the building. Mike scanned the area as they walked, looking for any sign they were about to be attacked. He started to relax as they reached the perimeter of the parking lot. There were very few cars, and he knew he was looking for a Honda. He chanced a press of the door lock button, and the lights flashed on a car sitting under a tree at the back edge of the lot. He jogged the rest of the way, pushing Amy ahead of him. Jackie was even faster and reached the car first, pulling open the rear door.

"Mike, she's starting to come around."

Mike was alarmed to see Amy looking at him, dazed but conscious.

Jackie held the chair while Mike quickly undid the restraints. He put one arm under her legs and the other around her back. She didn't weigh much, and he was able to quickly transfer her into the car. He arranged her limbs into a semblance of a seated position and clipped the seat belt around her waist and over her shoulders. Her hands were still free, so he pulled out his knife and began cutting the cotton sling into strips for binding.

I really should have done this before *we left*, he thought.

He managed to cut only two strips before he heard Jackie say his name in a tone of voice that elicited immediate alarm. Before he had a chance to move, a deep male voice said, "Out of the car, slowly." It was not loud, but it was deadly serious.

There was enough of a reflection from the passenger side window for him to discern a man standing behind him with a long gun, either a rifle or a shotgun. Mike considered the knife in his hand, quite long and quite sharp. He could hide it up his sleeve and wait for an opportunity to use it. Amy turned her head to look at him and her focus seemed to sharpen with every passing moment. There was not much time.

Mike withdrew from the car, keeping his hands by his sides and avoiding any actions that could be misconstrued.

There were two men, not one. The man who spoke, the man with the shotgun pointed at his face, was tall and heavily built. The other man was pointing a pistol at Jackie. He was short and fat and wore a baseball hat with a camouflage design. Jackie's pistol was jammed into the waistband of his dirty blue jeans.

"Get out of the car," the large man said. "Slowly."

"No!" shouted Jackie. "We need to get the girl to a hospital."

The large man looked over at Amy, disinterested. Her head lolled toward him, with her eyes taking a moment to focus on his face.

"What's wrong with her?" he asked.

"She's sick," replied Jackie, deliberately ambiguous.

The man took a step back. "*Sick* sick or some other type of sick."

"She has diabetes; she needs insulin."

Mike considered this to be an excellent choice of false information. There was a need for urgent treatment, it explained the symptoms, and it was a non-contagious condition.

The big man was unmoved. He jerked the barrel of the shotgun in the direction he wanted Mike to move. "Go stand over there with your wife."

He looked back toward Amy, who was shifting in her seat, trying to undo the seatbelt buckle.

"Hey! Girl in the car," he shouted over his shoulder. "You okay for a few minutes?"

Amy ignored him and kept working on the seatbelt.

He directed his attention back to Mike and Jackie. "She doesn't seem all that sick to me."

The shorter man looked Mike up and down, taking in the white lab coat.

"You a doctor or somethin'?"

Mike shook his head. "Only a lab technician."

The man just grunted, already bored.

"Let her go," said Jackie, pleading with the large man, the obvious leader. "You can take the car. We want the girl to stay with us."

The man ignored her and turned to his partner. "Abel, get behind the wheel. You two, move back. The girl stays with us until we get out of here. We'll drop her off on the next block down the street."

He kept his shotgun focused on them, perhaps surprised that they were not putting up more resistance. He slammed shut Amy's door and walked around to the passenger side.

Mike watched Amy closely. She appeared to have finally freed herself of the seatbelt, and it retracted into its receptacle.

As soon as the big man was seated, the car sped across the parking lot toward the nearest exit.

Jackie turned and glared at Mike. "I knew you didn't want the girl with us, but you could have put *some* effort into convincing them to leave her."

"It wouldn't have made any difference; they were going to take her whether I argued or not. I needed them to leave quickly."

"Why?"

"Because Amy was coming around really quickly, much faster than we expected." He hesitated. "And I left my knife in her lap."

"You *didn't*," said Jackie, sounding mildly impressed.

"I did. And I don't feel the least bit bad about it."

As they discussed what to do next, they saw a man walk around the corner of the building and approach the entrance. He looked unrealistically calm and casual, a demeanor that should have been unremarkable, but was now worrying. They decided not to re-enter the building.

Instead, they walked up the street in the direction the car had gone, with the carjackers and their not-so-innocent passenger. They found the vehicle three blocks later.

CHAPTER 21

The car had driven into a power pole at such high velocity that the engine was pushed back until it was almost against the front seats. There was steam and smoke coming from under the crumpled bonnet, although it did not look like a fire was imminent. The men may have been driving at a high speed because they were in a rush, or perhaps it was because the driver was being stabbed in the neck with a sharp knife. It was difficult to distinguish between the damage done by Amy and the crash itself. The driver's head was covered in blood, and the passenger was halfway through the windshield. For some reason, the airbags did not deploy. Both men were clearly dead, and Amy was no longer in the back seat. They looked around warily, but she was nowhere in sight.

There were numerous vehicles driving by them on the street but no pedestrians. Most of the vehicles were SUVs jammed with luggage and camping gear, and the drivers were ignoring the speed limit. One man flicked a quick, nervous glance in their direction, as if afraid to make eye contact.

"We need to find another car or get into a house or a building where we can hide," said Jackie.

Mike watched as a caravan of six SUVs rolled past. "I vote for finding another vehicle and getting the hell out of the city, just like everyone else."

Finding a vehicle was going to be difficult though. No car dealerships would be operating, private sales were out, and he didn't know how to steal a vehicle. That left finding one that had been abandoned with the keys conveniently left in the ignition, or perhaps breaking into a house and hoping to find the keys inside. Both options seemed more like wishful thinking than an actual plan, and either course of action might take a lot of time and a generous helping of good luck.

They continued to walk up the broad street, hoping for inspiration. They soon entered a business district with barricaded storefronts and uncollected garbage on the curbs. Mike was trying to look everywhere at once, like a meth addict caught up in the grip of paranoia. Except his paranoia was justified.

As they passed a five-level parking garage, Mike heard a scuffing sound that made him stop and look up. It was not a noise he would normally attribute to a vehicle, more like the sound of a shoe being dragged across pavement. It could be another survivor, like them. He scanned each level while Jackie walked on ahead, unaware of his investigation. After another fifteen seconds, a man's head poked out over the edge of the low concrete wall that ran around the perimeter of the parking garage's fourth level. The fellow had brown hair, but that was all Mike could see of him. The man looked up and down the street and then leaned over the wall and called down to Mike in a whisper shout, just loud enough to carry to Mike's ears.

"Hey, where are you guys headed?"

Mike did not know how to answer that question, because he and Jackie did not have a formal destination.

Before Mike could formulate a reply, someone came up behind the man and flipped him over the edge. The guy released a garbled scream that continued until the moment he made contact with the sidewalk. The impact was bone-crunching, and Mike knew he would remember that sound for as long as he lived.

He was very fortunate to have time to backpedal three steps before the man hit, just enough distance to avoid becoming collateral damage.

It does not take long for a body to drop forty-four feet, only one and a half seconds, but a one hundred-and-sixty-five-pound person falling from that height generates close to a thousand pounds of impact force.

The concrete was unforgiving. Bones splintered in the man's legs, and his head flattened and burst, not unlike what would happen to a pumpkin dropped from a similar height. Blood spray from the impact dotted the pavement all the way to Mike's feet.

Jackie was almost forty feet ahead, still unaware that Mike had stopped. She whirled around when she heard the body hitting the sidewalk and gave a startled cry.

"What happened?" she shouted. She looked up at the parking garage next to them. "Did that guy try to *jump* on you?"

"No, I think someone threw him over the edge."

They both looked up. Peering over the edge was a teenager with long, wavy blond hair, inspecting the body on the sidewalk with no apparent remorse. He shifted his gaze to them and suddenly pushed away from the wall, like someone in a hurry. They could guess who he was in a rush to reach, and they had no intention of being nearby when he descended from the garage.

They took a side street to throw off their pursuer and then turned onto a major thoroughfare they hoped would lead them out of the city. They covered no more than a block along the new street before Mike noticed a woman jogging slowly toward them while wearing a white wedding dress with a long train. Prior to the last few days, this would have been considered an unusual, perhaps even comical scene. Now, it was terrifying.

"Let's speed it up a bit," said Mike.

They broke into a jog as well, just fast enough to keep the gap from growing any smaller. Jackie stepped into the street and tried to flag down a vehicle as it drove past, but the driver simply swerved around her and leaned on his horn.

"Asshole!" she shouted after him.

The surreal footrace continued for another four blocks, until they noticed, several blocks ahead of them, two men and a woman coming from the opposite direction, toward them. The woman was young, in her twenties, and she had one of the men by the other hand, physically dragging him along. Her other hand held a leash, and a small black and white dog trotted along beside her.

The second man was elderly, and he was clearly having trouble keeping pace with his younger companions. The woman and the older man took turns looking behind them, toward a man in a blue suit carrying a length of metal pipe, like the type used when constructing a perimeter fence. He was about seventy yards behind them and closing fast.

Mike and Jackie were trapped between Wedding-Dress lady and Blue-Suit man, along with the two men and the woman. And the dog, a small terrier of some type.

"Shit," they said, in unison.

There were no side streets readily available either behind them or in front of them. Mike considered heading back the way they had come, trying to dodge the woman in the dress. She didn't look very fast, but she could be armed. A jeweled purse was clutched in one of her hands. When Mike looked back up the street, he saw that the older man had stumbled and was now sprawled on the pavement in the middle of the road.

The man lifted his head and shouted, "Go!"

The young woman seemed hopelessly torn between going back to assist or continuing with her efforts to get the younger man out of harm's way.

The man in the blue suit rapidly closed the remaining distance, prompting the woman into motion. Even from a distance, Mike could tell that she was crying.

"Phillip, I'm sorry," she shouted, the last word like a cry of pain.

The fellow with the pipe quickly reached the elderly man, who had finally managed to get up onto one knee. Blue Suit stood over the man and made a minor correction to his stance like a golfer finding the optimum position to hit a ball down the fairway. He then arched back with the pipe and swung it toward the helpless senior. The old man tried to block the swing with his arm but was only partly successful and the cost was heavy. The bones in his forearm snapped with shocking crispness, the sound causing Mike to recoil in sympathetic pain. The elderly man's cry of agony was abruptly terminated as Blue Suit struck him across the face with the pipe, knocking him onto his back. He continued to hammer the pipe into the man's head until the metal pipe was ringing off the pavement below.

The dog went berserk after the old man was attacked and eventually managed to free its leash from the woman's grip. It tore down the street toward the man in the suit.

"Milo, no!" the woman screamed.

The dog reached the man in seconds. Blue Suit watched it come and then smashed it in the head with the pipe as soon as it came within range. The dog gave a high-pitched yelp as it tumbled to the side. Its left leg twitched several times and then the dog's body went slack. It appeared to deflate as it died, a sad pile of black and white fur.

The man stopped, surveyed his handiwork, and then turned his head to look at Mike and Jackie and the young man and woman who were now just ten yards away.

The woman was crying even harder now but still moving.

Mike gave up on finding a side street and focused his attention on the buildings lining the avenue. Most were businesses with large plate glass windows that had protective security screens covering them. Even if they were to find one with an unprotected window and could smash the glass, their pursuer or pursuers could easily follow them inside.

On the other side of the street, situated incongruously between two staid business fronts, was a high metal fence that was both decorative and functional. Sharp metal spikes topped the barrier, but the gate had been left ajar. What looked like a red brick schoolhouse sat down a short, shrub-lined path. It appeared to be a private institution, with the words

Solomon Levy Institute engraved in stone over the entryway. The property was anomalous among the concrete and glass buildings on either side and had a well-kept flower garden and a burbling fountain off to the side. It was a far cry from Mike's own school experience, spent in a building surrounded by acres of concrete that bore more than a passing resemblance to a prison. The only grass close to his school was the stuff that pushed up between the cracks in the sidewalk. The school janitors killed the rogue vegetation with Roundup.

The young woman called to Mike and Jackie as she drew nearer, dragging her seemingly uncooperative partner behind.

"We need help," she shouted. "He's not going to stop."

Blue Suit man was not the only problem, although Mike deemed him a more credible threat than the woman in the wedding dress. She had slowed to a walk but was still making steady progress toward them. There seemed to be few options. He pointed toward the school that sat at the end of the path but did not wait to see if the woman and her companion would follow.

As they approached the building, Mike saw several shadowy faces duck out of view from the windows positioned next to the door. The entryway was formidable, with an ornate steel door equipped with viewports set high up. The glass appeared to be several inches thick and was cleverly configured to prevent someone from getting a clear look inside. The windows on each side of the door were protected by a decorative but substantial set of bars.

Mike repeatedly pressed on a doorbell button set into the wall next to the front door.

"Let us in, we need help," he shouted, echoing what the woman had said to him.

Jackie moved up beside him and knocked on the door, somewhat less aggressively. "Please, we have nowhere else to go."

The door remained closed.

The young woman who asked them for help appeared at the end of the lane with her male companion. She was about twenty-five, with a black ballcap covering straight brown hair tied into a ponytail. The man she was with was overweight, had short black hair, and appeared to have an intellectual disability. She had to steer him into the lane after he tried to continue walking down the street.

Mike could hear a heated but hushed argument being conducted on the other side of the door. The voices escalated in volume, and he was surprised when the door abruptly swung open, revealing a small woman with graying hair and glasses. The man behind her was large and beefy and glared at Mike and Jackie as if they were lice-infested junkies. He wore a plaid cotton shirt that strained against his substantial belly and had a large pistol strapped to his hip. His hand hovered next to it, indiscreetly close.

Mike pushed into the building before the man could intercede and jammed his foot against the door to allow access for the woman and her shambling male compatriot as well.

"You gotta be kidding me," the man said. "How many more of you are there?"

"Just the four of us. Although, I don't know these two."

"Joan…" The man appealed to the small woman, his voice a mix of whine and exasperation.

"Harold, we can take them. We have enough room."

A shadow in the shape of a man gathered in front of one of the side windows.

"Look," shouted Harold, "they led him right to us!"

The light coming through the door window flickered as the intruder moved about, trying to force the entrance. He had his head down, so it was difficult to get a good look at him. There appeared to be no play in the lock at all; it was like the door to a bank vault. That was good. If the door had been rattling a little in its frame, it may have encouraged the man to continue.

After another minute, the man gave up on the attempt and stood directly in front of the door window. The glass on the door was designed to allow a clear view of those outside while obscuring the details of those within the building. Although the man was dressed in a blue suit with a white shirt and a pale blue tie, his clothing looked rumpled and slept in. He had blond hair, neatly parted to the side, and light blue eyes that matched his tie. There was a black name tag with white lettering attached to his suit coat, but Mike couldn't read it. He could have been a Mormon missionary if Mormon missionaries had dead eyes and unsmiling faces.

The woman in the wedding dress was nowhere in sight, and Mike wondered why she was not at the door as well. In every movie and television series he had ever seen, the infected individuals always amassed in a mob. Perhaps they would join forces after a while, although he had never seen more than a couple at a time.

This one appeared to be staring directly at Mike's face, which creeped him out. Mike continued to observe him for a few moments and then tuned into the conversation behind him.

"The sick coming to our door is nothing new, Harold. The building is secure; you know that. They will give the doors a try, but they always lose interest very quickly."

The beefy man threw up his hands in frustration. "Well at least take their goddam temperature."

He stalked away, grumbling about how this was supposed to be a democracy.

The small woman waited until the man was out of earshot. "You will have to excuse Harold. He is not with the school. He was, like you, a person seeking sanctuary. Unfortunately, his idea of a democracy is when everyone agrees with what he thinks is best.

"The building *is* secure. We had an incident a few years ago which prompted some serious security measures to be implemented. The sick could cut their way into the building with a torch or use explosives, but the condition from which they suffer seems to make them disinterested in complex solutions. Or maybe it's just because they can't see us. They tend to go after the easy targets."

Joan walked over to a small side table and pulled out an electronic thermometer.

"Now, I will require each of you to submit to a temperature measurement. We have been keeping a close eye on the news, and we are aware that the presentation of violent behavior is almost always preceded by an illness. The most common symptom of this illness is a substantially elevated temperature, something above 102 Fahrenheit. It is our expectation that you submit to these measurements twice daily, for the safety of both you and the other guests and residents here."

"What happens if someone becomes sick and has a high temperature?" asked Mike.

Joan looked uncomfortable with the question. "We have been fortunate not to have that situation occur."

"But what if it does?" Mike persisted.

"On this subject, Harold and I are in full agreement: the ill person must leave immediately. We cannot risk spreading the disease, or worse. This is non-negotiable."

Joan frowned at the display on the device, pressed a button, and then stood before Mike. He could feel an anticipatory increase in his body temperature as the woman placed the infrared thermometer in front of his forehead. He released a pent-up breath when she examined the readout and then proceeded to the next person.

Everyone was clear, even the disturbingly emotionless and non-verbal young man who bore two of the common traits of the afflicted.

Mike sidled over to the woman with the ballcap while her ward —

because that was what he seemed to be— was having his temperature checked.

"We haven't been properly introduced," he said. "My name is Mike."

"Shannon," said the woman.

"What's his story?" Mike asked, nodding toward the hulking man-child. He would normally never ask such a question, but these were unusual times and he wanted to know what to expect.

"Johnny? He was in a car accident when he was four. The crash killed his mother, and he was trapped underwater for twenty minutes. It left him with severe brain damage. I take care of him when his father is out of town on business.

"They live in a condo a few miles from here, and Johnny and I always go down to welcome his father home when he gets back. We did that this morning, but then we couldn't get back inside. There was... stuff happening in the lobby. We've been wandering the streets ever since."

"That man who was with you, was that Johnny's father?"

She looked down. "Yes."

"I'm sorry to hear that. It was a terrible thing for Johnny to see."

He thought of something else. "Why didn't you take them back to your own place?"

"I live out of town and by the time we realized the extent of what was happening, public transport had been shut down and taxis were almost impossible to find. We have been trying to reach a hotel or a police station ever since, but those people are everywhere."

Mike didn't have to ask her what she meant by *those people*. He had another concern.

He nodded toward Johnny. "Does he ever have any violent outbursts?"

She laughed. "Never. He might give you a hug though."

Joan gave them a brief tour, although it was limited to just a few rooms. They did not have access to the classrooms, and the students who were housed at the school were kept isolated from the newcomers in a separate wing.

All the school's refugees were accommodated in the relatively large cafeteria. Most of the small white tables had been pushed into the center, effectively creating one very large tabletop, and leaving the perimeter available for cots and mattresses. Mike was alarmed by what he saw, not in the layout of the room but in the composition of its inhabitants. Almost everyone was armed, with rifles slung over backs, pistols shoved into waistbands, or shotguns held in the crooks of their arms. It was like a survivalist convention.

He turned to Joan, who was unfurling a sleeping bag on top of a small blue mat. "Is there anywhere else to stay?"

"I'm afraid not. The inn is full, so to speak. We have isolated the students in their rooms, and the staff have their own quarters."

"This looks," Mike gestured discreetly toward the guns, "almost as dangerous as being outside."

"It is not to my liking either. I abhor guns. However, it makes the people sheltering here feel safer, and the infected individuals with whom we are dealing are not receptive to de-escalation and other forms of peaceful resolution. As much as I hate to admit this, we may need people with weapons at some point."

"But any one of them could get sick and start shooting," argued Jackie. "The infected people are not mindless zombies; they act more like cold blooded killers. They use guns, knives, cars— whatever they have available."

"That is why we take temperature readings twice a day. Everyone who seeks refuge here must agree to the same condition— if they have an elevated temperature they must leave as soon as it is safe to do so."

It was not an arrangement Mike found reassuring, but he was not in a position to argue or demand a change to the policy. He was acutely aware that he and Jackie and the other two were the only new people to arrive over the last forty-eight hours. If anything were to happen or if anyone became sick, they would be the obvious scapegoats. The reality was, however, that with such a long latency between the original illness and the relapse into a *different kind* of sickness, anyone among the refugees could be next. The blood tests seemed to suggest that neither he nor Jackie were in any imminent danger of becoming brain-damaged killers, but he had no idea about the young man and woman who came in behind them.

The current situation, although not entirely satisfactory, seemed to be the best of a number of bad options. It was late afternoon, they were unfamiliar with this part of the city, they had no vehicle, and they had no plan. This refuge would give them time to consider their next steps.

They staked out an area on the floor next to a freezer that was pumping hot air. The room was already quite warm, so this spot was not considered prime real estate. Jackie preferred it for that very reason— there were no other refugees within ten feet of them. She was acutely aware that anyone in the room could be a carrier of the VHP-25 variant, and it would only take one person coughing to seed the air with the not-so-harmless virus. The cytomegalovirus sat within her like a delicate vial of poison, perpetually at risk of fracturing.

She had donned a double set of masks before entering the room, and most of the current inhabitants regarded these with undisguised hostility, as if she were intentionally attempting to provoke them.

For his part, Mike was relieved to see that Shannon and Johnny had located a spot on the other side of the room. The interaction with them had been cordial enough, but he did not wish to be saddled with them when he and Jackie decided to go. He knew what to expect with Jackie; she was nimble of mind and quick on her feet. That could make the difference between life and death in the next few days.

Jackie gave a delighted cry when she discovered a functioning internet connection, a guest account for Wi-Fi at the school. She rapidly logged on and began feverishly searching for information. The national and international news was bleak.

"It's everywhere," she said. "Occurrences in Great Britain, France, Germany, Japan, some in South America. No one seems to be able to put a lid on it."

"Have they mentioned the cause? It's hard to believe that we can be the only ones to discover the transformed virus."

Jackie scanned one article after another, speed-reading the content. Most of the stories were devoted to especially notable episodes of violence and only loosely speculated on the cause. All of them concluded that it was a virus of some type, hence the speed of the spread, although whether it was viral meningitis, a variant of influenza or VHP-25, or even a form of measles was not as well defined.

"Do you think some labs are aware of the viral transformation but may be afraid of mass panic if they release the information?" asked Mike.

"Don't you think we already have mass panic?"

"*Worse* mass panic, a complete breakdown of society."

She stared at him. "Conspiracy theories are unhelpful to our situation."

Mike realized she was right; they knew what they knew and needed to plan accordingly. Worrying about something beyond their control was a pointless expenditure of energy.

Jackie switched to the local news and let out a groan.

"The National Guard is setting up checkpoints for anyone attempting to get out of the city, trying to control the spread."

Mike made a sound of derision. "That won't work; it's far too late for it. I'm not an epidemiologist but even I know that. Plus, can you imagine how long it would take to check every single person?"

"The government wants to make it look like they are doing something. Roadblocks are already up."

"I don't want to be stuck in a car with nowhere to go if someone starts to go crazy. We'd be sitting ducks. We need to find another way out. They can't just trap us in here like some knockoff version of *The Hunger Games*."

"More like *Night of the Living Dead*, but I get what you are saying."

Mike sat back against the wall. "We are at a severe disadvantage because neither of us knows the city very well, but you should check the online maps and see if you can find a viable route."

Mike heard the metal shutters opening between the cafeteria and kitchen, signaling that a meal was ready to be served. He walked over to collect some food while Jackie worked away at her phone, pinching and expanding her thumb and index finger to shrink and expand the map.

"Anything?" he asked, after arriving back with a tray bearing bowls of soup, freshly baked dinner rolls, small bowls of canned fruit salad, and two bottles of water.

"Maybe. I don't think we can drive out of the city, much as that would be the preferable option. All the major highways leading out of the city are easy to block."

"What does that leave us? You're not suggesting we try to *walk* out, are you?"

Jackie gave him a sour look. "No, walking out would be a bad idea. But we may be able to take a boat."

"Out to the sea?"

She shook her head. "Too many other people will have had the same idea. The ports are going to be patrolled by the Coast Guard or the Navy. I think we should try the river. At the very least we can get out of the most heavily populated areas."

Mike had only a vague grasp of the geography of the region, but he knew that a river cut through the heart of the city. If he were by himself, exiting the city by boat would not be his first choice. He had very little experience on the water, limited to a pleasure boat ride in New York a few years back. However, the river here did not seem all that intimidating and appeared to be slow-moving when he crossed it by bridge several days ago.

Mike thought about it for a minute. The map showed a small town just ten miles down the river. Even drifting along at two miles an hour would get them there in five hours. With an engine on the boat, it could be as short as an hour. Still, he was not crazy about the plan. It pre-supposed their ability to safely get to the river *and* to find a suitable boat, two separate factors that were by no means a certainty.

"The National Guard may try to stop people from leaving by the river as well."

"They could, but I don't think they will. It's a matter of scale and resources. You can try to restrict 250,000 people from leaving by road or twenty-five people leaving by water. Where are you going to put your resources? Besides, we know how sick people can get before they turn violent. None of them would want to take a canoe or a kayak if they had the option of driving, and very few parents would take their sick child on a boat. Hence, I think most people going by boat will be healthy anyway."

Mike decided not to push it, especially since he didn't have a better plan himself. "Okay, but I think we should leave as soon as possible regardless, preferably first thing tomorrow. I don't like being around large groups; there's too much chance of something going wrong."

This assessment proved to be accurate far sooner than he expected. Sometimes he hated when he was right.

It was dark when it started, but it was not completely dark. Things might have turned out differently if the initial incident had been totally obscured, or conversely, well-lighted. As it was, there was just enough illumination from the various appliances and hallway lights for certain actions to be misinterpreted. People were already on edge; all they needed was a little nudge for them to act on that fear and paranoia.

This is what he knew: moments after being abruptly awoken by a panicked shout, Mike had propped himself up on his elbows and witnessed Johnny standing motionless on the other side of the room. He had no sense of how much time had passed since he fell asleep. It could have been minutes or hours.

"Oh my God, he's infected. HE'S INFECTED!" a woman screamed.

There were a number of valid reasons for Johnny to be standing there, several spaces from where he was originally stationed. He could have sleepwalked. But it was more likely that he had awoken with the need to urinate and took it upon himself to navigate his way to the washroom and back. On his return, he may have mistaken where he bunked down. Had he stepped on the woman? Tried to lie down beside her? Either scenario was possible, and in most cases this would have resulted in an awkward moment or two, to be laughed at later. But Johnny had a number of notable liabilities. He was big, he was non-verbal, and his default expression was vacant and unreadable. In this charged environment, that was about three strikes too many. The woman had likely looked up at Johnny, who would have appeared gigantic from her perspective, and assumed the worst.

Mike was neither pro-gun nor anti-gun. If pressed, he might describe himself as leaning pro, since he owned a firearm himself, a Glock 9mm.

Unfortunately, it was currently residing in a gun safe in his New York apartment. He had never needed to take it from the safe, but its presence was reassuring to him. If things ever started to get hairy, it was nice to know that he would be equipped. Of course, things *had* gotten hairy, but he had no way of knowing he would need the pistol when he traveled. The possibility never even crossed his mind.

Either the terrified woman or her husband took it upon themselves to be proactive and neutralize the threat by shooting Johnny without further delay. Johnny just stood there, staring down at them in the dark, a mute menace, unable to explain himself and defuse the situation. Even under normal circumstances, that type of behavior could cause someone to become alarmed and overreact.

Mike was just about to stand up, having risen to one knee, when the firing began.

Whoever fired the weapon managed to miss Johnny from a distance of five feet. They did, however, hit the man coming up behind Johnny with a pistol in his hand. The man cursed and tucked his left arm close to his body, like someone trying to squeeze through a tight spot. He then raised his weapon and fired multiple rounds at the source of the muzzle flash, either out of rage or the misplaced belief that the source of the gunfire was from an infected individual. He missed Johnny as well.

The second shooter hit not only the woman who sounded the alarm in the first place but also several people behind her.

A sort of madness descended upon the room after that, and everyone who possessed a firearm had it out and was firing at anything and everything. Shannon, the young woman accompanying Johnny, fled through the door and into the hallway. She may have visited the washroom too and returned just in time to be greeted by a hail of bullets.

Mike and Jackie squirmed across the floor toward the exit as well, being showered by pieces of plaster, shards of wood from splintered chairs, and the occasional spray of blood. It was insanity.

Mike was just a second away from exiting the room when he was kicked hard in the calf. He looked around to see who had attacked him, but there was no one there. He continued into the hallway, safe for a moment from the hail of gunfire. His calf was still smarting from the kick, and he twisted around and looked down at the spot. Blood had already soaked through his pant leg and was pooling over his shoe. He hadn't been kicked; he had been shot. He felt faint at the sight.

Jackie, unaware of his injury, grabbed his arm as if to hurry him along the hallway toward the exterior door.

Shannon was already working on the locks, trying to get the door open.

Her hands were shaking quite badly, plus she was turning the bolts in the wrong direction and trying to open the door before it was fully unlocked. She was out of her mind with panic, perhaps assuming that someone was trying to kill everyone inside the building.

Mike called out, "Wait!"

But Shannon paid him no attention, and it was very unlikely that she checked outside before attempting to open the door. She finally flung the door open only to be greeted by the sight of the blue-suited man. Blue Suit had either been waiting outside all along or been attracted by the sound of gunfire. He was upon her in an instant, stepping forward and bludgeoning her with the same length of steel pipe he had used on Johnny's father. There was dried blood, now black, along most of its length.

"Hey!" shouted Mike, trying to distract the man. But he could tell that it was already too late. Shannon's skull no longer sounded hard when the man hit it with the pipe; it was closer to the resonance one might expect when smashing a burlap bag full of apples. The end of the pipe was bright red and glistening, and there was a trail of blood spatter high up on the wall and ceiling from the backswing.

Blue Suit swung at Shannon's head one last time and then focussed his attention on them. They had nowhere to go, except back into the cafeteria, which now seemed to be a safer bet. The firing from within had ceased, replaced by crying and groaning and lamenting.

There were certain to be fatalities. Perhaps they could retrieve a weapon from one of the victims.

Just as they turned, Harold emerged from the cafeteria doorway. He was covered in blood, but it was impossible to tell if it was his. The pistol, an old revolver that he normally carried on his hip, was now in his hand. He looked wild-eyed and deranged, and he glared at Mike and Jackie as if daring them to make a move toward him.

They turned as one and pointed to the man in the blue suit. "That's who you want to shoot!" shouted Jackie.

Harold did not need any more encouragement. He raised his gun and fired at the man walking toward him.

Mike may have simply imagined that he felt the heat from the bullet as it passed by his face, but it was awfully close. The first shot missed the man, and Mike could sympathize just how difficult it was to hit a moving target with a pistol. Or, perhaps more accurately, how hard it was to hit a moving target that was moving toward you with the intent to inflict grievous bodily harm.

Harold pulled the trigger again, but this time the hammer fell on a spent round. If the first gunshot seemed loud, the sound of the revolver failing to fire on the second attempt was even louder.

Mike and Jackie shrank back against the wall, although the man was completely focused on Harold now, like a lion going in for a kill. Harold tried to fire again, but the result was the same. He kept pulling on the trigger of the empty weapon, seemingly unable to alter the course upon which he had set himself. The clicking stopped as Blue Suit swung the pipe and it connected with the side of Harold's head. The big man fell into a heap, as if all his joints had turned to butter.

Mike looked around for a weapon. Blue Suit would be done with Harold in short order and then turn his attention back on him. Mike did not want to fight, or take flight, with a bullet in his calf. Neither action was likely to be very successful.

A coat stand with a rain jacket hanging from one hook was the only feasible weapon in the hallway. It had a stylish design, with a circular wood base, a solid wood upright and four wooden pegs for coats. Mike stripped it of the jacket and grabbed it with both hands. It was awkward to lift and heavy as hell. A surprise attack was the only way this weapon would be useful since he would probably only get one swing. There was no way he could win a protracted battle, not with a forty-pound coat rack as a weapon.

He swung the stand back and then tried to accelerate it towards the man's head. It seemed to take an eternity. Blue Suit turned just as the stand was completing its arc. He attempted to block the object with his arm, but the stand brushed it aside and the circular base caught him just above his left temple.

The man collapsed, arms and legs akimbo. The steel pipe bounced and clanged against the stone floor when it was dropped.

The adrenalin released during the initial firefight in the cafeteria had worked wonderfully to blunt the throbbing in Mike's calf. But now that it was wearing off, the pain escalated rapidly, like someone was holding a blowtorch to his leg. He cried out involuntarily and hopped on one foot, trying to find a place to sit.

"What happened?" asked Jackie.

"I took a bullet in my calf," he said through gritted teeth. "Fuck it hurts."

She put his arm over her shoulders and guided him toward a bench by the front door. There was a collection of children's rubber boots underneath. She eased him down on top of the bench and took a look at his pantleg. There was a lot of blood, and he left a trail of it from their former position in the hall.

"I'll see if I can get a First Aid kit."

Jackie closed and locked the front entrance and then walked to the heavy door at the end of the hall that separated the cafeteria from the residence. She pounded on it and shouted her demands for a First Aid kit, but there was no response. Mike was not surprised. The principal had just heard a firefight that was followed by even more gunfire and would be justifiably reluctant to expose her wards to this type of danger.

Jackie repeatedly pounded on the door but gave up after another minute. She walked back to Mike and peered out through the bleary glass windows. It was still full dark, except for some distant streetlights.

"There's not much I can do for you without supplies. Can you wait until morning?" she asked.

Mike thought of himself as being fairly tough, with a high pain threshold. He had done some grueling workouts in his life. But this gunshot wound revealed to him that he had never truly experienced pain before. He couldn't fathom five more minutes of this, much less five hours. The pain had become worse, if that was even possible, and he had his eyes squeezed shut, trying not to whimper.

"No," he said. His voice was hoarse, as if he had been shouting. The truth was, he was willing to risk both his life and Jackie's life to find some relief. Pain can transform you into a child, selfish, and self-absorbed.

Jackie looked again at the dark window. "Okay," she said. "I'll be right back."

She disappeared into the cafeteria. Mike could still hear moans and crying from within and knew that there were many other people in need of Jackie's help. He didn't care. He could be ashamed of himself later when he wasn't in so much pain. She emerged a minute later, and he wondered if it was difficult for her to leave those people behind. She was a nurse, and her nursing instinct would be to stop and help. But there was also the bigger picture. At times like this, sometimes you needed to do the practical thing, even if it wasn't the right thing.

She pulled up her shirt and flashed a pistol that was stuck gangster style into the waist band of her jeans. She sat next to him, looped his arm over her shoulders and then helped him to his feet.

One of the other survivors came out of the cafeteria and stared down at the bodies of the two men.

"We're leaving," said Jackie. "Lock the door behind us."

She walked Mike to the window, and they both stared out into the darkness, looking for anything that didn't belong. The walkway was deserted as far as they could tell. She reached over and unlocked the door.

Going outside at night was scary at first, but the fresh air seemed to make Mike feel about ten percent better. That lasted until he tried to put some weight on his injured leg. The pain was so incapacitating that even his good leg started to buckle. Jackie had to work hard to keep him on his feet.

On the other side of the street was a large bundle of white. Mike didn't remember it being there before and eyed it with suspicion. It was only after they walked closer that he was able to distinguish some identifying features, the lace and the satin and the bunched-up train of a wedding gown. There was blood marring the white of the woman's dress, and she appeared to be dead.

"I wonder what happened to her?" asked Jackie.

"One less to worry about," said Mike. He realized that sounded cold, but his supply of empathy had just about run dry.

They were fortunate to come across a pharmacy about four blocks later. Remarkably, the protective metal grill had not been deployed *and* the windows were still intact. Perhaps the inevitable looters had been intercepted along the way. Jackie popped the trunk of an abandoned car and rooted around until she found a tire iron. The alarm sounded when she smashed the glass door, but she was no longer concerned about the police showing up. She helped Mike inside and sat him in a chair by the counter where they dispensed the medication.

The power was still on, so she was able to quickly gather the supplies she sought. However, the heavy-duty pharmaceuticals were locked away behind barriers that looked like they could withstand a serious assault. She settled for hydrogen peroxide and over the counter painkillers.

Jackie cut his pant leg away with a pair of scissors and gently probed at the wound with a large set of tweezers that she had disinfected with alcohol. Mike was writhing in pain by the time she was finished. It felt like she was examining him with a white-hot poker.

"The bullet is still in there. It's going to hurt like hell when I take it out, but your leg will feel better after it's been removed. Not immediately, but it will be much better than leaving it inside."

She was correct— it did hurt like hell. He may have even passed out once or twice while she worked the tweezers around inside the wound. At some point he looked down and she was bandaging his leg. Jackie was also right about one other thing; it did *not* immediately feel better. There was no more time for self pity, however; he needed to buckle down and accept the discomfort while they made their escape.

The pharmacy was equipped with a home health care section as well, including both walkers and a few folding wheelchairs. He gladly plopped into one of the wheelchairs once they were outside. Jackie immediately started to push him in the direction of the river, their presumed ticket out of this nightmare.

There was no traffic, and the sidewalks were so full of garbage and debris that it made their progress extremely slow. Three blocks later, Jackie decided to change tactics and roll Mike along the street instead. They passed under a streetlight soon after and were briefly highlighted by its glow. If Jackie had looked behind her at that moment, she might have glimpsed a spot of blue under another streetlight six blocks back.

CHAPTER 22

Their destination was the Finch River, which ran through the heart of the city and was less than a mile from the school. It passed under the Slocum Street Bridge, the so-called new bridge, which was completed in 2005.

Mike did not disagree with Jackie's plan, he just thought that the likelihood of finding a suitable boat within city limits was wishful thinking. To him, boats were something he associated with larger bodies of water, like a lake or the sea. But Jackie was a resourceful person and discovered that there was a boat club somewhere along the river that rented canoes and kayaks and paddleboards. They just had to get there without running into any of the infected.

The river had apparently undergone a dramatic transformation in the last fifteen years, with the closure of upstream factories that used to dump their waste products directly into the water, and a new wastewater treatment plant. It took a while, but recreational activities had begun to take place along its shores. Jackie had no direct knowledge of this, just her research online. The process was not without its doubters. There were a lot of old-timers with long memories who said they would never again let the water touch their skin.

Jackie pushed Mike in the wheelchair along the street until they reached the river and then she switched to a dual bike and pedestrian path that ran mostly parallel to the water. It sometimes ascended small overpasses or descended into tunnels when it came across infrastructure that was deemed too difficult or too valuable to displace.

There was no light in the sky yet, but the overpasses provided a welcome navigational aid, helping them get a sense of their surroundings and hinting at what was to come. The tunnels were the opposite, damp, claustrophobic, and blinding. Most of them were simply ribbed metal culverts with a concrete walking path. They were not well-maintained, and silt and gravel had accumulated on the walking surfaces over time, likely from the run-off from heavy rains.

It was in one of these tunnels, naturally, that they encountered the first person they had seen since leaving the school.

They were halfway through the passage when the feeble light dimmed even further. Mike looked up to see a man standing at the opposite end. He assumed it was a man, because the person was so large he seemed to block the entrance completely. That brief initial sighting was all he had to work with before the person ducked inside. The light was so scant that it made it impossible for Mike to see more than the curvature of the tunnel to his side, and the tops of his feet. All the lights in the tunnel had either burned out or been vandalized. The man was clearly tall as well as wide, because the tunnel had a clearance of almost seven feet. Mike's impression was that the size was due to muscle, rather than fat.

"Fuck," he said quietly.

"Should we go back?" Jackie whispered.

The tunnel was only thirty yards long and they were already ten or fifteen yards in. Walking backwards would be slow, especially with all the silt, and there was too little room to quickly turn the wheelchair.

"It's too late," Mike said. "Give me the gun."

Jackie fumbled the gun out of her pants and laid it against his chest. He grabbed it and pointed it forward at the space he expected the man to occupy. There was very little chance he could miss, considering the size of the target and the narrowness of the tunnel.

"Stop, or I'll shoot," he said. He still could not bring himself to take the offensive, not when he was still uncertain about the man's status. The man could be sick in some other way, or mentally ill but harmless. But Mike's reticence extended only so far; the odds were that the man was afflicted, and he had no intention of letting this giant walk right up to them.

"Last chance!" he shouted.

He did not provide an additional warning; he pointed at the dead center of the darkness and pulled the trigger. He planned to rely on the muzzle flash to tell him if his aim was off. He closed his eyes slightly In anticipation of the burst of light, but the trigger did not depress.

There was a sense of shambling motion in the darkness ahead of them, like a huge grizzly bear was rapidly advancing on their location.

"Shoot him!" Jackie shouted.

"I can't, the safety must be on!"

He desperately searched for the mechanism by touch, not knowing exactly where it would be located or how it would be configured. His weapon at home did not have one, but he knew there were different mechanisms for different weapons. Some safeties slid, some flicked, some depressed.

Before he had a chance to find it, the man commenced his attack. The decision to remain seated was a terrible tactical error, possibly fatal. For warding off an assault, being on one good leg was far superior to sitting in a chair with wheels. He was practically defenseless. He was functionally half the man's height, had limited reach and no ability to maneuver. Luckily, it appeared that the man was unarmed. His attacker's confidence in his physical ability must have survived the sickness, and it was possible that he had used his strength and size in the past, not needing to resort to weapons to subdue his opponents.

His chosen method of dispatching Mike appeared to be through strangulation. Mike could see the big hands converging toward his throat; with the man so close that he could smell his breath. The gigantic man had to lean far down to reach Mike, but he had plenty of arm length to spare. The arms were the only part of the man's body that Mike could reach, and he made a valiant effort to keep the hands away from his throat. All the while, the wheelchair was being pushed back, which seemed to render his blows powerless. He still had the pistol in his grip and was using it to smash against the man's arms, but there was no way to find the safety while he was employing it as a de facto hammer. Plus, he ran the risk of having the gun taken from him, although he suspected his assailant would not have much better luck getting it to work.

Mike thrust the gun behind him, at Jackie.

"Get the safety off," he shouted.

The hulking man took advantage of the momentary lapse in defence to wrap his meaty hands around Mike's throat. The man's hands were so large that they were able to completely encircle Mike's neck, with the fingers touching in the back. The power of the grip was immense. Blood flow to his brain and air flow to his lungs ceased immediately. Mike focused on getting one of the man's fingers away from his neck. If he could pull it back far enough, he believed he could eventually break the grip. But he had thirty seconds, at most. He dug into his own flesh in an attempt to worm his fingers under the man's pinkie, reasoning that it would be the weakest link. There was some progress, just some, but he was rapidly losing his strength.

Jackie must have given up trying to brace against the chair, because there was a sudden jerking motion as it rolled back a few feet. Unfortunately, this did not affect the man's grip in the slightest, and Mike could no longer distinguish between the darkness of the night and the veil of darkness descending over his eyes. One of those darknesses would last hours, the other would last forever.

Mike saw and felt the first shot simultaneously. Big as the man was, he was jolted by the impact of a high velocity round delivered at close range. Jackie was firing so rapidly that Mike lost track of the shots. The discharge from the pistol created a strobe-light effect, and the man appeared to jerk and spasm in slow motion. He finally slumped on top of Mike before sliding down to the sandy floor of the tunnel, his passage leaving a trail of hot blood against Mike's thighs. Mike tried not to think of it, how it was seething with potentially deadly contaminants.

It seemed a long time before either of them spoke. Mike's ears still rang from the shots fired at very close range, a high-pitched mosquito-like whine.

"Are you okay?" asked Jackie.

"I may never be okay again," he said. "But he didn't do any further damage."

He twisted around in his chair, but he couldn't see her face in the dark. "Are *you* okay?"

"Yeah," she said, but her voice was shaky. "Let's get to the river."

They only encountered one other person along the way, a man carrying a crossbow. It was so unusual that Jackie questioned what she was seeing.

"Is that a *crossbow*?" she asked.

"I think so. I've never seen one in person, just in old movies."

The Medieval crossbows from Mike's memory were small and handheld, like pistols. This was a highly advanced weapon meant for deer hunting, with a shoulder stock and a scope, a serious piece of equipment.

After the incident in the tunnel, they both shifted their perspective from presumed innocent to presumed sick and therefore a threat. The man with the crossbow made it an easy assessment by shooting at them first. When he put the crossbow to his shoulder, Mike and Jackie ran in opposite directions, looking for shelter. Whether he was sick or not, Mike felt completely justified in shooting back. After the first bolt thudded into the tree behind which he was hiding, Mike peered out, steadied his hand against the trunk, and returned fire.

He missed the first time, but the second shot connected, hitting the man in the upper right-hand chest, just above the nipple line. The man stumbled slightly but continued forward, although moving now at a slower pace. He may have been trying to improve his chances with the crossbow by getting closer, but it was a strategy outside the normal parameters of human behavior.

The man was wearing a long-sleeved gray shirt, and it was clear that the bullet had caused serious damage, likely hitting the upper part of his right lung. The shirt was already saturated with blood below the wound, and yet this had not succeeded in stopping the man. Some dramatic rewiring of his brain must have occurred for the desire to kill to be stronger than the instinct to survive. Even Mike's smart phone was smarter than that. If he left it lying in the sun for too long, it would shut down to avoid irreversible damage. The man with the crossbow passed that well-defined threshold after he was shot, and he kept coming back for more. Mike gave him more.

The infected man jerked spasmodically as Mike fired round after round, his body temporarily overriding his homicidal aspirations. Biology finally trumped whatever was left of the man's mind, and he finally collapsed just twenty feet from Mike, the crossbow falling from his grip.

After it was over, Mike sat on a tree stump and waited for the pain in his calf to subside. Jackie sat on the ground, her back against the stump.

He was still stunned by the man's dogged persistence even after being mortally wounded.

"My God, it's like fighting a crocodile," he said. "He just wouldn't stop."

"Do you think that everyone has this capacity in them, to do what these people are doing? Or is it just a few, with the new virus triggering something in them that is already part of their nature?"

"That's a good question. From the perspective of someone trying to stay alive, it's also very pertinent. Let's say that eighty percent of the population has been infected with the cytomegalovirus, and that six percent of those have already been infected with the new variant." He did some quick math in his head. "*Damn*, that's almost twenty million people."

"What the hell do we do if there are twenty million of these types out there?" asked Jackie.

Mike didn't answer. Couldn't. There was no way of dealing with that many infected. Twenty million was unthinkable and that number might continue to grow. Twice the number, forty million, was an extinction level event. Forty million infected with the sole directive of trying to kill as many people as possible.

Instead, he said. "I don't believe it can be that many. I think you're right; there's likely something distinct about a small percentage of the population, something that makes them prone to a violent reaction. It could be some kind of genetic predisposition, or an aberrant part of their psychological make-up. Like the difference between a happy drunk and a mean drunk."

"In vino veritas," said Jackie.

Mike stared at her. "My Latin is a little rusty."

"In wine is truth." She shrugged. "That's the only phrase I remember, but I think we all know more Latin than we realize."

"Huh. My father used to say, 'What soberness conceals, drunkenness reveals.'"

"Exactly. The response to the transformed virus may be to strip away all the restraints of normal civilized behavior, reducing the person to a predatory animal. Like alcohol on steroids, which is a terrible analogy, but you get the idea. And like alcohol, not everyone will have the same reaction."

Mike nodded in agreement. "We can only hope. Fewer mean drunks, so to speak. I don't know anyone who has become infected, so it's impossible for me to speculate based on personal experience. Does it make any sense from what you know about Martin?"

"I didn't know him either. Just met him yesterday. Even so, who's to know? I could have known him five years sober and never guessed either."

Even as she said this, Jackie knew that the comparison didn't properly reflect the current situation. The virus was not a bottle of rum. Inside, she was thinking about Dr. Gishar, who she *did* believe she knew. He was the one person who caused her to question their theory.

And Mike was thinking about the little girls, the one on the plane, and Amy. He wanted his theory to make sense, he really did, because the alternative was just too horrifying. But the two little girls would not fit into the box, no matter how hard he tried. In truth, he did not believe that only a small percentage of the infected became violent. The reality, he feared, was exactly the opposite.

Neither said anything to the other about their nagging doubts. It would not change anything, and the admission would be frankly unhelpful, serving only to extinguish what fragile hope that remained.

They sat only fifty feet from where the fellow with the crossbow had fallen, and Jackie stared at the man's crumpled form for a long moment. "It must be terrible to lose yourself like that, to lose who you are. I wonder how fast it happens, whether you can feel yourself slipping away, bit by bit, or whether you just wake up and you are simply…gone?"

She went quiet for a minute, and when she spoke again her voice was heavier, weighed down by a memory. "My mother started to show symptoms of early onset Alzheimer's when she was only fifty-four. I watched her world shrink around her, day by day, until she completely disappeared inside herself. Before that, during those times when she was still right-minded, she was very clear with her wishes. She didn't want to live like that, as a shell, and she asked us to arrange a dignified end for her. Do you understand what I'm saying? I don't want to live like that either, especially if I am at risk of hurting people."

She turned her face up to Mike.

"You have to promise me something. If you think I'm… no longer *me*, and that I'm a threat, I want you to do what you must. If that means killing me, you need to do it. Promise me."

Mike puffed out his cheeks as he exhaled a long, slow breath. "Jackie, that's a heavy thing to put on a person. I don't know if I can promise you that. The best I can say is that I will do what is necessary if I think you are about to harm me or others and there is no other alternative."

She did not seem entirely satisfied with that answer but it was the best she was going to get.

She said, "I want you to know that I would do the same thing for you."

Mike was not thrilled with the idea of someone pre-emptively killing him, for whatever reason.

"Thanks, I guess," he said.

They rested for another ten minutes before continuing their trek. The encounter with the man with the crossbow had forced them to expend their entire supply of ammunition, but they kept the gun in case they stumbled across another source. It made him very uncomfortable to realize that for the immediate future they had no way to protect themselves. The man had also run out of bolts for his crossbow, not that Mike had much confidence in his ability to operate it.

It took them a while to reach the boat rental operation, only to find that it was cleaned out, presumably by others who had the same idea of leaving by water. He had not been overly thrilled at the idea of paddleboarding his way down the river on his injured leg anyway, although a canoe would have been fine.

They decided to continue along the river, hoping to come across a residence with a dock and any type of vessel that would float. This seemed wishful thinking since there was little transition between the city limits and a landscape that could best be described as a bog.

There were both risks and benefits to maintaining their current course of action. There were fewer opportunities to find a boat, but with the limited number of people who had chosen to live out here, there were also fewer infected.

Mike soon needed to abandon the wheelchair and resort to using a long walking stick fashioned from a deadfall branch. Their progress was agonizingly slow.

Just about an hour later, they came across an abandoned boat. That was the good news. The bad news was that it was caught up on a submerged log on the opposite side of the river, and the intervening distance was a muddy expanse of approximately forty yards.

"I'm not excited to walk across that," Mike said.

"It's just mud," said Jackie. "Although we'll have to clean and re-dress your wound as soon as we get in the boat."

Mike's reluctance to walk across mud like this was not because he had never done it before; it was because he *had*. When he was thirteen, he and the family had loaded up their vehicle and visited relatives in Maine. His younger cousins, boys his age, did not much care for him, and the feeling was mutual. They considered him a soft city boy (only partly true— you had to be a different kind of tough in New York), and he considered them yokels. They talked constantly and enthusiastically about things of which he had no interest, primarily fishing and hunting.

"We can show you the best fishin' spot in all of Aroostick County," said the oldest one. He turned to the others and grinned, as if he knew Mike would not take him up on the offer, soft city boy that he was.

In truth, Mike did not want to go, but he would not give these hicks the satisfaction of confirming their first impressions.

"Sounds great," he said.

When they arrived at the "fishing hole", he discovered that it was a tidal river at low ebb, with a large expanse of mud to cross before they could cast into the stream.

The cousins dropped their heavy packs and extracted high rubber boots.

"Sorry, we didn't have an extra pair for you," the oldest one said. "You don't really need them, but there will be a little more hosing off to do when you get home."

A little more hosing off. The fuckers. So, this is what they had been smirking about, knowing he was going to be faced with a trek through the fetid black mud before he reached the river. He almost turned back then, almost. He thought he would be justified in making this decision, and an older Mike would have had the self-assurance to do so. But he was uncertain of the way back, and, of course, he didn't want to look soft.

"Whatever," he said. "It's just mud."

He removed his running shoes and left them on the grassy bank. The mud was thick and cold, and the sensation of it squirting through the gaps in his toes was distinctly unpleasant. But what happened next was much worse. It left him with a vivid, tactile memory that persisted well into his adult years.

He stepped on an eel. The eel thrashed wildly under his foot, whipping, and coiling itself tightly around his ankle. He let loose a scream that was involuntary, uncontrollable, and high-pitched in a way that only pre-pubescent boys can manage. He was oblivious to the hysterical laughter of his cousins until he was most of the way to the shore. They had played him truly and well, using a bit of reverse psychology. On his walk back, he reflected that his cousins had suggested fishing because they knew Mike *would* go, just to prove a point. And they had known about the mud and the eels and how he might react. The humiliation of it burned through him for months after, and he plotted improbable acts of revenge on his cousins. But his family never did schedule a return visit.

This river was not an exact duplicate but close enough to cause old memories to resurface and fill him with trepidation.

"It looks like the tide is coming in," said Jackie.

She seemed to have more experience with waterways, so he took her word for it. The immediate concern was that the rising water could dislodge the boat and send it on its way up the river. It had also started to rain, which would accelerate the process.

She turned to him. "We have to get out there, right now." She looked at his leg and at his walking stick. "I'll secure the boat and then come back to help you."

She took off her shoes and rolled up her pantlegs, although that was unlikely to save them from getting dirty. Her progress was slow despite the effort she was exerting. Each step took her at least mid-shin in mud, some to just below the knee. Mike wondered if he could wait until the tide was fully in, so she could maneuver the boat closer to the riverbank. The potential for another encounter with an eel was unquestionably a factor in his hesitancy, although of greater concern was his desire to keep his wound clean.

It took Jackie five minutes just to reach the river's edge and then another three minutes to wade across, with the muddy water almost up to her chest. Jackie was only five yards from reaching the boat when Mike heard a sound behind him. Forty feet away and walking fast was a backwoods-type man, lean and hard, perhaps thirty-five years old. He had thin brown hair that hung long and limp along the side of his head. Backwoods was blank faced, but his eyes were focused on Mike. And there appeared to be a filleting knife in his right hand. That was not good. The backwoodsman was wearing a dirty white tank top, although it was so filthy it was difficult to discern the original color. His arms were scrawny but muscular, like those of a person who has done hard manual labor their entire lives. His feet were bare, and they were practically black with dirt.

"Shit," Mike said, under his breath.

He hobbled toward the bank and into the mud, not having the time or the inclination to remove his shoes. Jackie was too far away to offer immediate help, but he reasoned he could make it close enough to the boat for her to assist him if necessary.

The rain was now torrential, the type of rain you realize cannot last for long because it is simply too heavy.

He called to Jackie but it did not appear she heard, with the raindrops slapping against the surface of the water like thunderous applause.

Each step through the mud was a titanic struggle. The vacuum created by his deep push into the thick sludge threatened to remove his shoes and made it very difficult to cover much ground. The walking stick was useless, penetrating even deeper than his feet and just as reluctant to dislodge when he needed to take another step. The mud stank of organic decay, a stew of bacteria that was surely to invade his wound. The cold mud dulled the pain in his calf slightly, but he could not push off effectively with his left leg. When he looked back to assess the progress of his pursuer, he was horrified to discover that the backwoodsman was less than eight feet away. He was stepping through the mud easily. Whether it was his lighter body weight, the absence of shoes, or some other factor, the man was able to make much faster progress than Mike.

Jackie had her back to him, rocking the boat off its perch.

He called to her again. "Jackie!"

Jackie finally wrenched the boat free and climbed aboard, apparently hoping to steer it to a more hospitable landing site. She turned her head toward him and shouted back, but he could not distinguish her words.

Mike redoubled his efforts, but it felt like the harder he pushed, the stickier the mud became and the deeper he sank. Perhaps the key was to treat it like quicksand, to be slow and deliberate. That would be a fine strategy were it not for the backwoods outcast lightly stepping through the muck and armed with a knife specifically designed to slice through flesh. Slow and deliberate might free him from the mud, but he would receive multiple stab wounds through the ribs before he was anywhere close to being clear.

Another quick glance back confirmed that he would not reach the boat before the man reached him, and certainly not before Jackie could make her way back across the river. It was much better to stop and face his pursuer rather than be taken down from behind.

He turned and waited for the man to reach him. There was something about fighting a person with a knife that was viscerally unsettling. Every person who has reached adulthood has accidentally cut themselves with a knife in the past. They know how much it hurts, and that foreknowledge adds to the anticipation of the pain they will likely experience while being stabbed. His internal organs constricted at the thought.

The backwoodsman proceeded toward him with his blank face, moving quickly but also appearing unhurried. Mike knew what to expect when the man reached him, although the visual cues were still off-putting. In the absence of the knife, he could believe that the guy was rushing after him to present him with a lost wallet.

Mike squatted as surreptitiously as possible, scooping up a handful of mud. When the man was less than four feet away, Mike flung the mud into his face, aiming for his eyes. He was only partly successful, hitting only one eye. But the man was sufficiently distracted for Mike to step forward and swing the walking stick at his head.

But the swing was weak, because he couldn't turn his hips into it, and the stick itself was quite light. Backwoods caught the stick one-handed, wrested it from Mike's grasp, and threw it off to the side. He was *very* strong, the kind of wiry strength that develops in a person after years of working with their hands. Whether it was from chopping wood or cranking on wrenches, his assailant had considerable power in his compact frame. But Mike had a weight advantage of at least forty pounds and enough adrenalin coursing through his veins to kill a small animal. The woodsman had dropped his knife while grabbing at the stick, and Mike managed to take a ponderous step forward before the man retrieved it. Mike grabbed the wrist with the knife as the woodsman straightened, fighting desperately to maintain his grip despite the mud and the wet. The only sounds the man made were involuntary grunts of exertion. Mike's attention was dually focussed on keeping the knife at bay and keeping the man's other hand away from his eyes. It was like an awkward dance, with them face to face, practically holding hands.

Mike suddenly pushed forward against his attacker, trying to catch him off guard. The effort caused him to cry out in pain as a fresh bolt of fire rippled through his calf. However, the surprise push produced the desired effect. The man was practically up to his knees in sludge and was not able to reposition his feet to counter Mike's action. He fell backward onto the mud, and Mike was forced to fall with him, lest he lose control of the knife hand.

The woodsman twisted his wrist aggressively, now slick with mud, and Mike could feel himself losing his grip on the man's arm. If the guy got his hand away from him, it would be all over. In such tight quarters, without the ability to dodge or counter the attack, the woodsman could stab him six times in three seconds, into his arm, into his chest, into the soft flesh under his ribs.

He let go of the man's other hand and punched him in the face. It was an awkward punch, with his left hand, but it left the other man momentarily stunned. Mike hit him again and again until his head was half-submerged in the reeking black mud. Still, the backwoodsman fought on. Mike was seconds away from losing his hold on the mud-covered wrist. He saw what he had to do, saw a way to end it. There was no other option. Jackie would be too late; and his current actions were not having the desired effect.

He pushed the man's head the rest of the way down, the thin hair producing a halo around the woodsman's head. In the last second before his face went fully under, Mike could see the black mud enter the man's mouth and block his nose. The man's free hand scrabbled at his face, and he turned his head away, shut his eyes, and waited. He held on like that until all the thrashing stopped, and then held the man's head down a little longer, just to be sure. It took a long time for the man to die, although he could not estimate the length with any certainty. Time like that cannot be measured in seconds or minutes; it has a special unit all its own.

He finally relaxed his grip and stared down at the murky water that covered the man's face.

How many people had he killed over the last few days, four? Five? He had lost count. Of them all, this one was easily the worst.

"Mike, are you okay!" shouted Jackie.

He was far from okay. He didn't even turn around, he just kneeled in the cold mud, exhausted in both mind and body. Foster was right about the act of taking a life. Killing a person took something from you in return, like dismantling the foundation of a building. Drowning this man felt far worse than that, as if he had just accelerated the process of his own decline. Holding the woodsman's head under the filthy mud until he suffocated was a savage act, animalistic in its violence. It was also personal in a way that shooting an individual could never compare, not even close.

He didn't know how much of himself he had left. If he went by

Foster's reckoning, he would soon fade away to nothing. This death would stay with him, and he knew he would remember the feeling of that man's face straining against his hand, his jaw working as he struggled to breathe, a vivid tactile memory, just like the one of the eel under his foot.

Jackie came up behind him and laid a hand on his shoulder.

"I am so fucking done with this," he said.

CHAPTER 23

The boat was just a small dinghy, probably used for fishing. Jackie removed his bandages and cleaned the wound as best she could with river water. Mike hoped that the waste treatment plant was still online. She then doused the injury liberally with hydrogen peroxide and iodine and then covered the area with a fresh bandage. Although reasonably confident that she had done her best, he hoped they would be able to find some antibiotics at their next stop.

As they were about to set off, Mike glanced toward the shore and saw a man exiting the woods. A man wearing a blue suit.

"Is that the same fucking guy from the school?" asked Mike.

The boat's small trolling motor was already carrying them down the river, away from the shore. Jackie looked back and squinted. "It can't be, can it?"

Mike watched him until they rounded a bend in the river.

"I should have shot him, just to make sure."

The little motor carried them down the river for miles, permitting them slow but steady progress. Once the battery died, Jackie relied on oars. She was considerably smaller than Mike but had far more experience, so he was happy to let her take the lead.

They did not stop anywhere they saw people.

Jackie finally angled the dinghy toward the shore, to a location with a small dock. There were no other boats there, and the spot seemed isolated. Over the trees, they could see the tops of a few buildings and the steeple of a church.

They made their way very slowly and carefully toward the main part of town, attempting to avoid any contact with the residents of the area, regardless of whether they were sick or not.

"We need to get you some antibiotics," Jackie said, echoing his earlier thoughts. "God knows what was in that mud."

"Let's see if we can locate another pharmacy. Maybe we can find one that doesn't have all their meds locked up."

"There are other options," she said. "A dentist's office may have some, or even an ambulance. Places people might not automatically try."

They were still on the edge of town when Jackie held out her arm in a stop gesture. A man walked by, gazing straight ahead, his expression impossible to decipher. Taciturn or afflicted? It was impossible to say. They let him stroll by, oblivious to their presence.

They found what they were seeking before they hit the heart of town, a veterinary clinic with a regal Labrador Retriever painted on the sign out front.

"They'll have antibiotics in here," Jackie said.

Mike made a small sound of disagreement. "For *animals*."

Jackie looked at him. "We *are* animals. They'll work, with the right dosage."

They knocked first, and then Jackie broke the front door window with a planter.

"Small towns. You gotta love them. They leave their break and enter tools right on the doorstep."

The medications were in a poorly secured room, in a simple cabinet. Once Jackie calculated the correct dosage (the package was for dogs weighing between twenty-five and fifty pounds), she gave him five pills with water.

The clinic's alarm started to ring as soon as Jackie broke through the door, but even if the police arrived to arrest them, it would be a considerably better alternative than trying to make their way through town on their own. However, they decided that the alarm might attract other unwanted attention, so they decided to relocate to a small bookshop, also closed, just four doors down from the clinic.

The book store's name was painted on a sign over the front entrance: *Read Into It*. Mike would have selected something different for the name of a book store, but not everyone thought the same way. In the front windows were slanted shelves displaying the latest hardcover releases. Mike gave them a cursory glance. He thought it was a sign that an author had truly arrived when their name was printed in significantly larger font than the title of the novel, as if the storyline of the book was secondary to the person who wrote it.

The store was not a great choice from a defensive perspective, with large glass windows in front, but the decision was made easy for them because the front door was inexplicably unlocked. They reasoned that unbroken doors and windows would attract little attention, and that very few people would loot a bookstore during a crisis.

They were pleased to discover a tiny lunchroom in the back, which they raided for food. They ate everything, even a stale loaf of bread that had spots of green and white mold. Mike could have done without that, but everything else was satisfactorily edible.

Other priorities soon came to mind. They had been awake all night and through a good part of the daytime hours as well. Once they finished eating, they immediately felt the urgent and impossible-to-ignore desire to sleep. In addition to books, the store sold plush toys. They bundled these into pillows as best they could and then laid on the carpet, bordered by the romance section on one side and the science fiction section on the other.

Jackie was already up when Mike woke in the morning. Judging by the quality of light coming through the front window, it was barely past dawn.

"I thought about trying for the coffee shop and bakery down the street," she said. "But there are too many people out and about. It's been too dark to tell who they are, friend or foe, but I'm going with foe. No one else would be crazy enough to be wandering the streets right now."

"We were."

She turned to him. "That's true, but I am sticking with my original assessment. Much safer."

Mike agreed with her evaluation, but his stomach growled at the thought of cinnamon rolls and baguettes. "How do you know there is a bakery there?"

"There are flyers on the front counter." She pushed back a little from the window.

A woman in a housecoat strolled by on the other side of the street carrying an axe. It looked like it had been used recently, but not for chopping wood.

After that, they just sat and watched the street and wondered what to do next.

"There's another one," said Jackie.

A man wearing a pair of dirty jeans and a denim jacket over a white t-shirt walked purposely down the sidewalk. He was of medium height with unruly dark hair, and he wore a pair of black glasses that were unfashionably large. Mike rated the probability of him being infected at nine out of ten.

They both shrank back from the window as he passed by, sneaking glances from between piles of books. On the other side of the street, a woman emerged from a building that appeared to be a private residence.

"Oh no," said Jackie. "Did she not check before she went outside?"

There was no way to warn the woman without exposing themselves to danger as well.

"What is that she is carrying?" Mike asked, leaning forward for a better look.

It appeared at first glance to be a cane with a hooked end.

"It's a field hockey stick," said Jackie.

As a potential weapon, a field hockey stick was not a bad choice. It was light weight, so it could be swung at high speed, and it had a bulbous hook at the end which gave it some heft. Aside from a baseball bat, it could be considered one of sport's most formidable dual-purpose implements. (Mike gave honorable mention to the javelin; it would be good for spearing people in the torso.)

The woman wielding the field hockey stick was older, with short grey hair, and stocky in a way that reminded him of his ninth-grade physical education teacher, Ms. Sears. She strode toward the man in the denim jacket with clear intent. The field hockey stick was already raised above her shoulder, and she looked like she knew how to use it.

The man stopped, pivoted on his heel, and headed across the road toward the woman. The woman, appearing far from frightened, chose to advance on the man instead of retreating back inside. In fact, the Phys Ed teacher, if that is what she was, showed no emotion at all.

"Interesting," said Mike.

He watched in fascination as they squared off in the middle of the street, like a couple of cowboys preparing for a gunfight at high noon.

"This is bonkers," he said. "It's like we're in an open-air insane asylum."

The woman may have been a good field hockey player in the past, but striking someone in the head —especially someone who was much taller than her— was quite different than hitting a ball at ground level. Her first swing was telegraphed much too far in advance and the man easily skipped away out of range. So, at least some semblance of self-preservation still existed.

It was also clear that being afflicted with the disease did not automatically convert the infected person into an efficient killing machine. Most were able to kill through a combination of surprise and aggression and diminished concern for their personal safety.

The PE teacher took another two steps forward and swung again, putting everything she had into it. But she missed, and the attempt left her off balance. Before she had a chance to recover, the man rushed forward and punched the woman in the face hard enough to dislodge several teeth. The two teeth hit the pavement and bounced in different directions. She staggered back several steps, and the man came at her again, grabbing onto her shirt and driving his fist squarely into her face. The woman collapsed in a heap, her legs twisting under her in an unnatural way.

The man stooped and picked up the field hockey stick, examining its striking surface. He then gripped the end of the shaft in both hands and proceeded to smash the woman's skull with her own weapon. The blows were delivered with such incredible force that the implement broke after just five hits.

The man dropped the shattered remains and then continued up the street as casually as if he were on his way to lunch.

"Jesus," said Jackie.

"Yeah."

"I wondered if this might happen," he said. "I mean, I don't think they have some kind of psychic link to help them distinguish between a regular person and a fellow infected. Maybe they have been killing each other all along, but we just never saw it or noticed it. A dead body is a dead body." He thought back to the woman in the bloody wedding dress.

Jackie said, "This could be the beginning of the end of it. Maybe we just need to stay out of their way and let them kill each other off."

They sheltered in the shop for the rest of the morning and were reasonably confident that most of the people wandering the street were sick. The majority who walked by were purposeful, like they were on a mission and in a rush to accomplish it. A few of them were armed, and these individuals appeared to be more wary, but at this point Mike and Jackie were just guessing.

Over the entire period that they watched out the window, they were only tempted to call out to one person, a thin man with a receding hairline who was carrying a hunting rifle with a scope. Joining forces with someone with a rifle might considerably improve their chances of making it through the day. But they debated too long, and the opportunity was lost.

At about one o'clock in the afternoon, Mike saw Jackie abruptly tilt her head to one side, listening, like an animal in the wild. Perhaps that was what they were becoming, hunted animals that were always on alert. Three seconds later he heard what she was hearing, a loud vehicle. Not just a loud vehicle but one that had been made intentionally loud with a modified muffler. It was somewhat unsettling to hear a sound of this volume after the nearly complete silence of the night before. Making any kind of noise now seemed irresponsible and dangerous.

A large black truck came into view about forty seconds after they first heard it, barrelling down the main street at an imprudent rate of speed. It almost certainly would have received a ticket if there were any police still around to dispense one. In addition to the modified muffler, the truck was also lifted, sitting almost a foot higher than a stock version. The tires didn't appear to be standard either, and they protruded six inches out from the wheel wells of the vehicle. The windows were heavily tinted, making it impossible to see the driver. As the truck roared past, they could see a Confederate flag decal on the rear window and a pair of rubber testicles hanging from the trailer hitch.

Jackie huffed a sound that might have been derision.

As they watched, wondering what the driver would do once he reached the end of the road, they noticed movement through the window of a door across the street. It belonged to a walk-up apartment that was located above a real estate business. Mike could see flyers for different properties taped to the large window at ground level.

A young woman with a pale face pressed her cheek against the door window as if trying to see where the truck had gone. She appeared to be in her late twenties.

"I wonder what she's doing?" asked Mike.

"Maybe she recognized the sound of the truck," Jackie said.

The truck drove almost to the vet clinic before it pulled a sharp U-turn and began to move back up the street toward them.

They returned their attention to the woman. She had pushed the door partly open, still looking through the window. She suddenly turned, reached down, and then walked out of the building, now holding the hand of a young girl who appeared to be about eight years old.

"*No,*" said Jackie, plaintively. The word encapsulated the horror and sadness and helplessness of foreseeing what was about to come. It seemed clear that the woman knew the person in the truck, or who that person used to be, and was hoping to be rescued. Jackie hoped that her hypothesis was incorrect.

It was not. The woman ran into the street, one hand waving in the air and the other hand dragging the child behind her, likely her daughter. The truck drove at high speed up the road toward them, still in the correct lane. It did not slow, and Jackie hoped that it would simply drive on by. However, at the very last second, it swerved into the opposite lane and slammed into the woman, the high bumper catching her at hip height. Even through the window Mike could hear the sharp snap of her pelvis fracturing. The young girl disappeared underneath the truck, and one of the rear wheels drove over her torso. The vehicle rocked slightly on its suspension but continued without slowing.

Both Mike and Jackie observed all this in quiet horror. There was no time to react, not that there was anything they could have done that would have affected the outcome. They would not have been able to convince the woman to change her plans, not in the ten seconds it took for the tragedy to unfold.

Jackie screamed at the window, practically incandescent with rage. It was a scream of both grief and anger, and once it was done, she sat and cried.

Mike screamed on the inside. The pain of seeing that little girl crushed under the wheels tore through his guts like a ricocheting bullet that could find no exit point. He gripped the window ledge so hard he thought it might snap off in his hands.

The truck disappeared from view, and the sound from its muffler eventually faded away until they were once again left in silence. The memory of what they had witnessed would stay with them much longer.

Over the next three hours they alternated between napping and sitting by the window. Hunger was starting to become a major issue. They had expended a great deal of energy between the point of leaving the school and arriving at the bookstore, and their bodies demanded to be fed.

"I should have grabbed some dog food at the veterinary clinic," Mike said.

Jackie made a face of disgust and then said, "Dry or wet?".

"Dry. And I'm not kidding. I think that food from the breakroom just made me hungrier."

Jackie's stomach rumbled in response to the reminder. "Okay, I know we said we were going to wait it out here, but we could just as easily wait it out in the bakery. It's *so* close."

Excessive hunger made people make poor decisions, and this seemed to be one of them. It didn't even matter that they were aware of it.

After an hour more of not seeing anyone, they decided to risk it. The thought of fresh-baked bread down the street was impossible to ignore. Its presence there was likely a fantasy, but the possibility proved too powerful to resist.

They could see the sign for the bakery almost as soon as they stepped outside. It was only a block and a half away on the other side of the street, sitting on a corner. They were armed with the stout legs of a small display table they had dismantled. The pieces of wood, no more than a foot and a half in length, seemed pathetically inadequate against what they might face.

They paused when they heard the booming sound of a shotgun being discharged toward the extreme end of town, at least a half a mile away. The sound echoed off the nearby hills, distorting their perceptions of location and distance.

The shots were intermittent, and Mike had trouble deciphering the intent of the shooter. Were the shots offensive in nature, or defensive? The timing between each discharge suggested offensive, although whether the targets were friend or foe was far less certain. In this case, any uninfected person was considered a friend.

"I think they are getting closer, whoever they are. We need to get inside."

There appeared to be no immediate threat, but they didn't want to be outside any longer than necessary.

Mike and Jackie scuttled along the sidewalk like nervous cats, taking quick glances inside the businesses as they passed and finding most of them empty. They startled one woman, an older lady who shrieked when they made eye contact with her, but they decided it was pointless to stop.

The bakery they visited was called *La Vie de Baguette*.

"Wand Life," translated Jackie. "It sounds much better in French."

The door to the bakery was locked, but Mike found a perfectly sized piece of broken concrete lying in the gutter and used it to punch a hole in the glass just above the lock. A small bell tinkled over the door as they made their way inside.

The shop was narrow and deep with single tables lining the wall next to the windows and a counter and display case taking up the other side. Every section of free space on the walls was adorned with prints from France: vineyards, narrow streets framed by stunning architecture, and, of course, the Eiffel Tower.

Angled shelves behind the counter displayed baguettes and sour dough breads. Mike's mouth began to water. He didn't care how stale they were.

A dark corridor to their left led to a set of washrooms. A sign posted on the wall by the corridor said: *Toilettes.*

To the right of the counter was a set of doors marked with a "Staff Only" sign, presumably the location of the kitchen.

They walked over to a display case that had a glass top and front and gazed longingly at the pastries and cookies lining the shelves. The food was likely days old but still looked a damn sight better than the moldy bread they had eaten the day before.

They had just about decided on their choices— who were they kidding, they were going to eat it all— when they heard a scream from out in the street. They hurried to the window, although were careful to stay out of sight.

The older woman they had seen earlier, the shrieker, must have been emboldened by their passage and decided to venture out as well. Unfortunately, she had not chosen a wise time to do so.

The man whom the woman encountered was unknown to Mike but strangely familiar, like a character from a B movie. There was something about his size, his clothing, and his facial hair that made him think of the famous pirate, Blackbeard. Perhaps it was the voluminous white shirt, open at the collar, and the overly broad brown belt holding up his pants. And then there was the beard, black and substantial, and wild. The long steel machete he held in his hand was the finishing touch, not quite a sword, but close enough to one that it didn't make any difference.

Mike wanted to go to her aid, but he knew it was too late to change the outcome. Blackbeard had already started on the woman before they reached the window, and he continued hacking away at her as dispassionately as someone ridding themselves of brambles. Several of the woman's fingers lay on the pavement, lost while trying to defend herself from his merciless attack. There were deep gashes on her arms, and she could no longer lift them to protect her head.

Jackie peeled away, not able to watch to the inevitable conclusion. Mike wished he had joined her. There are certain things that you can never unsee, not in whatever time you have left.

He and Jackie did not want to venture deeper into the shop, along that dark corridor, lest they get trapped. So, they both sat behind the counter with their backs to the display case, hidden from a casual examination of the shop, but not much more. They looked at each other and reached an unspoken agreement that they would wait in that spot for as long as was necessary. They sat very still, barely breathing.

The bell jingled again over the door, and the innocent sound filled them with dread. The person who entered had a heavy footfall and only took two steps inside the door before stopping. Mike could visualize Blackbeard sweeping his eyes across the seating area and counter. Had he seen them enter? If he had, he would start looking for them; Mike was certain of this. How long would it take him to find them behind the counter? Thirty seconds at most. They needed to be ready to run. Fighting a man of that size with a set of short table legs did not feel like a winning strategy.

The service area behind the counter was open at each end and Mike shared another look with Jackie to communicate his thoughts. It seemed most likely that the man would approach the counter from the left side first, the shortest distance from the door. Mike nodded toward the opposite end of the counter and hoped that she understood what he was trying to convey.

Ka thump, ka thump. Blackbeard took two steps forward, a two-note rhythm to his steps. First the heel contact and then the sole of the heavy boot.

Ka thump, ka thump, ka thump. A shadow fell over them, the big man looking at them from over the top of the display case. Mike had not been expecting that. The man braced himself against the countertop with his left hand and swung the machete toward Mike's head with his right. Mike was just barely able to sweep the blow aside with the table leg.

Blackbeard took a swipe at Jackie as well, but she had pushed herself across the narrow space and had her back to the wall, just underneath the angled shelves.

Mike quickly scrambled to his feet, narrowly avoiding another strike from the machete. The sudden effort caused a ripping sensation in his calf, and he knew he had done even more damage to the muscle. He couldn't easily go to his left since he was blocked by Jackie, and going to his right would deprive him of the protection provided by the glass display case, limited as it was.

The big man leaned over the display case, one hand on the back edge, but he was far too heavy for the fragile glass construction, and the countertop gave way with an enormous crack. The heavy top panel snapped in the middle and resulted in a pancaking effect on the shelves below it. Glass splintered and showered the floor on both sides of the display case, and their attacker was left floundering in the jagged remains.

Mike pulled Jackie to her feet, and they moved past the man as he struggled to extricate himself from the shattered case and the crushed pastries. His white shirt bloomed with blood in several places, there was a cut on his face just above his beard, and his hands were severely lacerated. Despite all his injuries, he still held onto the machete and managed to get to one knee before Jackie and Mike were out the door.

There were more of the infected outside, although none of them were close. In the direction from which they had originally traveled, from the bookstore, a young man who looked like a farm hand was carrying a pitchfork. It was like an old-time horror story, but they were the monsters, and the villagers were coming to vanquish them.

Far down the side street they saw another individual who was dragging a sledgehammer across the asphalt surface, the metal ringing as it bumped along. No one could be seen on the west end of the main street, so they hurried in that direction, Mike hobbling badly. He could barely put any weight on his leg at all and there was no way he could run if the need arose. They tried the doors of the businesses they passed, hoping to duck inside.

They heard the tinkle of a bell as Blackbeard exited the bakery. They were close enough to the storefronts that he could not immediately see them, but he only needed to step out a few feet for them to be visible.

Jackie pulled Mike into the alcove of a flower shop that was only a few steps away. The storefront was designed with the door set back from the street to increase the display area of the windows. The flowers that were artfully arranged behind the angled panes of glass were now wilted after days of neglect.

From Mike's current position he could lean slightly forward and see out through the glass at the front of the shop via the angled side window. The view was slightly distorted as it passed through the two panes of glass that were at odd angles, and the arrangement did not afford him a large field of view. But it was clear enough for him to see that Blackbeard was walking up the street in their direction.

"He's walking this way," Mike whispered.

Jackie tried the door again, a formidable barrier that they were unlikely to breach in the time they had remaining. Going through the window seemed like an equally unviable course of action. They were trapped.

The big man looked around as he walked and there was no chance he would not see them as he passed by. Mike estimated they had twenty seconds before they were spotted.

"You should run while you have a chance," he said. "He doesn't look very fast."

"No!" said Jackie. "We are going to fight him together."

They still had their table legs to use as weapons, although Mike did not have a lot of faith that they would stand up well against a machete with a fearsomely long blade. But the two of them against a lone attacker would help his odds of surviving the encounter.

"Let's get out of here before he reaches us," Mike said. The only way they could hope to defeat him would be in an open space where they could maneuver, Jackie being the nimbler of the two.

He started to move but she put a hand on his shoulder.

"Wait."

She pulled him back a step and pointed out the window in the opposite direction.

Striding up the street was a new player on the scene, a tall man wearing Ray Ban sunglasses and sporting a buzz cut. He was fully clad in camouflage gear and had heavy black boots on his feet. Mike reflected that he was likely wearing the outfit *before* he became sick, which suggested that he was either a hunter or a paramilitary type, like a survivalist. This theory was supported by the rest of his gear. There was a holster hanging from the utility belt around his waist, but it was empty. A large Bowie knife hung from a sheath on his left side. More significantly, a pump-action shotgun was held at waist level. A bandolier to hold shotgun shells was draped over his left shoulder. Most of the slots were empty.

The absence of shells made it reasonable to assume that this man was the source of the shots they heard earlier.

Mike and Jackie looked to their right to see the reaction of the man with the machete. He kept coming, walking even faster. They switched back to watching the Survivalist; it was like following a life-or-death tennis match. The camouflage-clad man brought the shotgun up to his shoulder and fired in one smooth motion. There was no need to aim when the target was only twenty feet away. Blackbeard staggered a few more steps forward, and the shotgun boomed again. The big man spun and dropped, his chest and face suffering the brunt of the damage.

The Survivalist continued up the street unhurriedly, bringing him directly in front of their hiding space. He stopped and fired again, this time at an unseen target.

There was a moment where they thought he might simply walk by, and one or two more steps might do it, but he turned his head at the last second as if sensing their presence. Up to this point it was not yet clear whether he was among the infected or simply a well-armed citizen meting out vigilante justice. The presence of the sunglasses made it more difficult to distinguish the difference. Jackie was hoping for the latter. She lifted her hand in a wave and tried to force a semblance of a smile on her face, but she knew it was likely a grimace.

The Survivalist's response was to lift the shotgun to his shoulder, take aim in their direction, and pull the trigger. Jackie closed her eyes, not wanting to see it coming. There was a barely audible *click* as the hammer fell on the empty chamber.

Jackie let out a strangled breath, halfway between a sob and a sound of relief.

The man patted his bandolier and then pulled it up to look at the bottom slots. Those were empty, but Jackie could see that three shells remained at the very top.

To their right, just coming into view, was the man dragging the sledgehammer.

The Survivalist located the shells at the top of the bandolier and began to insert them into his shotgun, appearing unhurried.

The sledgehammer stopped ringing against the pavement as the man brought it up to waist height and quickened his steps.

"The other side of the street," Jackie shouted, without any further elaboration.

This would take them on a path directly behind the man with the shotgun who tried to kill them in cold blood just seconds before. It was a bold move and not one that Mike was keen to attempt, considering his locomotion was limited to hopping on one foot. But the survivalist was temporarily occupied with loading his weapon and would soon need to deal with the imminent threat posed by a twelve-pound sledgehammer.

They walked past him just as he was prying the last shell out of its neoprene holder. He was only an arms-length distance away at their closest, and Mike caught a whiff of body odor and unclean clothes, and ketosis.

Could the survivalist load the shotgun and deal with the sledgehammer guy in the time it would take them to cross the street? That seemed likely.

Mike could now see the building that Jackie had chosen as their destination— a pawn shop with a reinforced door and metal slats over the windows. There was a man in a suit wedged in the doorway, clearly dead.

Mike turned his head to the right and looked down toward the veterinary clinic at the edge of town. What he saw made him pause midway across the road, and he turned and stared along the length of the street.

Jackie ran back to him and pulled on his arm. "What are you doing? Come on!"

They hustled the rest of the way across and arrived at the door to the store, Edgerton Pawn Shop.

Jackie stooped and grabbed the left wrist of the man in the doorway. "Help me!" she shouted.

Mike grabbed the other wrist, cold and fleshy and a little slimy, like the skin of a dead salamander. The sensation filled him with revulsion.

Despite their intense effort, eons seemed to pass before the doorway was finally clear. They heard a ratcheting sound of a shotgun shell being chambered and realized they were out of time.

The boom of the shotgun sounded again, and Mike flinched, but the spray of pellets was not directed at them but against the man with the sledgehammer. They both took a quick look back, just long enough to see the last victim sprawled on the ground and the survivalist turning the shotgun in their direction. Mike slammed the door shut, turned the deadbolt, and dove to the side in one continuous motion. His leap sent him crashing into a display table on which sat a collection of cowboy hats and belt buckles.

The first shot caused the glass in the front door to explode inward and slice into a rack of guitars which then fell to the floor, producing a discordant mix of musical notes. The second shot ripped into a display of digital cameras and watches, showering the shop with additional pieces of shrapnel.

After thirty seconds of silence, Mike risked peeking over the edge of the window display.

"What's he doing?" asked Jackie.

"Well, I think he must be out of shells by now, but he's walking toward the door with the sledgehammer. *And* the machete. Let's see if we can find another way out."

The survivalist wasted no time beginning on the door. It was reinforced to discourage easy entry, but it was never intended to be impenetrable. It was designed under the presumption that no thief would spend minutes of time bashing away at an entrance in plain view of other residents who would be calling 911 to report the break-in. The door began to splinter.

The shop was narrow and deep and there was no other door except for the one behind the front counter. The place had the distinct smell of *old*, like the combination of an antique book repository and a second-hand clothing store. They made their way around the counter to a door with an "Employees Only" sign tacked onto it. Glass and plastic crunched underfoot with every step.

The door was unlocked, and Mike pushed it open. It was very solidly constructed and had a square window with reinforced glass, the type with wire strands running through it.

Behind the door was a narrow storage room lined with numerous heavy metal floor safes and other receptacles that looked equally impossible to breach. Some of the safes looked to be a hundred years old, with rotary dials that required the correct combination of numbers to access. A heavy red fire extinguisher hung from a rack next to the door.

This was clearly where they kept the good stuff, or items they wanted to lock up at night.

The exception to this was a wooden crate with a handwritten label pasted to the side. It simply read: Broken/Junk. Mike peered inside. There were four wine glasses that had been completely shattered, the pieces too small to be used as a cutting weapon. A porcelain doll with its face smashed. A vacuum cleaner with an old, ribbed hose that had cracked with age. Two wooden picture frames with broken corners.

Mike lifted out the metal tube attached to the flexible vacuum cleaner hose. It was far too light to be used as a club. He tossed it back in the box.

The storage room was windowless, as was the tiny washroom located in the back. The door to the washroom was fragile, simply for privacy.

He had hoped for firearms —and there were some— but they were secured behind heavily fortified racks that were locked up tight. The owners of the shop were evidently very serious about security.

Mike heard the front door give way with a resounding crash. He and Jackie went to the storage room door and peered out through the little window. The survivalist came into view and made his way toward the door behind which they were now standing. He took off his sunglasses and stood directly in front of the window, staring into the room.

It was disconcerting to look into the eyes of the infected. The saying, 'the eyes are the windows to the soul' either did not apply to those who were infected, or their souls were dead and gone. The eyes held no more emotion than those of a rattlesnake. There was simply nothing there, an absence that was fundamentally disturbing.

The survivalist lifted the sledgehammer above his shoulder and began to batter the door. There was nothing in the storage room that could be considered a weapon, although Mike unracked the heavy fire extinguisher and carried it with him away from the door. Spraying the man with non-toxic powder might buy them a few seconds, if nothing else.

The door was already showing signs of impending failure, with an increasing amount of play in the hinges.

Jackie said, "You know, we had a guy come into the emergency room from a frat party once. One of his friends jammed a pencil into the hose of a fire extinguisher and thought it might be fun to fire it off." She paused and looked toward the door again. "The doctor had to surgically remove the pencil from the guy's abdomen."

The blows against the door suddenly ceased. The man could be tired, Mike supposed. He had just battered down one reinforced door and was now working hard on a second.

After a few more moments, both Mike and Jackie crept forward and looked through the window. The survivalist had his back turned to them and was looking toward the entrance.

Mike inched closer, adjusting his position to allow him to get a glimpse of what their attacker was seeing. He thought he knew. Five minutes earlier, when Mike was crossing the street, he had seen a man wearing a familiar shade of blue. The man had been all the way down the street, down where he and Jackie first emerged from the woods. Mike had stopped in the middle of the road and faced him. He wanted the man to get a good look.

It had been a dangerous and deliberate gambit, one that was intended to act as a diversion while he and Jackie located an escape route. This was not how he saw it playing out.

Blue Suit had traded his length of pipe for a long-handled carpenter's hammer. There was a patch of dried blood all the way down one side of the man's face.

I did that, Mike thought.

The survivalist dropped the sledgehammer and pulled out the machete he had slipped through his utility belt. He moved out from behind the counter, his eyes never leaving the man in the blue suit.

Blue Suit charged forward, closing the distance between the door and the man at the counter in six steps, already bringing his arm back to deliver a blow. The hammer and the machete clanged off each other. Blue Suit swung again, the faster of the two men and the bearer of a more agile weapon, albeit one with shorter reach. It hit the survivalist on the left arm, just below his shoulder. The pain from the blow must have been extreme, but the big man barely grunted. He responded with a slash to Blue Suit's torso, the blade slicing through his jacket and probably scoring a few ribs as well. The survivalist slashed at him again, missing entirely, and Blue Suit moved in close. This allowed him to deliver crippling blows to the survivalist's legs and knees while simultaneously reducing the effectiveness of the machete as a slashing weapon.

The survivalist hit the storage room door with such force that Mike was concerned that both men could tumble into the room.

Mike checked the pressure gauge on the fire extinguisher. Full. He looked back at the weakened door. "Now would be a good time to have a pencil," he said.

"We don't have a pencil, but we *do have* broken glass and a length of pipe."

Mike examined the box with the junked items. "Let's be quick."

CHAPTER 24

Jackie smashed the wine glasses into even smaller pieces while Mike removed the short metal pipe from the hose. It wasn't a perfect fit with the fire extinguisher nozzle, but it was close enough for a one time shot.

Jackie poured razor sharp pieces of glass down the tube and tamped them down with a strip of cloth.

The sounds from the fight had ended, and they had not stayed at the window to see who was victorious. Ultimately, it didn't matter who came through the door.

The wood of the door frame squealed as if in pain as someone once again applied the sledgehammer to the area around the lock. With a final agonizing shriek, the lock gave way, and the door burst open to reveal Blue Suit. Mike was not surprised; the dude seemed dead set on being the one to end his life.

The man calmly set the sledgehammer on the counter and picked up his hammer, the head of which was now covered in blood and what looked like scraps of hair.

Mike took a step back. Jackie stood directly behind him, holding the fire extinguisher. He pressed the nozzle hard against the length of tubing, readying himself. He assessed the odds at 60:40 that the contraption would not blow up in his hands.

Blue Suit moved quickly, closing to within eight feet of them in an instant, the hammer raised and ready to strike. Mike thought about the old man and the dog and the young caregiver, Shannon. This man deserved every bit of hurt coming his way.

"Now!" he shouted.

He felt an explosive rush of gas and powder through the pipe held in his hands. The kick was even stronger than he expected, and he quickly lost the tenuous connection between the nozzle and the pipe. But not before he heard pieces of glass hit the wall on either side of the door at high speed.

Jackie released the handle once she saw that the nozzle was no longer aligned with the pipe. That, and the fact that the room was so full of powder that it was becoming difficult to breathe.

Blue Suit was completely obscured in the dust cloud for a few moments. As the powder settled, Mike saw that they had failed. The man was covered head to toe in white dust but otherwise did not appear to have a mark on him. But that initial impression was incorrect. Spots of red began to appear underneath the white on his face, like a statue weeping blood. Red also bloomed across his chest. There were at least twenty separate points of injury. Even so, Mike wondered whether it was enough. Superficial cuts to the face and chest were unlikely to stop the man, unless both eyes had been damaged as well. The points of blood started to amalgamate into larger pools, red continents on an ocean of white.

It did not stop him. Blue Suit took a step toward them, but the movement caused just enough of an increase in his blood pressure to dislodge an arrowhead of glass that must have punctured his jugular vein. Scarlett blood spewed down the front of his body, a torrent. He took two more stumbling steps before collapsing to the floor.

Mike and Jackie both stared down at the body, not quite believing that it wasn't some ruse to trick them into walking closer. They waited another minute and then walked by him, carefully avoiding the blood.

Jackie scanned the street as soon as they were outside the main door, her eyes settling on the only vehicle that was close, an old Subaru Outback, off-white.

There were several people headed in their direction and they all carried items of some type. However, it was impossible to tell if they were holding weapons or something innocuous.

"See if he has any keys," said Jackie, nodding to the man they had pulled out of the doorway. "I'll keep my eye on these guys."

Mike was not optimistic that he would find the keys to the vehicle. The SUV could belong to anyone in town, not necessarily to the guy in closest proximity to it when he died. But a set of keys was in the first place he looked, the right-side jacket pocket. He pulled them out and pressed the unlock button on the fob. To his astonishment, the *chunk* of locks disengaging reached his ears.

Jackie tried to snag the keys from his hand, but he tucked them into his fist and held them close to his body.

"I'll drive," he said. He knew Jackie had an innate desire to be in control, but so did he. He locked eyes with her a moment, resolute. She sighed and walked around to the other side of the SUV without a fight. He climbed in and turned the key. It was an enormous relief when the engine started on the first try. The rear seat of the car was packed with what looked like junk, but the owner may have been trying to get something for it at the pawn shop. There was a pile of fast-food containers and cups in the foot well of the passenger seat, and he was doubly glad that he held on to the keys.

As soon as Jackie was seated, he backed out of the parking spot and looked left, right. He turned right, driving toward a person wandering along the main drag about a hundred yards away.

The fellow was carrying something that Mike hoped was a baseball bat —it was not— and the person raised it to his shoulder and fired. A bullet starred the window just above Jackie's head. She ducked and cursed.

Mike spun the truck around and headed in the opposite direction. Another bullet pinged off the rear hatch.

He only made it sixty yards before he was forced to brake again. There were people heading toward them from every direction, including two that were almost directly in front of the SUV. The guy who killed the physical education teacher with her own field hockey stick had made a reappearance and was now armed with a pair of gardening shears. He was the closest. Slightly behind him and to the right was a woman with a spade.

Mike hesitated, pondering how to proceed. There was a man with a rifle behind them, getting closer by the second, and a semi-circle of potentially dangerous individuals in front of him. But only *potentially* dangerous. It had been his position to only take aggressive action when he felt his life was in danger and there was no other option to avoid the encounter. It was not a policy to which he had given a lot of thought, it was simply a byproduct of his natural disposition. Yes, there was a man walking toward him while holding gardening shears, but this did not seem like a sufficient reason to run him down with the SUV. His moral compass had taken a beating over the previous few days, but this action felt like a step too far. He looked in the rearview mirror, considering taking his chances with the guy with the rifle.

"Oh, for fuck's sake," he said.

Speeding toward them, no more than a block away, was the lifted black truck. Mike thought he could see something on the chrome bumper in addition to the blood that stained it red. It did not bear closer inspection.

Jackie whipped her head around to look behind them.

"Go!" she said, apparently at peace with any moral dilemmas she may have been grappling with. Of course, that was fine for her to say; she wasn't behind the wheel.

He did not wrestle with his conscience for more than a heartbeat. Mike knew for sure that the man in front of him had already committed murder, ignoring for a moment the question of whether he could be held legally responsible. That made the decision easier. He floored the accelerator.

The SUV hit the garden-shears man at fifty miles per hour, and the vehicle was just high enough so that the fellow disappeared underneath the Subaru instead of being flung across the engine bonnet. Small favors. The SUV jerked and rocked as it rolled over the body, and Mike gripped the steering wheel and clenched his jaw so hard that he heard his molars grind.

There appeared to be only one other viable route out of town, a street to his right. A large green sign with a number and an arrow pointed toward the road, but that was all he saw before they rocketed past. The official-looking markings on the sign suggested that a major highway existed somewhere along its route. He turned hard to the right and the car sank deep to one side on its aging shocks. Items in the rear seat and trunk creaked and shifted and he was fortunate to keep the SUV on all four wheels. He gained a little distance on the black truck after the surprise turn, but the vehicle caught up to them less than forty seconds later. The truck was so close he could no longer see the bumper.

Their pursuer hit them straight on and gave them a resounding jolt, but Mike was able to regain control quickly. He pressed down on the accelerator, pushing the vehicle up to 80 mph. He didn't normally drive a car in New York, and it had been many years since he had driven at this speed, and even then, it had always been on a highway. This was a narrow two-lane road, and it made 80 mph feel like one hundred. A light but persistent rain that had begun almost as soon as they hit town limits was only going to make things worse. He barely felt in control as it was. He hadn't noticed the state of the tires but based on the condition of the rest of the vehicle, he had to assume that they were in poor shape.

The big truck hit them again, harder this time, and the hatch popped open in the back. A maelstrom of paper and food wrappers and disposable cups formed inside of the car and many items were sucked outside from the resulting vortex.

Mike fought for control of the car on the rain slicked roads, and the *Check Engine* light started to blink on the dashboard.

"Piece of shit car," he said. "I think the engine may quit before he has a chance to run us off the road."

Jackie, see if you can find anything to dump out the back, maybe we can slow him down a bit."

Jackie was not at all keen to disengage her seatbelt and climb into the back, but she knew they were in a desperate situation.

"Fine," she said. "But try not to crash before I get back there."

It was difficult to find much space in the rear seats to begin to sort through the collection of material, but she eventually wedged herself between the door and a box containing books. They smelled of mildew. She whipped them out through the hatch like frisbees until the box was empty, and then she threw the empty box out as well.

"I'm too far away to throw anything heavy," she shouted over the wind.

Not that there was much in the way of heavy items to throw. There were two lamps without shades, a footstool, a guitar with no strings, a mantelpiece clock, a framed landscape painting (poorly done), and various other lightweight objects. What she needed was a crate of hammers, or a collection of antique bowling balls. Even a box of long nails would do.

"He's coming again!" she shouted.

The grill of the truck filled her entire field of view before it struck for the third time. The hatch crumpled upon impact, spraying glass from the broken window into the SUV. The rear tires may have come completely off the ground for a moment, and the car fishtailed wildly. The front wheel on the passenger side veered off the asphalt and tried to drag the vehicle into the ditch. It would have been a good chance for the truck to finish them off, but a vehicle coming from the other direction attempted to ram them both. It missed the Subaru entirely but delivered a solid blow to their pursuer, just behind the driver's door. The big vehicle lost considerable momentum but was functionally unaffected. The smaller car spun back into the opposing lane; its front end smashed.

"Jesus!" shouted Mike. "I didn't even see that guy coming."

The small car, dark gray, make unknown, disappeared behind them.

Jackie had been knocked down into the foot well of the rear seats, in amongst trash and the footstool, one leg of which was jabbing into her side. She extricated herself as quickly as possible to check on the location of the truck. It was behind them by about sixty yards but closing again.

She still couldn't see the driver and the windshield of the truck was pebbled with rain. It was a wonder that the driver could see where he was going.

She propped her elbows over the rear seats and investigated the small trunk. The cargo space cover had been removed, which gave her easy access to whatever was stored there. It seemed clear that this trip had been primarily reserved for a grocery run, and it looked like the man had planned to hole-up for a while. There were bags of rice and flour, a jar of yeast, a bag of sugar, flats of water bottles, some canned goods, dried fruit, bags of cashews and peanuts, and bags of chips and candy.

She worked her way over the seats and into the little space, feeling very vulnerable. If the truck hit them again, she would be right there, maybe a foot or two away from that massive grill.

She hefted one of the cans of tuna in her hand and threw it sidearm toward the truck. It bounced off the Subaru's twisted and compacted hatch and hit the road. She tried it again, but the can landed on the road well before the truck. She couldn't throw properly in the confined space, and the angle was all wrong. The windshield would be her primary target, but by the time the truck was close enough, it would be impossible to complete the throw at the necessary angle.

"There's a flatbed truck stopped in the road about a half mile away," yelled Mike. "I need to get into the other lane."

Jackie looked at the collection of food in the back and at the rain-drenched truck and then turned to assess how much time she had before they reached the flatbed. The flatbed was carrying what appeared to be a large yellow bulldozer.

"Hold on," she said. "Don't move over until I say."

"What? Why?" asked Mike.

"Just wait!" she yelled.

She grabbed the bag of flour, 20lbs All Purpose, and ripped open the top.

The truck was coming at them hard now, ready for a killing blow. Thirty yards. Twenty yards. Ten yards.

When the truck was ten yards away, Jackie emptied the entire bag of flour into the slipstream behind the SUV. It billowed over the incoming truck, blanketing the grill and the hood. And the window. After a few seconds, the windshield wipers were activated, but they just smeared the flour over the glass.

"Switch now!" yelled Jackie, and she turned to see that they were perilously close to the flatbed truck.

They passed safely by on the left, but the big black truck did not. It hit the heavy flatbed straight on while traveling at more than 80 mph. The truck stopped almost instantly, while the driver, apparently not wearing a seatbelt, continued at the same speed as before, through the windshield and into the sharp edge of the bulldozer blade. Jackie saw just a splash of red before the flatbed was lost from view. She did not feel a single shred of remorse as she climbed back into the front.

They drove for ten more minutes before reaching the highway. Jackie looked at a large green sign with opposing arrows. North or South? The simple choice suddenly seemed momentous. She laid her head back against the seat.

"I need a vacation," she said.

"I know where we can go," said Mike. "It's a place in the woods not too far from here. What do you think? A couple of weeks of peace and quiet and this could be all over."

"That sounds... perfect."

The drive took longer than expected and if they had waited a couple of days, they may not have made it at all. There were numerous wrecks on the highway, caused by either inattentive driving or excessive speed, or by drivers using their vehicles as weapons. They narrowly avoided a few of those themselves.

At about ten past six in the early evening, on a secondary highway in the north of Florida, they came upon a narrow lane on the right-hand side that was so rough and overgrown it looked like any vehicle larger than a motorcycle would get stuck if it tried to enter. It was unmarked, and anyone driving by would be inclined to keep on driving. Mike would not have noticed it either if not for the GPS coordinates programmed into his phone. However, he was careful to check in both directions before turning off the highway. He wanted to ensure that their sudden exit from the main road went unnoticed. There would be fellow travellers looking for a safe place to hide, and other drivers, hunters, with a far less innocent objective.

The SUV was swallowed up by the trees and invisible from the highway within a hundred yards. Branches scraped along its side. Three minutes later Mike and Jackie arrived at a clearing in which sat a rustic cabin with a small deck in front. A slight wisp of smoke drifted out of its brick chimney. Incongruously, there was an array of solar panels on the roof. Beside the cabin was a large garden that was flourishing in the subtropical climate.

Mike pulled up next to an old brown Volvo, its paint faded and its fenders beginning to rust. The *Check Engine* light stopped blinking on the SUV's dashboard console, but he doubted he would ever use the car again. It had done its job, and it could now retire in peace.

A sudden movement caught his eye as the front door of the cabin was pushed open. An aluminum crutch emerged, followed by a slipper-clad foot, followed by the rest of the person, a man in his sixties bearing a cast from ankle to knee. He squinted at the vehicle but did not appear to be overly concerned.

Jackie took it all in; the house, the yard, the lush expanse of greenery surrounding them. "I like it here already."

"I knew you would," he said, as he opened his door. "Let's go and see my dad."

ABOUT THE AUTHOR

Peter Lord lives in Truro, Canada and graduated from Dalhousie University with a Master of Science degree.

Author contact: petersterlinglord@gmail.com

The author's other novels, AN ALTERED STATE, THE ARTIFACT, THE CULL, and TRIAL 48 are available in e-book and paperback format through Amazon.

The author's page on Amazon: Amazon.com: Peter S. Lord: books, biography, latest update

Goodreads page: Peter S. Lord (Author of The Artifact) (goodreads.com)

www.ingramcontent.com/pod-product-compliance
Lightning Source LLC
Chambersburg PA
CBHW030348200626
46808CB00022B/609